CRASH INTO ME

L.A. FIORE

For Anthony...

I couldn't write it with you, so I wrote it for you.

What started with words... ❤

PLAYLIST

Empire…Shakira
You Won't See Me Cry…Wilson Philips
Lost Without You…Freya Ridings
Rise…Katy Perry
A Reason To Believe…Wilson Philips
Come By Me…Harry Connick Jr.
I Dare You…Kelly Clarkson
New Normal…JJ Heller
Here Right Now…Lindsey Ray
The Heat…Need To Breathe
Pictures of You…Lauren Ruth Ward
Serenity…David Foster
Right Round…Flo Rida
Rock Bottom…Hailee Steinfeld
Break My Heart…Victoria Duffield
Safe Inside…James Arthur
The Look…Roxette
True Colors…Anna Kendrick and Justin Timberlake
Don't Forget Me…Katharine McPhee
Hands…Jewel
Blackout…Freya Ridings
Sad Song (Featuring Elena Coats)…We The Kings
Afterlife…Hailee Steinfeld

PREFACE

My hands wouldn't come clean. Scrubbing the blood off, it just smeared. Tears pooled, but my anger was stronger, rage burned through me. My hands were raw, but still, I saw the blood.

"Molly."

"It won't come off."

His hand covered mine, as he turned off the water. "I have to get it off."

"Molly."

I turned to him, then pushed him away from me. The screaming in my head spilled from my mouth and echoed around the bathroom. He made no move to stop me when I used him to let the frustration and pain out. I stumbled back, hitting the wall. Before I slid down it, he was there…holding me up. His hand curled around my chin. "Tell me what you need, Molly."

I held his intense stare, my breathing coming in hard pants, the anger giving way to the pain. I fisted his hair, pulled his mouth to mine. He didn't respond, at first, until I begged against his lips. "Please."

Twisting my hair around his hand, he yanked my head back, those eyes I loved stared back, with concern and heat, before his mouth slammed down on mine. I clawed at his clothes, but his arm banded around my waist, holding me to him, as he consumed me with just his kiss. My muscles loosened, my body giving in to him. He pulled at my jeans, dragging them and my panties down my legs, my tee and bra followed. He turned the shower on, stripped, then pulled me under the spray, before pressing me against the wall. His hand moved down my body, his fingers played with me. His mouth replaced his fingers.

"Oh god." I fisted his hair, spread my legs wider, and moved my hips to take him deeper. His fingers dug into my ass, as he brought me swiftly to orgasm, before he stood, turned me to the wall and ran his hand up my back and between my shoulder blades. He pressed down, bending me at the waist. He placed my hands on the wall and pushed my legs apart. In the next breath, he was slamming into me.

"Yes!" I scream.

He wasn't gentle. I didn't want gentle. "Harder," I begged.

He fucked me almost brutally; his hand fisted my hair, pulling my head back, again, for his ruthless kiss. I came so hard it brought new tears to my eyes. He broke the kiss, our gazes locked. New tears fell. "If it was you," I said brokenly.

His voice was a harsh whisper. "It wasn't me."

He pulled out of me, drew me against him and held me, as I broke down. Three months ago, I didn't know him, and now I wouldn't survive the loss of him.

ONE

It was cold, the temperatures were still dropping in the evenings, but the nights were getting shorter. She knew it wasn't safe to run through Central Park at this hour, but she'd missed her run that morning and needed to work off the alcohol she'd consumed at the reception.

Her muscles felt good; the sweat rolling down her back was welcomed. She hadn't been in the city for long; work had brought her here. She wasn't sure she'd adjust to city life, but she had. She loved everything: the hustle and bustle, the shops, the culture, and the people. She'd been interviewed; sure, it was an off the beaten path online publication and the journalist was more interested in hearing about her boss, but the interview had been conducted over tea at The Plaza.

When her assignment was over, she was seriously thinking about staying. An acquaintance set her up with a potential interview. Just thinking about it, more specifically, the man she'd be working with… Not only was he one of the most prominent men in the world, he was also the sexiest man she'd ever seen. It was unlikely she'd get the job; there were far more experienced publicists, but if she did, she was taking it.

Her footfalls were the only sound, as she jogged along the path. She didn't listen to music; she wanted to be alert, so it was a shock when strong arms wrapped around her waist. She screamed, but it was cut short by the hand that covered her mouth. She tried to flail her arms, tried to get traction like she'd been taught in her self-defense classes, but she couldn't budge her attacker. He dragged her behind a tree and slammed her up against it. Her head hit hard, her vision turning blurry. She couldn't see his face; he was shrouded in shadows, but he was big and strong.

His hand moved from her mouth. She filled her lungs, so she could scream, fearing he was going to rape her, but then she saw the knife. His hand closed over her mouth again. As he leaned in, a familiar scent hit her, his face coming into view, one she'd just seen earlier that night. Confusion accompanied fear when he plunged the knife into her heart.

TWO
MOLLY

It was disgusting, and like a train wreck, I couldn't look away. I cringed, wanted to cover my eyes, but I was morbidly fascinated. My filet sat untouched on my plate, the baked potato with butter and sour cream likely cold. When it was delivered, it'd made my stomach growl. My stomach was now churning for an entirely different reason. Maybe if the steak wasn't rare, or if he had even the slightest bit of table manners, the scene opposite me, at the small table, wouldn't be so horrifying. But bloody juice dripped down his chin, as he wiped it away with the back of his hand.

The back of his hand. I was tempted to roll my eyes, but I'd miss the show.

This was my third date, in as many weeks, a setup from my partner. My partner sucked.

"You gonna eat that?" My date asked, but he was already reaching across the table and stabbing the meat.

Looks were definitely deceiving when it came to my dinner companion. When I stepped into the restaurant earlier, I couldn't lie, I'd felt a tingle. He was beautiful: dark blond hair, bright blue eyes in a face like that of a fallen angel. He wasn't a big talker, but then, he looked so good, he didn't need to talk. Then the food came. He went from fallen angel to feral dog. Eating his food like he hadn't eaten in decades, course after course, shoveling the food in like there was a time limit. I didn't think I was particularly picky, but this was just...I was done.

"Excuse me." I didn't wait for an answer, not that I got one, except for a grunt, since his mouth was full of cow.

I found my waiter, paid for my meal, that I didn't even eat, and left the restaurant.

It was spring, but the nights were still cool. I could be home by eight, watch a movie before I went to bed. It had been far too long since I'd done something as lazy as watching a movie. The idea was growing more and more appealing. I hailed a cab, walking would take too much time. I might even have some wine at my apartment with the leftover pizza from the other night. This evening could be saved. Then my cell went off. Seeing my partner's name, I knew I wasn't going to be watching that movie.

"We got one in the park," Zac said, without preamble. "I'll text you the location."

STARING DOWN AT the young woman, it never got easier seeing death. A part of me was glad for that, not growing immune. Zac was hunched down next to the coroner; the crime scene unit was processing the area.

"Stab wound, one to the heart," Julia said. "No signs of sexual abuse."

I looked up the path then down. There were lights along it, but not enough. Why did people insist on running at night when they knew the dangers? "We got a time of death?"

Julia glanced up at me. "Based on liver temp and lividity, about an hour ago."

That got my blood flowing; Zac's, too, when he stood, looking around the scene. "So it's possible he's still here if he gets off on the chase," I said.

"He's strong and has experience," Julia added.

"How do you know that?" I asked.

"The wound. It's not easy pushing a knife through the rib cage into the heart. He did and with only one attempt. No hesitation wounds, either."

"And the victim?" I asked Zac.

"ID found with the body is for a Samantha James. Preliminary search, works for Milton Teller PR as a publicist. Here on assignment. Home is Chadds Ford in Pennsylvania."

"How long has she been here?"

"Two months."

She either had really bad luck or…"Seems remarkably bad odds for this to be random."

Zac glanced over at me. "I was thinking that, too."

I exhaled, then looked back at the body. "As soon as you have anything, Julia."

"I'll call you."

I started away from the body; Zac fell into step at my side. "So who'd be gunning for a visiting publicist?"

"Good question. Time to retrace her final hours," Zac said, then called to one of the crime techs. "Her cell. I want a list of numbers she called in the last week, and I want her calendar." He looked back at me. "We'll stop for coffee on the way to the station."

"My apartment first. I need to change."

"Right." He grinned. "The big date with Blake."

Sometimes, I just wanted to punch him. "The only thing big about the date was that it was a failure." I stopped walking and poked him in the chest. "Where the hell did you meet Blake?"

"Fantasy football."

Figures. "Don't fix me up again," I said, and started for Zac's car.

"That bad?" There was concern under the teasing.

"Worse," I said, yanking open the door. "I'm hungry."

"Didn't you go to dinner?"

I was climbing into the car, but stopped and glared at him from over the roof. "I…" No point in retelling the tale, so instead I said, "My apartment to change, food, coffee and no mention of Blake again."

He put his hands up. "Okay." Then muttered, "Someone's grumpy."

An hour later, my feet were up on my desk, and I had three cups of coffee and four slices of pizza in my stomach. "She was at the Rothschild reception earlier. That's pretty fancy for a publicist based out of Chadds Ford. What did you learn about Milton Teller PR?"

Zac folded his pizza and ate half in one bite, while tapping the keys on his keyboard. "Milton Teller was a big shot back in the eighties and nineties. Had quite the client list from actors to politicians. Established his business with headquarters in LA and New York, downsized about a decade ago and moved the operation to Chadds Ford and opened a winery."

"Still has clout, though, if his publicists are representing people attending the Rothschild reception." Sinclair Rothschild was a philanthropist. Made most of his money illegally, and then, allegedly, had a morality shift and had been pursuing philanthropic pursuits ever since. Every year, he hosted several receptions, inviting the who's who to raise money for whatever the cause du jour was. And our victim had been at one of these receptions.

"Guess who Samantha's client was?" Zac asked.

"Who?"

"Desiree McKenzie."

My brows rose at that. An A-list movie star who couldn't act, but she was beautiful, and her dad was wealthy. "Definitely still has clout."

"Yep. We're going to need the list of attendees from last night, but that shouldn't be hard to get," Zac said, reaching for his phone. "Every newspaper likely has the list."

He wasn't wrong about that. Sinclair's receptions were like the Academy Awards for the Hollywood set, a big deal. "We need to call her family." I hated that part of the job. Looking down at death was difficult, but having to share that death with the loved ones was brutal.

Zac sounded as solemn as I felt, when he said, "We'll wait until the morning."

MY HEAD DIDN'T hit my bed until three and at exactly six, Salem was purring in my ear. I reached for my pillow and pressed it over my head. I wanted another twelve hours of sleep, but Samantha needed us. Climbing from bed, I went to the bathroom and took care of business, before heading to the kitchen; I hit the Keurig first, and while that brewed, I fed Salem. Reaching for a slice of pizza in the fridge, I took my coffee to my bedroom and got dressed.

"I'll be home…" I started to say to Salem, as I yanked open my door, then remembered I had another date tonight. I should cancel it, didn't know why I'd scheduled one so close to the last one. I needed time in between the staggering disappointments that were my dates these days. "I'll be home to change. Going to dinner again; hopefully, I eat this time. I'll bring you something back." He turned, his tail going in the air, as he walked away. I knew he was going back to bed. Fucker. It's where I wanted to be. My neighbor, Ethan, was just leaving as I was locking up. He was in his twenties, was still working the Goth look, all black, even his hair was black and spiky around a face that couldn't be called beautiful but definitely had you looking twice. He was a stoner, but he was good about not smoking in the building. He knew I was a cop. I knew I should be writing him up, but he was a good neighbor and growing into a friend, so the rare times he did smoke, I turned a blind eye.

"Hey, Detective."

"Morning, Ethan."

"How was your date?"

My apartment building wasn't super big, and most were elderly who loved to talk and crack open their doors to snoop on their neighbors. "I'd like to forget it."

"That's too bad. You know…" He knocked his shoulder into mine. "You and me really should get a bite."

I played along, even leaned into him a bit and said, "And when it's over, we'll live right across the hall from each other."

He went pale, and I laughed out loud.

He was a charmer, and there was always a different girl leaving his place in the morning. He wasn't hurting for company. And me…I had my cat. We stepped outside, a breeze brought goosebumps to my skin. "Catch ya later, Ethan."

"You make a valid point, but I'm not discouraged, Detective." He called back, walking backward, so he could keep me in his sights.

I laughed, turned from him and waved my hand over my head.

I'd been a homicide detective for six years. I wasn't the first woman detective, didn't want that responsibility. I didn't have a traumatic childhood or life-changing event that got me interested in law and order. I liked puzzles, liked solving them to uncover the story. And I liked being a voice for those who no longer had one. It wasn't the easiest job, downright sucked at times, but when we brought the perp to justice, it felt damn good.

It was my turn to bring in coffee, so I caught a cab and stopped at the corner café, before meeting up with Zac. He was already at his desk, head down, pen scratching over paper. I placed his large black coffee on his desk. He didn't even look up. "Thanks."

"What are you working on?" I asked.

"Retracing Samantha's last steps."

"Did you call her parents?"

He stopped working, his head lifted. It hit him hard, too. "Yeah." He leaned back in his chair and pulled a hand through his hair. "They're making arrangements, coming into the city to identify…" He blew out a breath. "Julia said she'd greet them when they arrived."

I dropped my hand on his shoulder. "It never gets easy."

"No, it doesn't. The story is out, too, printed in time for the morning run."

That was fast, but, sadly, a stabbing in the park wasn't uncommon.

My desk faced his. I sat down and took a sip of my coffee. "Why was she out running last night? Those receptions go well into the evening."

"Don't know, but she had a salon appointment yesterday and met someone by the name of Frank Harris at The Plaza for tea."

"The salon makes sense because she did go to a fancy reception. What did you learn about Frank?"

"Reporter for some online publication." Zac leafed through his notes. "Daily Examiner."

"Never heard of it. So what's his interest in Samantha James?"

"We'll have to ask him, but first, let's go to her apartment."

Zac drove. Traffic wasn't too bad because it was early. I'd called ahead; the super was waiting for us, an elderly man, kind eyes. "Is Sam okay?"

Zac and I shared a look. Samantha James had only been in the city for two months, but her super knew her, which meant she was either a pest, based on the concern looking back at us that was unlikely, or she was social…friendly.

"I'm sorry, but Samantha is dead. She was found last night in the park."

His expression fell; he reached out for the wall to steady himself. "I can't believe it."

"Did you know her?" I asked.

"She'd only been here a couple of months, but she had that kind of personality, you couldn't help but like her. Always had a smile and a hello. Nice kid."

"Do you know why she might have been out running last night?"

"She did it often. I warned her, but she was religious with her exercise. She liked to run in the morning, but if she missed it, she'd run at night. Yesterday, she said something about a salon day when she was leaving." He took a deep breath. "You'll find out who hurt her?"

"Yes," I answered, without hesitation. "We'd like to see inside her apartment."

He pulled the key ring linked to his belt and unlocked her door. He stepped back, and I handed him my card. "You remember anything, please call me."

"I will."

I closed the door, Zac was already moving through the apartment that was remarkably neat. "Whoever killed her wasn't looking for something, or if they were, she was carrying it," Zac observed.

He was right because otherwise the place would have been tossed. I strolled around the living room. It was pretty lived-in for someone who was only here temporarily. "He corroborated the salon appointment, but we'll call and confirm she was there and establish the timeline. When was she meeting Frank?" I asked.

Zac checked his notebook. "12:30pm."

"So she pampers herself at the salon. Goes to tea at the Plaza, spends part of her evening at the reception and ends her night with a run." At least her last day had been a good one.

"Her laptop is here, files," Zac said, using his pen to lift the cover on the top file. "We need the team to process this like yesterday." He reached for his phone to get an ETA.

"I'll call the salon to confirm when she was there, and then I say, we hunt down this Frank Harris," I suggested.

"Works for me."

THE DAILY EXAMINER office was actually an apartment in a walkup in Queens. There were boxes of papers lining the walls; the windows hadn't been cleaned in a while. A desk sat in the middle of the room, an old laptop on it. Frank Harris was in his forties, looking like a throwback to Woodstock. His hair was long and greasy, his glasses sliding off his nose. How did a man like this afford to take Samantha James to The Plaza for tea? One thing that was clear, whatever Frank's involvement, his shock at hearing that Samantha was dead was genuine. What I found curious was that I saw fear, too.

"I can't believe she's dead," he said, rubbing the back of his neck, as he paced in front of his desk. "I just talked with her yesterday."

"Where were you from eight to ten last night?" Zac asked.

"At home."

"Can anyone verify that?" I asked.

Frank clued in when his eyes went wide. "You think I hurt Samantha?"

"You were one of the last people to see her. We need to rule you out, so can anyone confirm your whereabouts?" I asked again.

"Yeah, my neighbor. She came over, and we watched a movie."

"Name?" Zac demanded, pulling out his notepad.

"Emily Duncan. Lives across the hall, apartment ten."

"Why the interest in Samantha?" Zac asked.

Frank stood and paced, not that he got far with all the boxes. For an online publication, he sure kept a lot of paper.

"Her boss," Frank said.

Zac didn't hide his surprise when he questioned, "Milton Teller? Why are you interested in Milton Teller?"

Frank stopped pacing and looked at us like we'd just beamed down from a spaceship. "Katrina Dent."

The name seemed vaguely familiar.

"Who's that?" Zac asked.

"You don't know…" Frank started to pace again. "Katrina Dent, the movie star." He stopped pacing. "None of this is ringing any bells?"

Zac and I shared a look. "Why are you interested in her?" I asked.

"Because she's dead."

Were we dealing with a potential serial killer? "When did this happen?" Zac had his pen to the paper.

"1989."

That was when Frank lost me. It took effort to hide my exasperation. I was all for conspiracy theories; I had a few of my own, but there was a fine line, and I suspected Frank, here, was on the wrong side of that line.

Zac was more patient. "Katrina Dent was murdered?"

"It was ruled a suicide, but I believe she was murdered."

And that's where he lost Zac.

While Zac rolled his eyes, I sought confirmation to my suspicions. "And Milton represented Katrina at the time of her death?"

"Yes," Frank said, then added, "I hoped that Samantha knew more about it, working for Milton. It was really big news back then."

"Did she?"

He hesitated, before he said, "No."

He wasn't telling us everything.

"Why do you think Katrina Dent was murdered?" Zac asked.

"Because she was terrified of razors. Had a bad experience as a kid," he said, waiting for us to connect the dots.

"And she was found—" I started, but he finished.

"Slit wrists. There are countless ways to kill yourself, ways that are more effective than slitting your wrists." He moved to one of the boxes, rummaged through it and pulled out some crime scene photos.

"How the hell do you have those?" Zac demanded.

"Case is closed, so the reports and photos are public record. Look," he said, but I already was. Katrina Dent looked like a movie star, even in the final picture of her life. Pretty and young, a life cut short way too soon. "There's no hesitation and the cuts were deep. Someone afraid of razors would have needed a few tries."

He made a good point, but then, in my experience, when someone was truly ready to end it, they had no hesitation. Almost like they were already gone and were just tying up the loose ends.

"And do you have theories on who killed her?" Zac was encouraging him. It was his way; he liked puzzles as much as me, but sometimes, it was best not to feed the delusion. To say Frank was mildly obsessed with Katrina Dent was fair since I was pretty sure all the boxes around the room were related to her case. He might not be playing with a full deck.

At Zac's question, Frank closed up. Like he didn't want to get scooped on his own story. "Nothing concrete."

Like hell. He probably had at least ten running theories, likely a crime board for each of them, but Katrina's death had nothing to do with Samantha James. We were done here. I touched Zac's arm. "You ready?"

"Yeah." He reached for his card and handed it to Frank. "You think of anything else about Samantha, call me."

Frank moved back to his desk, sat down. "Yeah, okay."

We stopped at Emily's to confirm his alibi, but she wasn't home. I waited until we were outside on the curb before I said, "You didn't need to encourage him."

"I know, but I couldn't help it. We've got detectives on the force who don't put that much effort into active cases, and he's still digging on a closed case that's over three decades old. Obsessed much."

"I'll confirm his alibi with Emily, but he was holding back."

"Yeah, he was. We need to talk to Samantha's parents."

"Alright, I'll schedule some time with them. What's next?"

Zac got that look, the one that meant he was going to stir shit up. "I say we go to the top, work our way down."

I just knew he was going to say that. "We need to tread lightly," I warned.

"We're just asking him a few questions."

"Alright, let's warn Cap," I said, reaching for the door of Zac's car. "You know how he gets about getting calls from the commissioner."

"Yeah, yeah. Call him, let him know we're paying Sinclair Rothschild a visit."

Zac hadn't drunk the Kool-Aid when it came to Sinclair Rothschild. Despite the man's good deeds, Zac didn't like him. A man with his wealth, Zac argued, tended to think he was above the law. He wasn't wrong, but Sinclair Rothschild's altruistic ways had helped so many in the city. Whatever Zac thought of him, the man did good things. That wasn't debatable.

He walked around his car and tapped the roof. "One thing you gotta acknowledge. This job is never boring."

He could say that again.

IT BLEW MY mind the wealth of some. Sinclair Rothschild was a billionaire, many times over. Walking through his Brownstone, one of many properties he owned, the display of wealth was overwhelming… decadent.

His butler showed us into a room that had oak walls and a highly polished wood floor, covered, in parts, by rugs that I was sure cost more than I made in a year. A fire, warming the cool spring morning, was burning in the fireplace that was big enough for a man to stand upright in. Old paintings in thick gold frames hung from the walls and windows that went from floor to ceiling were draped with dark green silk.

Sinclair sat behind a desk that looked like an antique. His white hair was a little long, and he was dressed in a smoking jacket and pants. As he walked from around his desk, my eyes traveled to the black loafers he wore with a gold emblem stitched on the top. Rings of platinum and gemstones sat on a few of his fingers. When he smiled, though, it reached his eyes, which was unusual because most people we interviewed weren't happy to see us.

"To what do I owe this visit from New York's finest?" he said, gesturing to the chairs around the fireplace. "Can I get you coffee?"

"No, thanks," I said, taking the seat closest to the door.

"Do you know Samantha James?" Zac asked, not bothering to sit.

Sinclair didn't answer. Instead, he said, "I'm going to have coffee. Joshua," he called. The man had been standing right at the door because he appeared like magic. "Coffee and pastries, please."

"Very good, Sir."

He looked back at Zac. "I'm sorry. You were saying?"

"Samantha James. Do you know her?"

"I can't say that I do."

"She was at your reception last night," Zac added.

Sinclair brushed unseen lint from his pants. "Half of Manhattan was at my reception, Detective." His eyes lifted to Zac when he asked, "Has something happened to her?"

"She was murdered last night." Zac was blunt, looking for Sinclair's reaction.

He had one when his face paled. "Oh, dear. Who was she?"

"A publicist who worked for Milton Teller," I offered.

Recognition swept his face before he said, "Milton. Now that's a name I haven't heard in a long time. And this Samantha worked for him."

"She was at your event because her client was there, Desiree McKenzie."

"Ah, now Desiree I do know. Heart of gold," he said, before leaning closer and lowering his voice. "Not the best actress, I'm afraid." He wasn't wrong about that. "Since I've got homicide detectives in my study, I'm guessing there's more to her death."

We didn't answer and that was an answer. Joshua appeared, pushing a cart with a silver coffee pot, china cups and saucers and a plate of mouthwatering pastries. Joshua didn't serve it, though. Sinclair did. "Are you sure I can't entice you with something?"

I caved because I was hungry. "Coffee, please. Cream and sugar."

"Very good, and you, Detective?" he asked Zac.

"No, thanks."

"As you wish." He handed me my coffee that I placed on the table next to me, before he held up the plate of goodies. I took one of the sticky buns because they looked amazing…gooey with golden raisins piled on the top. A plate and a cloth napkin followed, before he settled back in his chair with his coffee.

The sticky bun was mind-numbingly delicious.

"I wish I could help you."

"You can. We need a list of attendees from last night," Zac said.

We were working on getting the list, but this would be faster, not to mention it was a test to see how cooperative Sinclair would be. "Of course. Joshua?" He appeared again. I kind of wished I had a Joshua. "A list of names from last night, please."

"Yes, Sir."

"Whatever I can do, Detectives. The idea that such a beautiful evening ended in tragedy… However I can help, you have it."

Joshua returned with the list. Sinclair gestured to Zac, and Joshua handed it to him. "If you think of anything…" Zac said. He didn't give his card to Sinclair because I was sure he already had our numbers. He probably knew more about us than we did.

I finished my coffee and stood. I was tempted to take another sticky bun, but I didn't. "Thank you for the coffee and pastry."

"Sweet Escape on Fifth Avenue," Sinclair said with a smile. "They make the best sticky buns."

They sure the hell did. "I'll remember that," I said.

In the car, Zac was shaking his head. "You were having a mini love affair with that sticky bun."

"It was the best thing I ever tasted."

Another head shake.

"I like food. Sue me. Besides, we were doing good cop, bad cop."

"No, we weren't."

"And yet, it worked out that way. Look at us go."

"You're ridiculous sometimes."

"But awesome all the time."

He chuckled. "Who is on that list? Any names stand out?"

I reached for the list, scanned it and, oh, there was a name that stood out. "Kade Wakefield."

That turned Zac's head. "He was there?"

"He's on the list. Whether he attended is another story."

Kade Wakefield was an enigma: money and movie star good looks. He ran a multi-billion-dollar corporation with interests in everything from national security to toasters, but he hated publicity. Probably why the paparazzi loved him, his face showing up in countless tabloids every week. It also was known, but not proven, that his businesses weren't a hundred percent legal. To say the Feds were watching him, would be accurate.

"What are the chances we get a sit down with Kade Wakefield?" I asked.

Zac didn't miss a beat when he replied, "There's a better chance of Desiree McKenzie winning an Oscar."

THREE

Kade stood by the windows in his penthouse, his hands fisted in his pockets. Samantha James. Her name first mentioned to him last night, and this morning, she was dead. The cops loved connecting the dots, particularly when his name was in the mix. He'd have to entertain their questions, despite the fact that he couldn't pick Ms. James out of a lineup.

He didn't do anything on a whim, but agreeing to Penelope's suggestion of having Samantha interview for a position in the public relations department had been just that. Penelope had been with him from the beginning, his trusted right hand. She was also a bit of a Hollywood freak, and Samantha had worked for Milton Teller, representing Desiree McKenzie. Penelope saw stars. She'd argued that bringing in young blood to the public relations department might help pull in the younger generation, not that they had trouble with that demographic, since he owned several of the most trendy night clubs in the city, but he knew part of Penelope's suggestion was getting the chance to meet Desiree, someone Samantha would no longer represent if she'd gotten the job. He wasn't sure Penelope had thought her idea through, not that it mattered now. Samantha James had been a kid with a promising career and now she was dead.

"Mr. Wakefield. Levy is bringing the car around." Benson, like Penelope, had been with Kade from the beginning. He'd offered to set Benson up with his own place, offered him any job he wanted, but he wanted to tend to Kade. He understood. They had history; they were family, and Benson believed in earning his way.

"I'll be down in a minute. Thanks, Benson."

Kade turned back to the window. It was a beautiful day, but he suspected his day was going to be anything but beautiful. He crossed the room to the elevator; reaching for his jacket as he did, while wondering how long it would be before the NYPD was knocking on his door.

Two hours later, he had his answer. A detective Zac Ashton was requesting a meeting. He begrudgingly had to give it to the homicide detective. Samantha James wasn't high profile, but he wasn't letting any flies settle. That would be of some comfort to her family. He'd asked Penelope to send the detective in when he arrived. It wasn't going to be a long conversation because there was little Kade could tell him. Not taking the meeting would raise suspicion and he didn't have time for that bullshit.

He heard the knock before the door opened. He didn't look up from his papers when Penelope said, "Detectives Ashton and Donahue."

He glanced up then, his focus passing the tall man with dark hair and cop eyes, dressed in a cheap suit, and an even cheaper overcoat, and settled on the woman with him, a female homicide detective. She, too, was in a suit: a black pantsuit, a white button-down that looked like it might be a man's cut. Her black hair was pulled up into a knot. She wasn't wearing makeup and had the biggest, bluest eyes he'd every seen. Most women in his presence got that look. He wasn't being arrogant; he knew the appeal he had on women. He played on it sometimes, but this woman looked at him like he was, well, a suspect…cold and calculating. If she was sweating under her cotton shirt, he couldn't tell.

He stood and gestured to the chairs in front of his desk. "Please have a seat."

Ashton was the senior partner; it was subtle, the two played off each other well, but Ashton was the first to move. And when they sat, he was the first to talk.

"We're here about Samantha James." There was a touch of arrogance in Ashton's tone. Kade knew the type: hardworking, middle class, and not a fan of the rich, the entitled or the pampered. For a detective, making blanket assumptions was a hazard, but then Kade knew most of the time that assumption was right.

Not one to allow another to set the tone of a meeting, he ignored Aston and turned his attention to his partner. "Can I get you something to drink?"

Her eyes were mesmerizing. Not just the size and color, but, despite his earlier observation, there was a spark in them. Not so cool and calculating, but smart because she knew what he was doing.

"We're good, thanks."

On the outside, Kade had no reaction to her husky voice, but on the inside, it was like taking a hit to the gut. He held her stare, waited and wasn't disappointed to see interest…just a spark of it, but her pupils definitely dilated. He'd bet money she was sweating under her clothes now. The idea of peeling her out of them, so he could lick…

His reaction to her surprised him, but he shut it down and turned his attention to Ashton. "I can't tell you much about Samantha James. I'm aware she was at the reception last night, but our paths didn't cross. My assistant was working on getting her an interview for our public relations department. You might want to talk with her."

Ashton pulled out a notepad and jotted that down. "We'll do that." His eyes lifted. "Where were you between eight and ten last night?"

"The reception. Penelope can give you a list of people who can verify that."

The way Ashton snapped closed his notepad, he'd been hoping Kade would be less cooperative. The idea that they thought he was in anyway involved in the woman's death pissed him off, but he held that in, too. "May I ask what happened to her?"

"It's an active investigation," Ashton replied curtly.

The party line, he wasn't surprised by the reply. He was surprised when Donahue added, "She was stabbed in the park last night during a run."

Her partner was surprised, too, when his attention snapped to her. She didn't care, her focus lingering on Kade. She then took lead when she stood and offered her card. "Thanks for taking the time to see us. If you think of anything, please call me."

Kade didn't look at the card; his focus was on her. Her partner stood and walked to the door. She didn't move, deliberately waiting a beat, before she smiled and turned for the door, not looking back until she reached it. "We'll just have a word with your assistant and then we'll be on our way."

Kade nodded, and waited until the door closed, before he looked down at the card. Detective Molly Donahue. He ran his thumb over the embossed print before he slipped the card in his pocket. Taking his seat, he didn't get back to work. It sounded as if Samantha James had been a victim of a random killing. It was possible the detectives were just dotting the i's and crossing the t's, before the case went cold like so many did, or was there something more about her case that piqued their interest? Penelope was linked, however obscurely, to the investigation. He was, too, and he'd learned early on to never find yourself in a situation where you didn't know all the players. He reached for his private line and made a call. It was answered on the first ring. "Find out everything you can on Samantha James. Yes, the murder victim from last night." He almost ended the call, but then added, "Find out everything on homicide Detective Molly Donahue, too." He didn't wait for a reply and hung up. His first request was business, and it was smart. The second request was to appease his curiosity.

BRIDGET DUBOIS PICKED at her salad, had turned down the stuffed mushrooms, and the chicken parmigiana that had been the best he'd ever tasted. She was a super model, exquisite bone structure, long platinum blonde hair, lips that had been augmented but worked with her face, but she needed to eat a hamburger, a bacon double burger and fries. A milkshake wouldn't hurt, either. Kade reached for his glass of Duclot Bordeaux, studying his companion from over the rim, as he took a sip.

He couldn't keep the smile from his voice when he asked, "You'll not be wanting dessert I'm assuming."

"No, I've eaten too much already."

She'd eaten next to nothing.

"If you'll excuse me." Bridget didn't wait for him to reply. He knew she was going to the bathroom to purge. It was sad. He wouldn't be seeing her again. Trying to fix other people's problems wasn't his business, and he, honestly, had no desire to do it.

He'd picked this restaurant because he was contemplating becoming a silent partner. Several associates mentioned the place to him. After his first visit, he dined there regularly, toured the kitchen, and studied their financials, but the selling point for him was the food. He'd been to the finest restaurants in Italy, and this place could hold its own. Anita Valentino, owner and mastermind behind the recipes, was having trouble with the increased rent and taxes. It'd be a crime for the city to lose this little gem. He'd have his lawyer draw up the papers in the morning.

A woman at the bar caught his attention, or, rather, it was the black bandage dress she wore that showed off her curves to perfection. His eyes moved to her legs that were long and toned, ending in black stilettos that screamed sex. A jolt of heat raced through his veins. He rarely experienced so visceral a reaction to someone. He was around beautiful women all the time, but there was something about the curvy, raven-haired beauty that made his blood burn, and he hadn't even seen her face. She wasn't alone, a man stood at her side. From their body language, he was guessing it was a first date. He'd bet his bank account she wasn't into him by the way she held herself at a distance. A woman who dressed like that was open to the idea of connecting. She wanted to connect, and she had put the effort into the date. He found himself annoyed for her because the same couldn't be said of her companion. That had him studying the man. He was definitely out of his element. His clothes weren't his size, he kept pulling a hand through his hair and then he picked his nose. Kade wasn't surprised by a lot, but watching a grown ass man, on a date, picking his nose, what the fuck. The woman turned, Kade almost spit out the wine he'd just sipped. At first, he thought he was seeing things because he'd been thinking about Detective Donahue far more than he'd like to admit, so seeing her again, so soon, seemed serendipitous.

He couldn't help the smile because she was looking for an escape. He didn't act without weighing the options, but apparently, he was having a problem with that lately because he reached into his pocket for his phone. He didn't let himself think about the fact that he'd memorized her number. It rang, and she reached for it like a lifeline.

"Detective Donahue." There was hope in her voice, a murder to get her out of her date.

"Detective." He enjoyed the color that rose on her cheeks, her hand going to her hair, tucking a lock behind her ear. He liked it even more that she knew who he was by his voice. Oh yeah, there was definitely interest.

"Mr. Wakefield."

"Kade," he corrected.

He caught the grin before she replied, "Kade."

"Look to your right."

Her spine went stiff, seconds before she turned, her eyes roaming the dining area, growing wide when they landed on him. Her focus then shifted, and he followed it to see Bridget walking toward the table.

"Is that Bridget Dubois?" she asked, but not with the awe that Penelope would have had. It was simply stated.

"Yes. Do you need a rescue?"

That got him her eyes again, and a smile followed. His own moving to her lips, as something elemental burned through him. He wasn't taking no for an answer.

She said only one word, but all the scenarios that she could say that word to him had his pants growing snug. "Please."

He stood and disconnected the call, reached for Bridget's arm and escorted her to the door. "Something's come up. My driver will take you home."

Levy was already holding the door open for her.

"When will I see you again?"

She wouldn't be, but to her, he said, "We'll see if we can get something on the books."

She smiled at him. He kissed her cheek. Once she was in the car, he turned back to the restaurant. "I'll text you when I need you, Levy." He reached the door, glanced over his shoulder and added, "Thank you for taking her home."

Levy nodded, before climbing into the car. Kade didn't linger, strolling into the restaurant with determined strides. He caught sight of Molly, the stark desperation on her face. He could have played it in any number of ways, but he settled on taking her hand, not even acknowledging her date, and pulling her from the restaurant. She went willingly, almost running to keep up with him. He waited until they were halfway down the street before he looked over at her because feeling her small hand in his brought on a wave of protectiveness. The sensation was a foreign one.

Her face was flush, and her eyes bright. "I owe you," she said, her husky voice a little breathless.

He studied her face. She wasn't wearing much makeup: just a little mascara and her lips were tinted. Her hair was down, falling in soft waves around her face. He'd just dined with the hottest super model of the time, but the woman at his side was the one who stirred his blood.

"You didn't eat." He wasn't asking.

"I didn't. Two nights in a row."

His brow rose at that.

She waved it off. "I think I need to take a break from dating."

The almost primal reaction he had to that alarmed him. He ignored it. "I know a place."

She stopped walking. "But you just ate."

"You didn't."

"I'll order a pizza."

He let his eyes wander over her body, and the luscious curves that were on display for his viewing pleasure. There was no way he was letting her go home. Not yet. "You're already dressed."

Her mouth opened to object, but he could see she didn't want to. He made it easy for her when he said, "You owe me."

Her eyes narrowed before she smiled. "And taking me to dinner is what you want."

He let those words hang in the air between them, for a few seconds, before he replied, "Please."

The heat behind those blue eyes had him clenching his jaw because, fuck, he wanted her. He didn't even know her, but he wanted her. He should be going in the other direction. He knew better; instead, he held her hand tighter. When he started walking, she was right there with him.

FOUR

MOLLY

I felt his eyes on me, those intense gray eyes that shared nothing. He watched me almost dispassionately, and yet, he'd rescued me from another horrible date and insisted on feeding me. I focused on my food because I couldn't actually believe I was here. In his office earlier, the man seemed almost untouchable, and, undeniably, beautiful with his chiseled features, dark hair that a woman just wanted to pull her hands through and those stormy gray eyes. The way he read the room, picking up on Zac's penchant for jumping to conclusions when it came to the wealthy. He'd agreed to see us, didn't make us wait, and had been forthcoming. We couldn't have asked for more. Hearing his voice on the phone, deep with a hint of an accent I couldn't place, was one I'd know anywhere. I'd been desperately looking for a way out of my evening. I never in a million years would have thought my rescue would be at the hand of Kade Wakefield.

The heat of the curried shrimp lingered on my tongue. I was tempted to scrape my fork over the china to get the last drop of sauce, but I controlled the urge. Placing my fork down, I lifted my gaze to his. "That was amazing." He was studying me, the only word to describe it. I felt self-conscious, but I pushed past it and looked around the club. He'd brought me to Polar. I'd heard of it, had never been inside. There was dancing, a bar that was shoulder-to-shoulder, waitresses in tight tees, skirts and three inch heels walking around balancing trays loaded with drinks, but we were on the other side of the club. A jazz ensemble was on the stage, the tables covered in linen cloths, and the waitstaff were dressed a bit more formally in black and white.

I reached for my glass of wine and turned my attention back to the man opposite me. "Thank you for the rescue." I took a sip, holding his stare.

"Anytime."

I grinned, couldn't help it, because it was just something people said, but the thought of calling Kade Wakefield, every time I needed rescuing from a date, held its appeal, and considering my string of bad luck, I'd be calling him a lot.

His focus was on my mouth, and I swear his eyes looked darker. He didn't move his gaze when he stated, "He wasn't right for you."

"Those dating sites are not all they're cracked up to be," I said, taking another sip of wine.

His focus jerked to my face. "Why are you using a dating site?"

There was a bite to his words, and I couldn't lie, it felt nice hearing disbelief in his voice. "I don't have a lot of free time, and my circle is pretty limited." I shrugged and placed my glass down. "Those sites open up my circle."

He reached for his whiskey; his accent, a little more pronounced, when he said, "Whatever site paired you with him doesn't know shit."

Those words shouldn't have had the effect on me they did, but I actually felt them, a slow wave of warmth that moved from my head right down to my toes. I shook myself out of it. This was Kade Wakefield. The man had just dined with Bridget Dubois. We didn't move in the same circle; hell, he wasn't even on the same plane.

"Bridget is even more beautiful in real life," I said.

He didn't reply, just placed his glass on the table.

The waiter returned and asked, "Would you like dessert?"

Kade looked at me and waited for my reply. I'd love dessert, but there was no way I could eat it. It was with regret when I said, "No, thanks. I'm good."

Kade studied me again, reading me perfectly, when he said, "The spicy chocolate cake to go, and the check."

"Very good."

"You're very good at reading people," I said on a chuckle, looking around the club again.

He had no reply, but he did ask, "Why a homicide detective?"

I dropped my elbows on the table, meeting his stare. "I like puzzles. As a detective, I have the final image, but I have to go back and figure out how all the pieces come together."

He held my stare and asked, "But why the dead? Why not something less brutal?"

"Because all the beauty of a life is overshadowed when someone is murdered. It's like their whole life is summed up with how they died and not who they were. I give them a voice, and, hopefully, peace when I bring their killer to justice."

"You grew up in the city?" he asked.

"I grew up in Jersey, Marlton. Went to Columbia and stayed. I love it here."

"Siblings?"

"No, it's just me. Mom and Dad had me later in life. They had all but given up on having children, and then they had me. My birthday is in December, so they call me their miracle." I liked the way he listened, the way I held his undivided attention, as if there was no one else in the room. What would it feel like to be his? The thought came out of nowhere, but it lingered. "Where are you from? Your accent, I can't place it."

The waiter appeared to drop off my dessert and the check. Whatever spell had been weaving between us broke. Kade reached for his wallet, dropped a few bills in the black folder, then stood. "I should get you home."

I was disappointed, sure, but then I never thought I'd be here, so I really couldn't look at the evening as anything but what it was, unexpected and awesome.

He had me precede him from the club. Stepping outside, a black car was waiting. A man was holding the door open. "Levy will take you home."

I thought Kade was joining me, but he didn't move from his place on the sidewalk. "Are you not coming?"

"No."

I wondered what brought on the change. It was tempting to ask him, but I could read people, too, and knew it'd be a wasted effort. I didn't immediately climb into the car, lingered longer than was polite, because how often would I be this close to this man. He really was beautiful. I wasn't in his fan club, didn't follow his every move like so many did. To me, he was much like the stars…beautiful and completely untouchable. Our paths crossed under unfortunate circumstances, but whatever it was that had us bumping into each other tonight, fate or just plain old luck, I knew I'd always remember the evening. "Thank you for dinner and the rescue."

He said nothing, just watched me. I smiled then climbed into the car. He was standing there, his hands in his pockets, his focus on me. Our gazes locked when he said, "Good night, Miss Donahue."

The door closed, but the glass was tinted. I didn't want to look away, so I didn't. I'd have really liked a few more hours, hell, days, weeks, months to get to know the man, under the stoic image, but that was as likely to happen as Bridge Dubois becoming my new best friend.

Levy folded himself behind the wheel. I gave him my address, keeping my eyes on Kade until we pulled away. I even looked back, and he was still there. I didn't settle back on the seat until Kade was out of sight. Despite how abruptly the evening had ended, it had been amazing. I watched as the scenery changed, my smiling face reflecting back at me.

TOM AND GRACE James tried hard to control their tears, but they weren't successful. I'd brought in a box of tissues and some coffee. The interview was taking longer than we planned, but Zac and I didn't push them because no parent should go through what they were.

"I'm sorry," Mr. James said. Wiping at his eyes.

"Take your time," Zac said softly.

"No. You need to find the man who did this." Right before our eyes, we watched strength infuse him, tapping into his reserve for his daughter. I was having trouble holding back my own tears because the James family reminded me of my own. Samantha was an only child, was conceived later in life. She'd been a decade younger than me, and now, she was gone. We'd find out who did this.

"Samantha had been with Milton for about a year. She was initially covering a few local businesses, but Milton said she had the personality and the drive to move into one-on-one representation. He still had a few clients from back in the day. He was taking it slow, giving Samantha a client at a time. She'd been representing Desiree for four months, and Milton was right. Samantha was a perfect fit. And she loved it." His voice broke with that last part.

When we went through Samantha's phone, she had quite a few correspondences with a man we had trouble locating. "Do you know Terence Baker?"

"He was an acquaintance of Samantha's," Mrs. James said. "They met in a chat room or something. Common interests. He works in public relations, too."

"Did you know that Samantha was planning on interviewing for a position that would have kept her in New York?" Zac asked.

Both of their faces lit up before they fell. "No, but she would have loved that," Mrs. James said on a sob. She pulled it together and added, "We could tell when we spoke with her how much she loved Manhattan."

"Do you know Frank Harris?" Zac asked.

"No." Mr. James' expression shifted to fury. "Is he—"

"No. We're just linking all the pieces," Zac said, cutting him off.

"When can we take our daughter home?" Mr. James asked.

"I'll walk you down to Julia. You can make the arrangements," Zac offered.

"Please keep us in the loop," Mrs. James whispered.

"Absolutely."

"WE'VE GOT NOTHING," Zac said, as he paced behind his desk. "We've got no suspect, no motive." Zac stopped moving and pulled a hand through his hair.

"We're missing something," I said, flipping through our file.

"You think so, too," Zac said, yanking out his chair and dropping down into it.

"It's her cause of death. Methodical. A random attack wouldn't have been so precise. She hadn't been unlucky; she was the target." I leaned back in my chair and met Zac's gaze. "But why?"

"No fucking clue." He reached for his coffee. "So I heard something earlier."

I knew what was coming because nothing ever went unnoticed in this city.

"We ran into each other."

"I've never run into him," Zac said, taking a long drink of his coffee. "Not once. And if memory serves, you've never run into him before either. Funny, how on the day we visit him, during a murder investigation, you run into him."

The thought had crossed my mind. I wouldn't be much of a cop if it hadn't, but my gut told me Kade Wakefield had nothing to hide. Well, he had a lot to hide, but not in regards to Samantha James' murder.

"He's not involved," I said.

"Doesn't look like it, but it's a hell of a coincidence, and you know me and coincidences."

"He didn't have to see us, he didn't have to point us to his assistant, but more to the point, he's smart…building the empire he has, he has to be. And he reads people well; you noticed that I'm sure. So him running into me, he'd know how that would look. He wouldn't make such a mistake."

"All valid points. Still."

I glanced at my watch. "We gotta go," I said, standing and reaching for my jacket.

"Where are we going?"

I flashed him a smile. "We've got ten minutes with Desiree McKenzie."

Zac was out of his chair. "How the hell did you manage that?"

"It was easier than you'd think. I called her. Her assistant fit us in."

"Nice job, Molly."

"I have my moments. Not sure we'll get anything from her, but maybe she can tell us more about Samantha."

"Yeah, I've got a call in with Milton Teller for that reason," Zac added; his steps a little hurried.

I couldn't help the grin when I asked, "You in a rush, Zac?"

He flashed me a smile when we hit the elevator. "Desiree McKenzie."

Another star falling from the heavens…I understood completely.

SOME MOVIE STARS could pass as mere mortals, when they weren't all dolled up for movie sets, and then there were some who stood out, no matter what. Desiree was the latter. She greeted us in yoga pants and a tee. She wasn't wearing makeup, her hair was pulled up into a pony-tail, and still, she could stop traffic. Zac was feeling a little tongue-tied by the way his normally fast-paced questions were dragging. I made sure to take notes because I suspected he was missing half of what Desiree was saying.

She wasn't much of an actress, and I'd always thought she was a bit of an airhead based on interviews I'd seen her give, but that was all part of her image because the woman sitting with us now was articulate and thoughtful and also sad.

"Samantha had only just started representing me. We'd been together for only four months. She was good, though. On top of every-thing, always looking for new ways to promote me." She sniffled and reached for a tissue. "She was trying to get me to change my image, encouraged me to think about being more than a face."

She'd be offered more roles if she showed this part of herself to the world. Was it possible she couldn't act because she was being something she wasn't? I moved on from that. "Samantha was with you at the recep-tion?" I asked.

"Yes. We didn't leave together, though. I had an early morning, so I really only made an appearance. She was having fun, her first celebrity event. When you're around it all the time, you forget what it's like… the glam of it."

"We've learned that she was approached about another position," Zac offered.

Desiree's surprise wasn't feigned. "I didn't know that, but I can't say I'm surprised. Milton took me on as an unknown child actress because he and my dad are friends. He's been moving away from the Hollywood scene. His publicists now support local politicians and businesses. His influence and foothold in Hollywood has dwindled. Samantha loves—" She looked down and corrected herself. "Loved the part of the job that Milton is moving away from, so I'm not surprised she was looking for something else. She really loved the city, the life…all of it."

"Can you think of anyone who would want to hurt her? Did she have trouble with anyone?" I asked.

"Publicists don't have an easy job, but she never mentioned anything. Milton would know better than me, though."

"Did she have a boyfriend?" Zac asked.

"No. Her focus was her work, and she was good. She had a way about her that you couldn't help but like. She could get her way but have you smiling as she did." Her eyes grew bright. "She had a hell of a career ahead of her. It's just so horrible and senseless."

"If you think of anything…" Zac said, handing Desiree his card. "Thank you for seeing us."

"Find whoever did this to her," Desiree said.

Zac nodded. Her assistant appeared to see us out. Like Rothschild's man, Joshua, she had to have been waiting at the door.

Outside her Brownstone, Zac looked back at the apartment when he said, "She's not what I expected." His focus lingered for a second before he started for his car.

"More than a pretty face," I said.

We got into the car; he started it up. "We got to find the piece we're missing."

I knew what he was thinking because I was, too. Murder was awful, a young victim made it even worse, but when they were good, decent… it was a triple hit.

"We'll find it." But I wasn't so sure we would.

SALEM WAS CURLED up in my lap. It was late. I needed sleep, but my mind wouldn't rest. I'd been thinking about Samantha's case, but for the last hour, my thoughts were on Kade Wakefield. My blood heated just thinking about him. Untouchable and out of reach, but for a few hours, he hadn't been. Funny how someone I'd never really thought about now lingered in the back of my mind. He had stoic down, and you couldn't help but watch him, waiting for him to give you something. And he had, a few times, a flash in those eyes, the slightest curving of his lips. Even just hearing him say *please* had my pulse jumping.

He'd asked quite a few questions about me, but when I asked one about him, he ended the night. Why?

I reached for my laptop, stirring Salem who jumped off the sofa. He'd be back. That was his way of telling me he was displeased with being disturbed.

I did a search on Kade Wakefield, tons of paparazzi pictures popped up, pictures taken from wide angle lenses: Kade getting into his car, going into buildings. There weren't many of him with women, but the women he socialized with were all celebrities.

For a person in the spotlight, there was surprisingly little on him. That was consciously done, took a lot of effort, but then he had an incentive to keep things close to the chest since, allegedly, his business dealings weren't all above board. Were any of those relative to the case? My gut was saying no.

I shut my laptop. I could dig deeper. I had the resources, but it felt wrong to invade his privacy, particularly since I had no credible reason to dig, except curiosity, and I was curious about Kade Wakefield.

A story on the news pulled my attention. Reaching for the remote, I turned up the volume. "CyberTech will be unveiling their new bionic division, with far reaching revolutionary science." The newscaster turned to her co-caster. "It's like something right out of the movies."

Salem jumped back up on the sofa and curled into me. "Bionic division? Technology catching up to fiction," I said. "That's pretty damn cool."

A picture of Carmine DeLuca filled the screen. "In other news, Carmine DeLuca was seen attending an event for presidential hopeful Brian Gaines. The charismatic DeLuca, who allegedly has ties to organized crime, is putting his money behind young front-runner Brian Gaines in his run against the incumbent President Baker."

Carmine was charismatic and loved, despite his possible link to the mob, a true New York icon. Still, if he was mob connected…"History is repeating itself, Salem. Alleged crime bosses helping get a candidate in the White House. Didn't work out so well the last time." I hoped that wasn't the case, this time, because I liked Brian Gaines. The story reminded me of the function on Friday, and I bit back a moan. I didn't get into politics, but the NYPD was hosting a fundraiser for some of the local politicians, and as a detective, I was required to be there. Fantastic.

IT WAS UNSEASONABLY warm, so I was taking advantage and walking through the park, but first, I needed lunch. I didn't know what it was about vendor dogs, but they were so good, with spicy mustard and relish, hard to top that.

A fancy black car caught my attention. I could admit I looked for it because despite not moving in the same circle as Kade Wakefield, I'd enjoyed the time I'd spent with him, and I sure as fuck liked looking at him. It pulled up across the street, moments before he stepped from the building. He was dressed in a dark gray suit, with a shirt and tie that matched his eyes. I still had trouble believing that I'd had dinner with him. That he had, not only saved me from a horrible date, but had bought me dinner. I wasn't sure how the stars aligned for that to happen, but I wanted them to align again. He had said I could call him, anytime. I bit back the laugh because I wanted to call him.

His head lifted, his eyes catching mine from over the roof of his car, and I swear my legs went weak. I'd never experienced anything like it, but to say I was attracted to Kade Wakefield was an understatement. He didn't smile or wave, I hadn't expected him to, but getting those eyes, knowing that, on some level, he was aware of me, too, it felt good.

I was smiling when I turned to the vendor to order my lunch. I was just adding the relish when I heard, "Detective."

I almost dropped my hot dog. Turning around, Kade Wakefield stood behind me. He'd lost the jacket and tie, the top two buttons of his shirt undone, drawing my gaze to the tan skin of his neck. I had the strongest urge to kiss him there.

"Lunch?"

That voice, I almost closed my eyes and imagined him saying a few choice things with that deep tenor, but instead, I asked, "Would you like a hot dog?"

His gaze drifted to the street vendor; he looked skeptical.

I made the decision for him. "Another dog, Bobby."

"You know the vendor by name?"

"I make it a habit to know the people who feed me."

"You like food."

"I love food, and with my schedule, I'm usually dependent on others to make it for me. Learning their names is a small way for me to show I appreciate them."

"Here you go, Molly." I turned to Bobby, took the hot dog and gave him a five. "Keep the change."

I handed the dog to Kade. "What's your poison?" I asked, and gestured to the condiments.

"Usually ketchup." The thought of him eating something as simple as a hot dog was hard to imagine, but he hadn't always been the man he was now.

"May I suggest spicy mustard and relish?"

His brow rose slightly.

"Trust me. It's heaven."

To my surprise and delight, he took my suggestion, and then in unspoken agreement, we headed to the park.

I took a bite, looked over at him and waited. He took a bite, chewed, glanced over and said, "Better than ketchup."

It was silly, such a small concession, but coming from Kade Wakefield, I couldn't help but smile because I suspected he didn't concede often. His focus moved to my mouth and like Pavlov's dog, my body reacted to that look when my heart slammed into my ribs. Was it possible he wanted to taste me as badly as I wanted to taste him? Needing to change the subject, I asked the first thing that popped into my head, well, that didn't involve us naked. "What's your favorite meal?" I resisted the urge to roll my eyes. I asked questions for a living and that was the best I could come up with?

Silence followed. I glanced over; he was watching me. "Why? You going to cook for me, Detective?"

If I got him alone, food would be the last thing I'd be thinking about. His eyes grew darker, his voice rougher when he said, "Steak and potatoes. You?"

I focused on my hot dog, bite, chew...the attention to the mechanics helped keep me from traveling down a mental path that led to us getting naked, a reaction to a man I'd never experienced so viscerally or so early. It was during the routine of chewing that I realized he'd asked me a question. I was kind of abrupt because I really liked the thought of us getting naked. "I'm on a salmon kick, love a nicely grilled piece of salmon." I took another bite, kept myself distracted with thoughts of food and remembered the cake he bought me during our dinner. "Oh…" I glanced his way, "That spicy chocolate cake was life changing."

His eyes showed the humor before his lips tipped up. "Life changing?"

"It changed my life." And, in a sense, it had because, however loosely linked, he was the one to introduce me to it, the same man I was now walking through the park with, while battling the headiest attraction I'd ever experienced.

"I'll have to let Carrie know," he said.

It was only then it dawned. "You own Polar." He didn't answer, but he didn't need to. "Well, yes, then please tell Carrie that cake is the best cake I've ever tasted. And I'm a sweet loving kinda gal."

He studied me before he said in a low drawl, "I'll have to keep that in mind."

I felt chills, from my head right down to my toes, that this man was keeping anything about me in mind.

We finished our lunch. I studied him from the corner of my eye. The man was a mogul, one of the richest men in the world, with the responsibilities to match, so did he get times like this to shake off that responsibility? "Do you get to do this often?" I asked, earning me his attention. "Doing nothing more than strolling through the park eating a hot dog."

"No." But I heard the weight of that word.

"Well, next time, I'll introduce you to the gyro man on Fifth Avenue. It's all in the spices."

Warmth moved into his gaze. So distracted with him, I didn't realize we were back on the street. His car was waiting. "Can I give you a ride?" he asked.

With how I was feeling, I wasn't sure being in close quarters with him was wise. "Thanks, but I'm going to walk. Enjoy the weather."

He nodded, turned to get into his car but stopped, looked back and said, "Thank you for lunch."

"Anytime, Kade."

Silence settled as the air practically zapped between us. His voice was a rough whisper when he said, "Noted."

I didn't move, wasn't sure my legs were up to the task of walking just yet, so I watched as his car mingled with the midday traffic, before getting lost in it.

IT WAS FRIDAY; I dragged my feet through the halls of the hotel where the fundraiser was being held. Entering the banquet hall, it was like a wall of blue. I was in my dress blues, surprised they still fit me because it had been awhile.

I recognized a few politicians, Brian Gaines being one of them, talking to the captain and the commissioner. I saw Rothschild with his man, Joshua, and spotted Carmine DeLuca talking to a tall gentleman who I recognized, Gregory Enzi, the son. It was a who's who; both sides of that line in the sand that represented law and order were in attendance. My focus shifted to the buffet and bar. Alcohol seemed like a good idea.

"I hate this shit."

My attention turned to Zac and then I took a step back and checked him out from head to toe. "Damn, Zac. You look good."

He pulled at his collar. "I'm not staying long."

"I hear that."

"I'm getting a drink. You want one?"

"Yeah, wine, red."

I watched Zac beeline to the bar, then looked for a dark corner we could hang out in, and it was while scanning the crowd that I saw Kade Wakefield. He was talking to a few circuit court judges, but his eyes were on me. In the next breath, he was crossing the room. I didn't hide that I was checking him out because no one should look that good. He was in a tux, and wore it so naturally. And the way he moved, controlled and deliberate, damn, he was sexy as sin.

"Detective."

And that voice. "Kade."

His lips tipped up, as his gaze drifted down my body. "That's a good look on you."

My blood wasn't just racing, it was heating up.

"I was thinking the same about you."

Those eyes went stormy before he said, "You've created a monster."

I wasn't sure where that was going, but I loved the note of humor I heard in his voice. "How so?"

"I've had hot dogs for lunch for the last two days."

"They're good, right?" I said, and then took the risk and added, "Besides my gyro connection, there are a few other choice places I'll share with you, so you can switch it up a bit."

He didn't miss a beat. "I look forward to it."

Oh my god. I had the green light. He could just be saying that, but I suspected, Kade Wakefield only said what he meant, which meant he wanted to see me again, too. I almost pinched myself because this couldn't be happening.

Someone called his name; he glanced over, before his focus shifted back to me. "Enjoy your evening, Molly."

"You, too, Kade."

Zac returned. "Were you just talking to Kade Wakefield?" he asked, handing me my drink.

"Just saying hi."

"Hmm, he doesn't just say hi to me."

I glanced at Zac and grinned. "Jealous?"

"Of his bank accounts? Hell, yeah."

"Alright, let's finish these drinks and then I say we ditch this and go for pizza," I suggested.

"Right on, partner."

FIVE

Frank pushed his glasses up on his nose and flipped through his notebook, his fingers tapping on his keyboard. His heart was pumping, his pulse racing, because he cracked it. He loved journalism; he loved putting the pieces together. He loved how pulling on a string could lead to the story of a lifetime. He knew there was more to what happened to Katrina Dent. He knew no one believed him. They thought he was a crackpot, a man so desperate for a story, he was willing to create one, but now, he had the proof.

His fingers flew over the keyboard, as he transcribed his shorthand, trying to get the story on paper. Katrina Dent's death had been just the tip of the iceberg. Never in a million years would he have thought the story he was working on, the one he'd spent the better part of a decade researching, would be so juicy. He smiled, as sweat rolled down his back. He'd get the Peabody Award for this story; fuck, he might even get the Pulitzer.

It wasn't just murder, but conspiracy, blackmail…he was practically salivating with the juice he'd dug up.

He didn't hear the lock to his apartment turning. Didn't see the figure in black slip soundlessly into the room. He saw the shadow too late, feeling the cold steel pressed against his neck; he didn't even have time to scream before he died.

The killer left the knife, but took the hard drive and notebook, before he doused the room with lighter fluid and lit it up. He made one other stop in the building before he left by the backstairs. In the alley, he saw the smoke bellowing out of the window. He was two blocks away when he heard the sirens.

SIX
MOLLY

They didn't care if they took out the whole fucking building," Zac hissed, as we looked at what remained of Frank Harris' apartment. Luckily, the firefighters had been able to put it out fairly quickly, before it caused devastating damage.

"Throat was slit. I'll know more when I get him on the table," Julia said.

"Hard drive is gone," I observed, looking around at the boxes that were all charred now. "If he was working on his computer, probably a notebook was taken, too."

"Then they torched the rest," Zac said, then added, "Just strolled into his apartment, slit his throat, and lit the place up." He turned to me. We were thinking the same thing. "He meets with Samantha. She ends up dead, and now, he's dead. That's not a coincidence."

"No," I agreed. "Shifts the investigation. Maybe he really was onto something with Katrina Dent."

"My thoughts, too," Zac said. "How the hell does an old suicide case of a Hollywood starlet fit into this?"

"We've got another body," a uniform said from the door.

Julia moved, and we followed her. Zac caught my eye. Apartment ten was Emily Duncan's apartment, Frank's friend.

Her apartment was across the hall from his, so it had some fire damage, definitely would have gotten smoke. Her body was face down in the living room. It looked like the smoke got to her.

As soon as Julia looked up at us, we knew. "Her neck was broken."

Shit. There was no longer any question that the deaths now were related to Katrina Dent.

There was one person on our list who had known Katrina. We needed to talk to him. Looking at Zac, I knew he was thinking what I was. "We need to pay Milton Teller a visit."

Later that afternoon, we were pulling into the Chadds Ford police station. It was a courtesy, since we weren't on our turf. Captain Jamison was waiting for us.

"How was the drive?" he asked.

"Long," Zac said.

That earned a chuckle from the captain, but then he sobered. "You've got three bodies."

"Yeah, and, somehow, one of Milton's former client's death is related."

Captain Jamison didn't hide his interest, and on purely an investigative standpoint, the case was fascinating. "I'm curious how this plays out."

"We'll keep you posted," Zac offered.

"Did some recon. Milton is at his winery." Jamison handed Zac a post-it. "That's the address. If he's not there, call me. We'll find him," Jamison offered. "He's a good guy. Decent. A little scattered, but he makes a hell of a Cabernet, well, at least according to my wife."

The drive to the vineyard was beautiful, lots of open land and stone farmhouses. The entrance to the vineyard was understated, two stone columns and Teller Vineyard over it in metal. The driveway was long and then opened to grapevines, for as far as the eye could see. There was a huge stone house to the right and a large building for the winery to the left. We parked and climbed from the car.

Zac looked around. "Nice place."

He wasn't wrong. Two golden retrievers greeted us when we entered the winery. I'd never been to a winery before. There was a long bar and some tables, the tasting center, based on the woman who was pouring wine into little cups and talking to a few guests. Her attention turned to us, when the guests started sampling the pale, wheat colored wine she'd just poured.

"Can I help you?"

"We're looking for Milton Teller," Zac said.

"Is he expecting you?" she asked.

We flashed our badges. "It won't take long."

Her eyes went wide before she glanced at the guests. My guess, she didn't want to bring any more attention to us when she disappeared in the back, returning a few minutes later. "This is Eddie. He'll take you to Milton."

We nodded then followed Eddie. I was fascinated. I liked wine but never saw how it was made. There were large stainless-steel canisters, rows of them, and tucked off to the side were stone rooms filled with barrels. We found Milton there, sampling wine right from a barrel. He glanced over at us. He knew who we were by the look in his eyes. He had just lost an employee. It wasn't a leap that he'd be getting a visit.

"I'm Detective Ashton, and this is my partner, Detective Donahue. We have some questions."

He handed his glass to Eddie. "Let's walk," he offered.

We stepped outside; the dogs joined us, as we strolled through the vines. "I'm sorry I didn't call you back. Honestly, I was processing the news of Samantha's death. I've..." He looked down and took a deep breath. "It's been a long time since I've gotten news like that. Have you found her killer?"

"Not yet."

"When will you release her body?"

"Not sure, but her parents are in the city."

"Poor Tom and Grace. No parent should ever have to get such news. Anything I can do, please let me know."

"Thank you. What can you tell us about Katrina Dent?" Zac asked.

Surprise moved over his expression. "Why do you want to know about Katrina?"

"We have reason to believe the cases are somehow linked," I offered.

He looked how we felt. Incredulous. "Seems unlikely. Katrina died so long ago."

"What do you remember about her death?" Zac asked.

"It was the first and only time I had a client die." Milton's focus shifted to the line of grapevines as he remembered. "I won't lie. I was surprised by her suicide because Katrina had just gotten the role of a lifetime, one that screamed Academy Award." Zac glanced my way, as Milton continued, "But Katrina did have mental health issues. She'd suffered her whole life, and back then, doctors weren't as good with identifying mental illness. A new role that brought with it added pressure and anxiety, not to mention her pending marriage, I guess it was just too much for her."

Zac jumped on that tidbit. "What was the name of her fiancé?"

"Jason Benjamin." Milton's face twisted a bit. "Don't know what happened to him. After Katrina died, he kind of fell off the face of the earth."

My cop senses perked up with that bit of knowledge. "What did Jason do?" I asked.

"He was very involved with Katrina's career, but before that, I don't know."

"And they lived in LA?" Zac asked.

"Katrina was from Brooklyn, but when she hit fame, they moved to LA."

"And Jason?"

"I don't know very much about him, which is unusual, considering I represented Katrina."

"I wonder if the investigating officer knows more about Jason Benjamin?" I was thinking out loud.

"Well, he might, but he isn't in law enforcement anymore," Milton offered. "He's a senator now. Still lives in LA, though."

"I wonder if we can get his files on the case," Zac said, pulling out his phone to have someone at the station make the request. Frank had them, so I didn't see a reason for us not to.

"May I ask why you think what happened to Samantha is related to Katrina?"

Maybe Milton knew Frank. Frank had certainly been interested in Milton. "Do you know a man name Frank Harris?" I asked.

Milton thought on it before he said, "No."

"Frank Harris was working on a story, Katrina Dent's story. He was convinced she was murdered. He took Samantha to lunch to pepper her with questions because of her link to you."

"Okay."

"Frank Harris was murdered last night, as was his friend," Zac stated.

Milton paled, but he was following the logic. "Which makes Katrina's death of interest."

"Yes."

Shock shifted to anger. "So you're thinking Samantha was murdered because she'd been out with this Harris fella?"

"We had no motive for her death. Frank showing up dead, his friend's death—the only other person who could possibly have known about the story he was working on. Knowing that Frank met with Samantha, her death on the same day of that meeting. It's weak, but it's motive."

"Poor Samantha," Milton whispered. His voice grew stronger when he asked, "You will find who did this?"

"Yes."

"Anything I can do," he offered.

"Thank you," Zac replied.

MY FEET WERE up on my desk. Tossing coins into a cup, as I rolled the facts around in my head.

"Samantha meets Frank for lunch. That night, she ends up dead. Frank Harris then shows up dead a couple of days later. Emily too. If Katrina Dent's murder plays into this, why didn't they take out Frank before he met up with Samantha?"

"That's bothering you, too?" Zac asked.

I stood and started to pace. "Okay, so let's say Katrina Dent was murdered. The killer got away with it for three decades." I stopped pacing. "Samantha worked for Milton Teller, Katrina's publicist. She comes to Manhattan and has lunch with Frank Harris." I rustled through the case file. "Frank Harris' cell records. Look up this number." Zac got on his computer. I gave him the number. *New York Times*."

"And this one?"

"*Huntington Post.*"

We went through the last eight calls Frank made, and all of them were for news outlets. My gaze collided with Zac's, just as he said, "He figured it out."

"Yeah, he got his story," I added.

"And someone is watching him closely. He goes to lunch with Samantha. They look into who she is and discover she works for Milton. The killer doesn't think it's a coincidence," Zac says.

My heart dropped. "They thought she was Frank's source."

"Yeah. Take her out. Days later, Frank starts calling around, preparing for his story to hit. Confirmation to the killer they were right about Samantha. But they wait to see what he knows. If they were watching him, and you know they were, he was very hushed about his story. He clammed up on us. But maybe not the girl across the hall he watches movies with," Zac reasoned.

"So the killer wasn't worried the story would go any farther than Emily," I added.

"Exactly. The only way that story was getting out was Frank's article, one he wanted every outlet to pick up."

"Killer discovers the phone calls to the media, takes out Frank and Emily, takes the hard drive and torches the rest of the research and the secret of Katrina Dent's death is, once again, buried."

Zac and I had the same thought when I said, "There's a chance that Milton could be in danger." But Zac was already reaching for his phone.

"Jamison is going to put a car on him," Zac said, as he disconnected the call.

I dropped down in my chair. "So, if Samantha, Frank and Emily were all murdered because of Katrina Dent, then was her death a suicide? And if not, who the hell killed her? Why did they kill her? And how is it still relevant thirty-one years later?"

"All good questions," Zac said. "I think we need to take a trip."

"Another one?"

"This all went down in LA. Seems like we need to start at the beginning."

"Will the captain clear that?" I asked.

"We've got three deaths and the only thing that links them is an old case from LA. I don't see how he can't clear it, but let's go ask."

DONALD DARLING HAD been a semi-professional boxer, who took too many hits to the head, so he changed career paths to law enforcement. He worked his way up from beat cop. He was hard and he was fair and he had his officers' backs…always.

He was on the phone when we reached his office. He waved us in. "Make it happen," he said, before he hung up. "You read my mind," he said, gesturing to the chairs in his office. "Talk to me about this case."

The captain's once brown hair was mostly gray, but his face looked younger than his age of sixty-one. He was tall, over six feet, and big in the shoulders and chest. It wasn't hard to believe he'd once been a boxer. He had dark blue eyes that were sharp, intelligence burned behind them.

Zac gave the captain a rundown.

"So the only link is this old case?" Cap asked.

"Yeah. It's thin, but it's all we've got right now," Zac replied.

"Katrina Dent's case was ruled a suicide," Cap confirmed.

"Yeah. The investigating detective was a Laurence Breen. He's a senator now."

Cap stood and paced. "So our three murder cases are linked to a thirty-one year old suicide case that may have been a murder." He rubbed a hand over his head. "That *is* thin."

"Very, but it's all we got. We'd like to go to LA. Katrina Dent still has family there. We can ask around. Get the files on the case, maybe even talk to Breen and get his gut feeling on it."

"There are no other leads?" Cap asked.

"Nothing. Emily was collateral damage. Frank and Samantha have no other points that cross. We've already talked to Milton Teller. He wasn't able to give us much, and, digging deeper into him, there are no links to Harris," I offered.

"But we've got a killer who isn't afraid of taking out an entire apartment building to destroy evidence," Cap said. "Okay. I'll call the LAPD, to clear the way. And will work to get you in with Breen."

"How you going to do that, Cap?" Zac asked.

"By calling in a few favors." He moved back to his desk, reached for his phone. "Make the arrangements."

"Thanks, Cap," Zac said, as we stood.

We were halfway to our desks, when he called after us, "Economy class!"

Zac grabbed his chest in feigned pain. "So close."

LOS ANGELES WAS like a different world. A uniform officer met us at the airport. LAX was pretty spectacular, and the drive to headquarters was incredible: palm trees, beautiful people, and the Hollywood sign. I couldn't help looking into some of the fancy cars we passed, hoping to see celebrities. We pulled into a building that was all glass and looked like a high-tech computer firm. Inside was light and spacious, nothing like our station house.

We were brought to the homicide division, stopping at the break room. Whereas ours had vending machines and old coffeemakers that burned coffee if it sat too long, theirs had an espresso machine, a smoothie maker and plates of pastries. I looked at our escort and asked, "What's the occasion?"

I knew by the way he glanced back that there was no occasion. They always had fresh pastries.

"I think I might need to make a change," I teased.

We got our coffee before we were led to their captain, a Timothy Carson. He greeted us with a smile. "Welcome to Los Angeles," he said, offering his hand.

"Thanks for having us," Zac said.

"When your captain called, I must admit, I was intrigued by the case. We've pulled the case file."

"Thanks."

"The coroner who worked on the case is retired, but…" He reached for a folder on his desk and handed it to Zac. "His name, number and address. I reached out to him, told him you'd be stopping by. The information on Laurence Breen is in there, as well, as is the address and number for Katrina Dent's parents."

"This is great. Thank you," Zac said.

"Like I said, this case is curious, but if we got it wrong, all those years ago, we need to do what we can to set it right." Timothy Carson was alright. "You need anything, you've got my resources at your disposal." He gestured to the officer who brought us to the station. "Officer Dobbs will take you to your hotel. There's a car there for you. All I ask, if this gets dicey, call us in. The paperwork involved in shootings from officers out of their jurisdiction is tedious."

"Will do," Zac replied.

"Thank you," I said.

He took his seat and smiled. "Happy hunting."

Zac waited until we were outside before he said, "I say we get some shut eye, start fresh in the morning." It was eight in the evening, our time, but in LA, it was only five. We'd been on the go for over twelve hours. Starting fresh was smart.

"Sounds good to me."

Our hotel wasn't far from the station. As soon as we checked in, Zac put the Do Not Disturb sign on his door. "I'll call you in the morning."

He had the right idea. "Night, Zac."

I got ready for bed in record time and was out seconds after my head hit the pillow.

"SHE WAS SUCH a beautiful child. Always happy. Always smiling." Ellie Dent touched a picture of a young Katrina, the following day during out visit. Her eyes were bright, a tissue clutched in her hand. "The camera loved her. Always had."

Tony sat across from me; Zac next to him. It had been thirty-one years, and still, their pain was clear to see. Looking around their spacious and elegant living room, it was a shrine to their daughter. Her picture was everywhere: framed on the mantel, over the hearth, the walls, a collection of shots covered the top of the white baby grand.

"Why are you looking into this now?" Tony asked, his voice unable to hide the pain.

"Katrina's case came up during our investigation into another crime."

"I don't understand how," Tony said.

"That's what we're trying to figure out. Is there anything you remember from back then? Anyone who was giving Katrina a hard time? Any crazy fans?"

"No," Ellie said, looking up from the photo album, "she was loved."

"What about her fiancé, Jason Benjamin. Do you know what happened to him?"

Zac and I didn't miss the look that passed between Tony and Ellie. We'd hit a nerve.

"We lost touch with him after…" Ellie didn't finish the thought.

"I know this is difficult, but was Katrina the type to take her own life?" Zac asked, as gently as that question could be asked.

Another look was shared between Katrina's parents, before her father said, "Katrina was a beautiful soul, eager to please everyone, to be loved and accepted. Hollywood is difficult, particularly for women back then. Did the pressure get to her?" He paused, as if he was forcing the words out. "Yes."

Zac handed Tony his card. Ellie didn't see us out. Her focus was on the photo album. "If you think of anything else, please call me."

The door closed at our backs with a decided thud. I stood on their front stoop and looked out at the acres of land surrounding their estate. Zac was looking at the Greek revival home we'd just walked out of.

"This place must cost a mint," he said. "According to what we learned, Ellie doesn't work, and Tony worked as a scientist. Retired now."

"You think they're using their daughter's money." That left a bad taste in my mouth.

"We need to look closer at Katrina's finances."

We started for the car. "That living room bugs me," I said. "It's a shrine. And I understand they lost their daughter, but she died thirty-one years ago. Took her own life."

Zac stopped at the car and looked at me from over the roof. "What are you thinking?"

"I got more of a guilt vibe than a mourning vibe."

Zac looked back at the house. "If they're living off of her dime, that might be why they feel guilty."

"Yeah, maybe, but it seemed almost difficult for Tony to admit that Katrina was capable of taking her own life."

"You picked up on that, too? We weren't getting the whole story. We need to find the fiancé," Zac said, climbing into the car.

I joined him and reached for the seatbelt. "He seems to have vanished."

Zac started up the car. "So he's either on the run because he had something to do with her death, or he's dead, too." It was like Pandora's box. Zac put the car in gear. "Let's go see the senator."

The show of wealth that we passed on the way to the senator's was insane, particularly knowing, only miles away, there was poverty and people struggling. The stark contrast was unsettling. The senator's house was a massive one-story rancher that sprawled over acres. Horses grazed in the distance. Palm trees lined his drive, a fountain in the center of the circular driveway. Large stone urns flanked the ornate gold door, overflowing with colorful flowers.

We knocked, and in seconds, a woman, wearing a black dress and white apron, opened the door. "You must be Detectives Ashton and Donahue. Please this way."

She walked us through the foyer of black and white marble tiles, a black concert grand piano tucked in the corner of it, and through a living room with windows along the back wall, bringing the sunlight into the space done in all white, to a door that led to an office of oak paneled walls and floors with book cases all around the perimeter. A massive desk sat in the center of the room and behind that desk was the senator, Laurence Breen.

And to think he was a public servant thirty-one years ago.

"He stood and smiled, gesturing to the leather chairs across from him. "Please sit. Can I get you anything?"

"No, thanks," Zac answered for us both.

"That will be all, Maddie."

The door closed quietly.

Breen leaned back in his chair and steepled his fingers. "You want to know about Katrina Dent."

"Yes."

"I still see it," he said, his focus turning to the window. "It's been so long, but I still see her in that bath tub. There were no signs of a struggle. There was no forced entry. The medical examiner said the wound angles supported self-inflicted. She had a history of mental illness. It was textbook."

Zac leaned up in his chair because he sensed the but, too. "But?"

Breen looked back at us, the expression in his eyes that of a cop. "It was almost too textbook."

Shit.

"So you think it's possible she was murdered?" Zac sought confirmation.

"Yes, but it was a high profile case and everything pointed to suicide."

"And the fiancé, did you look at him for the murder?" I asked.

"Unofficially, yeah, but he had an alibi for the time of death."

"Any idea where he is now?" I asked.

"No. That was another flag, one that was brushed under the rug. He disappeared shortly after Katrina's death. Cleaned out his bank accounts and disappeared. If you were to look into him now, you'd likely find nothing, no activity of any kind."

"Taking off so soon after her death makes him look guilty," Zac said.

"Or he was scared," Breen added.

"You think Katrina wasn't the target?" I said incredulously.

"I'm just throwing out theories because that's all it is after all this time, but her case was ruled a suicide, so why the hell would he run?"

"But if she was a warning…" I said, following Breen's logic. "What did Benjamin do for a living?"

"Outside of running Katrina's career, nothing stood out."

"So what was he involved in that made him a target?" I asked.

"That was what tripped me up, too. Can I ask why you're looking into this after all this time?"

"A case we're working on is linked somehow to Katrina Dent."

We both saw the curiosity burning in his eyes, the cop intuition kicking in. "I wasn't sorry to leave death behind. It's a hard job to do day in and day out, but I'm not going to lie. I am curious how your case links to a thirty-one-year-old one."

Zac held his stare and confessed, "So are we."

UNLIKE THE OTHERS we'd seen that day, the coroner who handled Katrina's case, Jackson Kilburn, didn't live in the hills. His modest apartment was in the city, not far from the Chinese Theater. We were settled in his small living room, drinking iced tea. The man was old, had to be pushing ninety. His hair was all white, but he still had a full head of it. His face was lined with wrinkles; he had a hunch to his gait, and he was sweet. Friendly.

"You're a long way from home," he said, as he pulled a blanket from the sofa and dropped it over his lap. "Have you gotten to look around?"

"We're hoping to see a bit of the city after we finish the interviews," Zac said.

"You should. All work and no play is not healthy," he said, reaching for his glass of tea. "I know why you're here. I've been waiting."

Zac and I shared a look.

"I worked as a coroner for thirty-eight years. Not an easy job, but every person who ended up on my table, I treated as if they were my own because, in a sense, they were." He took a sip from his tea.

"Why have you been waiting for this visit?" I asked.

He placed his glass down on the table and folded his hands in his lap, before his gaze shifted to Zac and me. "Because Katrina Dent's case is the only one of hundreds I worked on that I signed off on a cause of death I knew to be wrong."

Silence followed that confession because of the ramifications of such a declaration. Shit, we didn't have three bodies; we now had four, possibly five, if Benjamin wasn't in the wind but dead.

"Why did you?" Zac asked.

"I had no evidence to support murder. Everything suggested suicide. I had other coroners look at the body, and they all came back with suicide. It all fit."

"What made you think it wasn't suicide?" I asked, leaning up in my chair.

"My years of experience. I'd been on the job for over twenty-five years when Katrina came to me. She'd been drinking. A bottle of wine and glass were next to the tub. That coupled with the nerves one would feel knowing what they were going to do. The cuts were too neat."

"But the angle was right," Zac clarified.

"Yes, but if someone made her hold the razor and covered her hand with their own..."

Which shined a light on her fiancé. No forced entry, no struggle, because she didn't see it coming. Waited until she had enough wine in her...

"I always thought her fiancé was good for it, especially since he disappeared shortly after. He'd gotten away with murder, so why the hell not run. Start over elsewhere."

"But from all accounts, they were happy," Zac offered.

"It's Hollywood. You see what they want you to see." Jackson looked back out the window. "That case haunts me. She haunts me because, if I'm right, her murderer has gotten away with it for thirty-one years." His focus shifted back to us. "Find out what happened to her. Before I leave this world, I'd like to know she's at rest."

"THIS CASE IS from hell," Zac said, moving into the late afternoon traffic on the San Diego Freeway. "We've more questions than answers."

I turned in my seat to face him. "Both the investigating officer and coroner thought it was murder, so let's assume Katrina was murdered. If it was her fiancé who killed her, why did he? What was his motive? They weren't married, and even though they'd been living together for over three years, California isn't a common law state, not even back in the eighties. So he has no claim to her money."

"Yeah, and being unhappy seems like a stretch for murder," Zac added.

"Financially, she was the breadwinner. Murder usually does come down to money," I offered, then added, "But killing her, he takes out his source of income."

"Exactly, so even though he had means and opportunity, motive is sketchy…" Zac let that thought trail off.

"Alright, so the other option is Katrina wasn't the target," I theorized. "She was a means to an end. So what was Jason Benjamin involved in that led to the murder of his fiancée?"

"No clue because no one knows shit about him, and he's in the wind," Zac said. "We need to find Jason Benjamin."

For the rest of the ride back to our hotel, Zac and I were quiet, lost in our thoughts. We had one more day in Los Angeles and that would be spent poring over the case file, digging more into Jason Benjamin. We wouldn't be getting in any sightseeing. Whatever happened to Katrina, someone was willing to kill to keep it quiet, even decades later. Was it her fiancé, afraid of the truth coming out? Or, was it possible, whoever killed Katrina did so to get to her fiancé? And if so, why? What the hell were we walking into?

SALEM GREETED ME, as soon as I closed and locked the door to my apartment. "Hey, buddy," I said, hunching down to scratch his head. "Did you miss me?" He rubbed his head into my hand in answer.

My place wasn't much, but I was glad to be home. I unpacked, made sure I had clean clothes for tomorrow, then settled at my desk in the living room and consolidated my notes. The more people we interviewed, the more questions we had. What was perfectly clear was someone was willing to kill to keep the secret of Katrina's death. And now, we needed to figure out why.

I spent an hour getting my stuff together for the briefing the captain would want in the morning, and then I walked to the kitchen for a glass of wine. Dropping down on the sofa, I flipped on the television.

I caught the tail end of a story on the attempt on Gregory Enzi senior's life. He was a known crime boss, dabbled, some said too much, in politics. Meaning, he had people at all levels of the government in his pocket, though that was never proven. I had enough in my head, didn't need to think about the attempted murder of a crime boss, so I was switching to a movie when a familiar face filled the screen. My heart skipped, as I turned up the volume.

"Kade Wakefield's annual masquerade party has a date."

I entertained the fantasy of going to that for about three minutes, before I came back to reality and changed the channel.

"SO THE CORONER and lead detective weren't convinced it was a suicide, and yet, ruled it as such. And the one person who could shine some light on this mess is in the wind," Captain summarized.

"In a nutshell," Zac said. "For someone connected to the level of celebrity Katrina Dent had been, there is surprisingly little on Jason Benjamin."

"Maybe that was intentional. Maybe he planned his backout strategy," Cap said.

"Yeah, but why?" I asked.

Captain shook his head. "Good question. I'll get the forensic division on it. They can reach out to their counterparts in Los Angeles, see what they can shake out."

Captain stood and turned to the window. "What a crazy case, but we've got three bodies, so keep at it." He looked back at us. "You need more hands, say the word."

"You got it, Cap," Zac said, standing and heading for the door.

"Thanks, Captain," I said, and followed Zac out. He was itchy; the wheels were turning. He dropped down at his desk. "I'll start digging into people we know Jason dealt with as Katrina's representative. See if we can find someone who can tell us about this guy," he said.

"I'm going to finish the report on what we learned in LA," I said, then saw the black envelope, with my name in silver, sitting on my desk. Lifting it, I asked of the room, "Where did this come from?"

"A courier dropped it off yesterday," someone shouted back.

Pulling out my chair, I dropped down into it, turning the envelope around in my hands.

"Are you going to open it or are you practicing your x-ray vision?" Zac teased.

I flipped him off. Then ripped the envelope open and pulled out an invitation, also black, with silver writing, and a purple mask on the bottom right corner. I read it four times, my body growing warmer with each read through.

"What is it?"

I glanced up to see Zac watching me with interest. "An invitation."

He rolled his eyes before he said, "To what?"

"Kade Wakefield's masquerade party."

Zac stopped tapping on his keyboard, his curious stare fixed on me. "Really?" Then he leaned back in his chair, lifted a pen and rolled it around his fingers. "An invitation to the most sought after party of the year, hosted by a man we've got on our radar. Interesting."

I dropped the invitation, but I wasn't unaffected. Butterflies were going crazy in my stomach. I showed none of that to Zac because I'd never live it down. "You know as well as I do the likelihood that Kade Wakefield has anything to do with this case is slim to none."

"Still an awfully big coincidence."

Dropping my elbows on my desk, I didn't hide my irritation because, for as smart as Zac could be, he let his bias color his judgment far too often. "Did it ever occur to you that he might have invited me because he thinks I'm attractive?"

Zac opened his mouth, then closed it. "I guess, but you know enough about him and you're a detective. You think that's smart?"

What he meant was I maintained law and order and Kade Wakefield blurred it when it suited him, but this wasn't a date, this was a ball, a once-in-a-lifetime moment. Still, I was a cop, and he was most definitely a bad boy, elegant, rich and sophisticated, but a bad boy nonetheless.

"No," I replied honestly.

"Are you going?"

"No," I said, and then added, "I don't think so." This particular bad boy I liked more than I should.

He chuckled and got back to work. I tried to work, but I was distracted, my focus shifting to the invitation throughout the day. Even that night, I studied it on my kitchen counter like it was a living thing. I had nothing to wear. I really shouldn't go, but the thought of getting dressed up, seeing him dressed up made me really want to go. I couldn't go, shouldn't go. Reaching for my phone, I texted the number to reply with a no, my finger hovering over the button, and, at the last second, I responded yes. Dropping my phone, I stepped away from the counter, took a deep breath. It settled in slowly that I was attending the event of the year. I needed a dress. I'd go shopping over the weekend. As hard as I tried to not make it a big deal, I caught myself grinning for the rest of the night.

SEVEN

He stood in the shadows, eyes trained on the cop's apartment. Surveillance for now, but if she and her partner got too close, he'd have to throw them off the scent. If necessary, take them out. He waited until the lights on the third floor went out, before he pulled his hoodie closer and disappeared into the shadows.

EIGHT

MOLLY

I got home after a day that was just too long, kicked off my shoes, put my badge and gun in the drawer and poured myself a glass of wine. After a long sip, my eyes met Salem's. "Jason Benjamin has got to be dead. Nothing, there is nothing on him." I took another long drink. "So if he's dead but people are still willing to kill to keep Katrina's true cause of a death a mystery, why?"

It really was the case from hell, but I couldn't deny I liked it. All those strings to pull to see what happened.

I almost didn't answer the door when I heard the knock, and had I dropped onto the sofa, I wouldn't have. Looking out the peephole, it was Ethan. Pulling the door open, he grinned at me, but I was looking at the silver box with a black bow that he carried.

"Surprise!"

I stepped back to let him in. He chuckled when he placed it on the counter. "It's not from me. Courier didn't want to leave it at the door." He pushed his hands into his pockets. "You okay?"

I pulled my eyes from the box to Ethan. "Yeah, just tired."

"Want to talk about it?"

"It's just this case."

He lifted a brow.

"Do you think it's possible for someone to stay off the grid effectively for over thirty years?"

"Back in the seventies and eighties, I'd say yeah, but today. No. Not with all the technology. Everything we do leaves a footprint."

That was my thought, too.

"You picked up the apartment fire case?" he asked. Not surprising he knew of it, since it was on all the news channels.

"Yeah."

"Lucky it was only two deaths," he said.

He was the right. The fire could have taken the whole building. Sadly, for the two, it didn't matter.

Ethan did a chin lift toward the present. "You've got a secret admirer."

"It would seem."

"And one with some change."

"How do you know that?"

"I worked at Bergdorfs for a time. I recognize the box."

Who the hell would be sending me a gift from Bergdorfs?

"You going to open it?" Ethan asked, and then wiggled his brows.

"I need a shower first."

"Okay, fine," he teased.

"Thanks for accepting it."

"No problem, Neighbor." He started for the door, then looked back when he reached it. "That drink invite is still on the table."

He was adorable. "Maybe one drink."

His eyes lit up. "Well, damn, alright."

Chuckling, I walked to the door; he had his door open. "I'm holding you to that drink."

"I look forward to it," I said sincerely.

"Evening made. Night, Detective."

"Night, Ethan."

I locked up, then showered, before I returned to the box. There wasn't even a card. What I was thinking couldn't be, and yet, my fingers were shaking, as I worked off the ribbon. Lifting the lid and moving the tissue paper, my heart did a hard knock behind my ribs at the sight of the red silk and the masquerade mask resting on the top of it.

Kade Wakefield.

I didn't reach for it, at first, because it felt like I'd stepped into the middle of the most perfect dream, knowing the man who had bought this and that he'd been thinking of me when he had. I lifted the mask and studied it, a silver mask with delicate filigree work and crystal accents. It was beautiful and a touch mysterious, the whole point of a masquerade ball.

Placing the mask on the counter, I took the box to the living room, set it on the sofa and lifted out the gown. It had a deep v halter neckline and a long straight skirt; the back was completely open and, when on, would sit at the base of my spine. It was also red, like Little Red Riding Hood red. It was exquisite. I moved to my bedroom and held the dress up, as I stood in front of the mirror. It really was a fairy tale moment, and for not being one for fairy tales, since I worked in the trenches, I wanted this moment. I wanted to get dressed up. I wanted the magic and the mystery. I wanted him. Completely impossible, but maybe for one night, the impossible was possible.

THE BALL WAS on Friday, two days away. My beautiful gown was hanging on my closet door, and every time I walked past it, I felt a bit like Cinderella. I wanted to call Kade to thank him, but I wanted to thank him in person more. Two more days, I couldn't wait.

Real life pushed into my happy bubble. Zac and I were visiting Milton Teller again because he was someone who had actually met Jason Benjamin, which finding people from back then who were still alive and remembered anything was proving really hard. Calling his office, we were happily surprised to learn he was in Manhattan. We'd been penciled in for a few minutes. The man had back-to-back meetings.

We had tried to follow the money, namely Katrina's estate, thinking that might lead us to Benjamin, but we were hitting a wall with her financials. Zac put a call into the LAPD in the hopes they could cut the red tape.

We met Teller at his suite in the St. Regis. We settled in the opulent living room before Milton asked, "How can I help you, Detectives?"

"We're having trouble finding anything on Jason Benjamin, and given you were someone who actually knew him, we wondered if you could tell us about his background, where he grew up. Anything," Zac said.

"Like I told you previously, I really didn't know much about him."

"You represented Katrina, but from everyone we talked to, Jason had a lot of say in her career," I shared.

"He did, but I was the one who hit the pavement, made the calls to get her interviews, talk shows, on the cover of magazines. Jason helped create the star, but I got her in front of the public."

"Who hired you?" Zac asked.

There was a slight hesitation before he said, "Jason hired me. Katrina was well on her way to being a star. I was virtually unknown, but I was hungry, had put together a plan before I'd even been given the position. He liked that I was new, believed I'd work harder for Katrina. Knew I'd be a fraction of the cost of the big public relations' firms. He was right on all points. While he focused on money, contracts and filming locations, I worked on her public image."

"What do you think happened to Jason?"

"Jason worked Katrina too hard." Milton stood and started to pace. "He got caught up in it, the glamor, the money, the lifestyle, and Katrina was his link. She was a star, and he intended to keep her there. Her death, even self-inflicted, can be leveled at his feet. No one in Hollywood would touch him after her death. Particularly with Katrina being so loved. If he was smart, he'd have changed careers and names." Milton stopped pacing and leveled us with hard eyes. "Jason was very smart."

IT WAS THE night of the ball. I stood in front of the mirror, but I had trouble believing it was me looking back. The gown fit me perfectly, hugging my figure. Even the length was spot on. Did Kade make a habit of buying gowns for women? I didn't want to know. I'd bought the Christian Louboutin strappy silver sandals I'd had my eyes on. If ever there was an excuse to buy insanely expensive shoes, this ball was it. My hair was up, my makeup subtle, and my lips tinted red. I didn't have the mask on, but felt that rush of excitement for the moment I slipped it on and assumed a bit of anonymity.

I grabbed my silver clutch, mask and invitation and left my apartment. Ethan wasn't around when I knocked earlier. Stepping outside, I was pulling up the Uber app, when I noticed the car double-parked in front of my building and a man standing by the open door. Kade had sent his car for me.

"Evening, Miss Donahue."

My voice was a little off because talk about a fairy tale moment. "Good evening, Levy." My heart raced thinking Kade might be inside, but the limo was empty. A bottle of champagne was opened and chilling, a glass poured. I took several sips because I was practically humming with excitement.

We drove out of the city, urban gave way to rural. It was some time later when we pulled down a long drive. The estate at the end of the drive sat on a hill, a sprawling stone estate that if I used my imagination almost looked like a castle with its chimneys reaching up to the heavens. I tried to play it cool, but my face was almost pressed up against the glass to take it all in.

Limos waited in line to drop off their passengers. I slipped on my mask. When we reached the entrance, a man dressed in silver and black livery opened the door and offered his hand. Climbing from the limo, I took a moment to look around. I never knew there was any part of New York that looked like this.

I followed the other guests inside. Everyone looked so beautiful in their gowns and tuxedos, elegant masks covering their faces. I felt the need to pinch myself. I stepped over the threshold, and candles were everywhere, as if we had gone back to a time of no electricity. The high ceilings, the priceless art, and the furniture that was as old as the building that housed them. It was breathtaking.

I moved through the hall and stepped through double doors that opened into a ballroom of gilded thick moldings, a mural painted on the ceiling, and huge gold chandeliers holding white taper candles. The old wood floors were polished to a high shine. A bar was setup in the back, tables, dressed in black and silver, scattered around it. Exquisite floral arrangements—done in white: roses, peonies, hydrangeas, and freesia sprinkled with silver fairy dust, and a splash of blue from the campanulas that pulled in the color from the mural on the ceiling—were centered on each table. There was a string ensemble tucked in a corner, their soft music added ambience. Servers dressed in black carried silver trays of champagne flutes. A masquerade-themed tiered cake was setup in the other corner.

"Champagne," a server asked.

"Thank you," I said, taking one, before I looked around to those assembled. Even with their masks, it was a who's who of the rich and famous, everyone from Hollywood A-listers to senators. The usual suspects were in attendance, Sinclair Rothschild and Desiree McKenzie. Carmine DeLuca, even Milton Teller was present. A social circle I didn't belong but was lucky enough to get a glimpse into. I couldn't help think of Samantha James and how she'd attended an event similar right before she was killed. Feeling as I was, knowing she had to have felt the same, made her ending that much more tragic. I tried not to put myself in the shoes of the victim because I wouldn't be able to do the job, but thinking about her now...we would find out what happened to her.

I pulled my thoughts from that and looked around the room, captivated by a scene that looked as if it had been plucked right out of the eighteen hundreds. It was beautiful watching the couples move, the way the long gowns swished around their feet. A sensation of being watched tickled me. Scanning the room, my eyes landed on a man across it. He was hidden partly in the shadows. Leaning against the wall, at first glance, he looked like a man without a care in the world, but the way he held his shoulders and the rigidity of his jaw belied that observation. He was a predator on the hunt. A chill moved down my spine, and my heart skipped a beat because I knew who was staring, the same man who had dressed me for the evening. There was something erotic about the thought of him picking out my gown, especially holding that gray gaze and watching as he moved it down my body.

He left the shadows, closing the distance between us in long, sure strides. I couldn't move. Like a fly caught in a web, I was his captive. As he grew closer, I soaked up the sight of him, from his sensual mouth, with the heavier lower lip, to those eyes that were the color of storm clouds. Half of his face was hidden behind a wolf's mask. He was dangerous, a touch mysterious and absolutely beautiful.

Desire raced through me, a want so strong my body swayed toward him in anticipation. He stopped just in front of me; those eyes, the windows to his soul, were shuttered. Awareness moved through me in a long, slow, seductive roll.

He spoke no words, but took my glass and placed it on the tray of a passing waiter, before he drew me into his strong arms and held me tightly against him. My breath caught at the feel of his hard body against mine. It felt so perfectly right for me to be there, his touch stirring heat that went from a burn on my skin to a fire racing in my blood. His focus was unwavering, as if he was memorizing every one of my features. I knew I was memorizing his. He moved me around the dance floor, his steps sure and graceful, despite his size, but it was how he held me, as if I was both precious and his that had desire chasing that fire.

The song ended, but he didn't release me, holding me as if he couldn't let go. We stood in the middle of the ballroom, but everyone faded for me, my world becoming nothing more than this man holding me close. He brushed his thumb over my lower lip, his eyes turning darker, as he watched the movement. If he didn't have his arm around me, I would have swayed. As it was, I swayed into him. I wanted him to kiss me, even ran my tongue along my lower lip in anticipation. His hold on me tightened, heat flashed behind his eyes. My breathing grew labored, my body was on fire, but instead of putting me out of my misery, his hold on me loosened, then he released me when I'd found my balance. Without speaking a word, he turned and walked away, moving through the crowd, before disappearing altogether.

I didn't move, wasn't able to. Still caught in his seductive web because this really was like a fairy tale. I moved, eventually, grabbed a glass of champagne and walked out the French doors to the backyard. I took a healthy sip and allowed the flavor to coat my tongue...the effervescent yet dry taste. The moon offered enough light to see the yard, beautifully tended beds, mature trees, some of which were flowering. I touched my lower lip, thinking about the dance, about the man. I'd wondered what it would feel like to be his, and that small glimpse into just that was more intoxicating than the champagne I was sipping. I was attracted, but I was also fascinated. He was young to have accomplished so much, and with so little information available on him, yeah, I was captivated. And I was really fucking attracted.

"Evening, Detective."

I closed my eyes, enjoying the tingles that moved down my body from that voice, before I turned to face my host. Dressed in all black, he blended into the night. He'd taken his mask off, but still, I felt a bit like Little Red, at the mercy of the wolf, and wondered if he'd done it on purpose.

My voice was a bit breathy when I said, "Good evening, Mr. Wakefield."

"Kade," he said, those gray eyes locked on mine.

I felt the warmth on my cheeks, and with how fast my heart was beating, I was surprised I wasn't as red as my dress. His lips tipped up slightly on the one side.

I touched the skirt and said, "It's the most beautiful dress. Thank you."

"It suits you."

The man *was* dangerous.

"Why did you invite me?" I surprised myself that I asked, but it was a question that had sat in the back of my mind, since receiving his invitation.

He could be so still; his hands weren't in his pockets or crossed over his chest. He stood almost like a statue, even breathing seemed to be done sparingly. I wasn't sure if I was seeing things, and considering our surroundings I could be, or if this man did everything deliberately. It wasn't just my heart that pulsed thinking about him letting go, watching as everything he held under such tight control was freed. It would be an unbelievable sight.

"I suspect you spend so much time giving a voice to those who no longer have one that you forget your own," he said softly. "And I saw that dress and knew I needed to see you in it." Those words said as if they were dragged over sandpaper. I drew my lower lip into my mouth because I was so fucking turned on.

His gaze dropped to my mouth, heat flashing in his eyes, before they lifted back to mine.

"You make me forget where I am," I whispered.

Never in my life had someone looked at me like he was. He wasn't so still now, as he fisted his hands. His features sharpened as that control, he kept under tight rein, was pushing at the cage to break free. "You make me want to forget," he rasped, and though he didn't move, it was like being surrounded by him, when he added, "But I'm not a prince, I'm the villain." And for a second, I saw just how much he believed that, before he finished, "Enjoy your evening. Levy will see you home when you're ready."

He turned to go, and the words tumbled out of my mouth. "I didn't think you were a prince, but I do think you're beautiful." He looked back, that knot at his jaw as he clenched it was the only visible reaction to my words. I wanted to kiss him, but my feet wouldn't move, held spellbound by that dark gaze. Seconds passed before he broke the connection and walked away, the night closing around him, until he blended into it. Took me much longer to follow after him because I thought he was fascinating before, but now...what skeletons hid in his closet? I didn't go back to the party but out the front door. Levy was waiting for me, and somehow, I knew he would be because Kade Wakefield read me like a book, the first person who ever did. Settling back on the seat, I watched the scenery change, but my thoughts were on Kade, learning his story and wanting it to be him to tell me.

I STOOD AT the corner by my apartment on Saturday and wasn't sure how to get back into real life. Last night, even not lasting as long as I would have liked, had been every bit as magical as I'd hoped. I hadn't been able to pull my thoughts from Kade because he felt it, too. He didn't want to feel it, that was pretty clear, but he did. What was in his past that was so terrible he thought himself a villain? I had no doubt that to accomplish all he had so young, he'd had to cross the line, but the man he was now was no villain, and I doubted he ever had been.

I was edgy, had a constant humming in my blood, knowing that man was out there and was as curious about me as I was about him. I hit Fifth Avenue and saw Amar, my gyro connection. It was almost without thought when I ordered two. I wasn't even sure that Kade was working, but I caught a cab to his building. By the time I reached his floor, I was having second thoughts and then I saw the woman. She looked to be in her fifties, dressed in jeans and a tee. But she was working, which meant he was, too. I got butterflies in my stomach. Never in my life had someone stirred that feeling in me, but around Kade, I had them all the time.

"Can I help you?" she asked.

"I was hoping to see Kade, if he has time."

"Miss Donahue, yes?"

I was excited for about two seconds and then remembered she had seen Zac and me into Kade's office that first day. Working for a man like Kade, knowing names was likely a job requirement.

"Yes, Molly."

"One second," she said, then stood and disappeared behind the double doors. I wasn't waiting long before she stepped out and held the door for me.

"Thank you," I said, my focus turning to Kade, as soon as I entered. He was also dressed in jeans and a tee, standing behind his massive desk with the New York skyline behind him.

"Detective."

"Molly," I said, and witnessed just the slightest softening around his eyes. I crossed the room to him. "I brought you lunch," I offered, pulling a gyro from the bag but stopped. "Have you eaten?"

"No."

"Oh good. A gyro. I didn't get anything fancy because, honestly, the spices that Amar uses are enough."

He walked around his desk to the sideboard and got two bottles of water and more napkins, but instead of sitting across from me, he took the chair next to me. He handed me a bottle of water, and I handed him the gyro. He waited for me to take a bite before he did, the man had impeccable manners, but when he did, he smiled. "You're right, the spices are enough."

I took another bite. "I could live on this."

"Have you ever been to Greece?" he asked.

"No, I've never left the States, but it is on my bucket list."

"Bucket list?" He studied me a second before he asked, "What else is on your bucket list?"

For the amount of nerves the man stirred in me, talking to him was surprisingly easy, natural even. "Swimming with sharks. I know most want to swim with dolphins, but I'd love to swim with sharks." I reached for my water. "And skydiving, that moment of freefalling sounds terrifying, but I imagine, it's life altering. Seeing the pyramids, looking up from the bottom, something that is so old and yet still standing, still a reminder that we aren't the first and won't be the last."

He finished his gyro, reached for his bottle and leaned back in his chair. "What else?"

"I'd love to attend the Academy Awards, walking down the red carpet, getting all dressed up. I have absolutely no reason to be there, but I'd love to experience Hollywood on her special night. Staying in a castle in Ireland or Scotland, or really anywhere in Europe. And believe it or not, I've always wanted to attend a masquerade ball, so thank you for allowing me to scratch that off my list."

"Is that all?" he asked.

I had a new item, and it was to kiss him, but I wasn't going to share that. "Yeah. What about you?"

"I've never thought about it."

"Okay, well think about it."

He looked thoughtful, before he offered, "Drive in Nascar."

I placed my water on his desk, sat back and said, "Oh, that's a good one."

"Dive a sunken pirate ship off the Caribbean."

"I'd like to do that, too."

"Build a yacht with my own hands."

My focus shifted to his hands. Lucky yacht. He took a drink, my gaze moved to the line of his throat, and even that was sexy. He knew what I was thinking, by the way his eyes turned darker. "Eat a gyro in my office with a detective I can't seem to get out of my head." I went numb, but in the best possible way. He leaned closer, dropped his voice when he added, "Thank you for allowing me to scratch that off my list." I almost kissed him. My knuckles were white with how hard I was gripping the chair, so I didn't act on the one thing in that moment I wanted more than anything. The answering fire I saw burning behind his eyes hypnotized me. "Are you busy tomorrow?" he asked.

It took me a minute to break out of the trance. Busy? If it I were, I would cancel. "No."

"I'll come for you at ten. Dress casual and wear sneakers."

I answered a little too quickly. "Okay."

His lips tipped up on the one side. "Don't you want to know what we'll be doing?"

I answered honestly. "It doesn't matter."

The sexiest sound rumbled up his throat. "I'm not good for you," he said, but it sounded as if he was trying to convince himself of that as much as me.

"I don't agree."

His gaze moved to my mouth, lingered, before he lifted it back to mine. "Thank you for lunch."

That I didn't go up in flames was amazing because my blood was on fire. "Duke's sandwiches are next," I whispered.

He held my gaze. "Looking forward to it."

He walked me to the elevators, pushed his hands into his pockets, and why I had the sense he did that so he didn't reach for me, I couldn't say. But I wished he'd reach for me. "See you tomorrow at ten," he said.

Before I could respond, the doors closed. I leaned against the wall, worked on slowing my heart, but I was smiling because I was seeing him again tomorrow.

I didn't go right home. I stopped at my favorite store and spent an hour trying on jeans and blouses. I bought low-rise jeans that hugged my figure and a blouse that knotted closed, with a deep v neckline and open at the belly. And I didn't care if people judged. I was going out with the sexiest man I'd ever met, damn straight I wanted to look hot as hell. That was why I stopped at the salon after. I never did much with my hair besides cut the bottom, but I had the stylist actually give me a style with long layers and balayage highlights: a sun-kissed version of ombré. When she turned me to the mirror after she was done, it was me but sexier. I absolutely loved it. He would know I had it done for him, but that didn't bother me. I wondered where he was taking me, but didn't really care because I'd be with him, but the thought kept me up for most of the night.

IN THE MORNING, I was tying up my sneakers when the doorbell rang. I jumped up, but then forced myself to slow down, took a deep breath and pulled the door open. It wasn't Kade. It was Ethan. His mouth opened then closed, as his gaze moved from my head down to my toes.

"Damn, Molly, you look hot."

A tingle moved through me because that had been the goal. "Thanks."

"Where are you off to looking all…" He leaned against the door-jamb. "Sexy."

"I'm not sure," I said honestly. "Want to come in?" He followed me in. "There's coffee," I offered.

"What do you mean you don't know?"

I turned to him. "The man who sent me Bergdorfs is taking me somewhere."

He poured some coffee into a mug. "I wondered what happened to him." His eyes found mine. "What did happen with him?"

"I'm captivated, Ethan."

He was about to make a joke but took a good look at me and said, "You're serious."

"I am." I knew there were obstacles, the least of which being the man thought he was a villain, but someone who made me feel like he did was worth taking a chance on. "I never saw him coming, and I really don't know him, but I want to."

He leaned against the counter, took a sip of coffee, his eyes moving behind me. "He the one responsible for your new look."

I held his stare and answered truthfully. "Yeah."

"Lucky man."

It was then I felt the heat move down my spine and turned to see Kade in the doorway. And like he had the night of the ball, he held me hostage with nothing more than his hot gaze.

Ethan walked from the kitchen, stepped up to my side and kissed my cheek, before he headed to the door. "Have fun."

Kade and I didn't acknowledge him, and when Kade finally did speak, he said, "I am."

When his words finally registered, I asked, "You are what?"

"A lucky man." His gaze drifted down my body. "You're beauti-ful." Looking at me the way he was made me feel beautiful. "Are you ready?"

I so was. I grabbed my purse and keys; he waited for me to lock up, before he touched the small of my back and led me to the waiting car.

Once we pulled into traffic, I'd gotten some of my senses back and asked, "So where are we going?"

"You'll see." He touched a strand of hair that fell over my shoulder. "Beautiful." His gaze dropped, heat stirred. "You should have that shirt in every color."

I needed to change the conversation because what I wanted to do was crawl onto his lap, straddle him, kiss him, shit, I wanted to do a hell of a lot more than kiss him. "Do you always work on the weekends?"

I was sure he knew what was going through my head, but he took mercy on me. "Usually. I imagine you do, too."

"More than I like, and not that I mind working on the weekends, but..."

"It means someone's died."

"Exactly."

"How's the case?"

I didn't want to think about it because the case gave me a headache. "Complicated. Not that murder isn't always complicated, but the more we investigate, the less we know."

He was intrigued, but he didn't press.

"You're very good at that." His brow rose. "Reading people."

"So are you," he countered.

"I don't read you so well," I confessed.

"I think you do." When I said nothing, he leaned closer, his scent filling my nose. I might have moaned. His voice turned into a rough whisper. "Right now, I want to untie that fucking knot, cup your breasts and kiss your lip gloss off." Our eyes met, then he grinned. "See, you read me better than you think."

Oh my God. I didn't realize I said that out loud until his grin turned into a smile, and my eyes dropped to his mouth. "I definitely am buying this shirt in every color."

He laughed, and I thought his intense stares were my undoing, but holy shit. "You should do that more."

He ran his thumb over my lower lip, and though he said nothing, he didn't have to.

"MAYBE WE SHOULD think this through," I said, when we arrived at our destination.

He glanced back. "You can scratch it off your list."

I could. "You're going, too?"

"Absolutely."

I inhaled, letting it out slowly. "Okay."

A half an hour later, we were thirteen thousand feet up. "You can go separately or together," the instructor said.

"We'll go together," Kade answered. That was when I realized he'd done this before.

"This isn't your first time."

"No, Sweetheart." He touched my cheek. "I've got you."

He so did. He totally had me, and I hardly knew him.

He then threaded his fingers through my hair. I couldn't stop the moan. "We need to braid this." His voice was seductively soft. This man was going to be my undoing. He'd thought ahead when he pulled an elastic tie from his pocket.

His strong fingers twisted my hair; his touch lingered on my neck, like he was enjoying the moment as much as me. I was so wet and all he was doing was braiding my hair. The thought of his mouth on me had an ache accompanying the wet heat. He tugged lightly on my hair, but the thought of him pulling my head back for his kiss, caused more heat to pool between my legs. It was official, I had no control around him, and I fucking loved it.

I was then strapped to him, my back pressed against his front. If this didn't end well, I would die a very happy and extremely turned on woman.

His breath brushed across my ear when he asked, "Are you ready?"

I wasn't sure if my heart was pounding because I was so close to him or because we were going to be jumping out of an airplane or both, but I was ready. Very ready. "Yes."

We moved to the open door of the plane; staring out, it was a good kind of fear, liberating…freeing. And then we jumped. That feeling you get on a rollercoaster when you're going down a steep slope, but you don't scream, that's what I felt. And then I screamed, but not in terror. It was amazing. The world rushing past us, tethered to this man; it was the most amazing moment of my life. He wrapped an arm around my stomach, the signal he was going to pull the chute, and then my stomach dropped, the air rushed from my lungs and an entirely different sensation moved through me, gliding down to earth, watching as everything grew bigger. Kade nailed the landing, and for the first few seconds, when my legs struggled to hold me up, he did. His lips touched my ear. "Worth it?"

I wanted him. Life endangering moments stirred your libido and already wanting this man, I wanted to feel his cock inside me, hard and rough, right here, right now. It was pure lust in my voice, when I whispered raggedly, "Yes."

His hold on me tightened, for just a second, before he released me. He unstrapped us, but before I could move away, he was untwisting my hair. I closed my eyes, never imagining something as simple as unbraiding my hair could be so erotic. I heard the car, just as he turned me to him. He felt it, too, his eyes almost black with want. If he didn't make a move, I was so totally jumping him in the car. He read my thoughts; his thumb touched the corner of my mouth, moved slowly along my lips, then pressed in, so I'd part them, my tongue touching his thumb, but wishing it was his cock. He brought that thumb to his mouth, his tongue touching where mine already had. Fuck, but he looked like the villain in that moment. I was completely at his mercy. He could do with me what he wanted. And then his phone rang. I watched as the mask slipped back into place, his hand moved, reaching into his pocket for his phone.

"Kade." Something dark moved across his expression. "I'll be there in an hour." He disconnected and said with regret, "I have to cut the day short." He cupped my chin to hold my gaze on him. "I'll make it up to you."

Disappointed wasn't a good enough word, but to him, I nodded and said, "Thank you for today. This was amazing."

He studied me; his voice lower when he said, "We'll pick up where we left off."

I was breathless when I replied, "That plan...definitely on my bucket list."

NINE
MOLLY

The following morning, I was on fumes. After Kade dropped me at home, I spent some time in my room with my vibrator and fresh batteries, taking the edge off my lust. Then I worried about what had called him away because the change in him was not just notable, but a little alarming. I hadn't heard from him, though I wasn't expecting to. After a sleepless night, I was grateful for the case to get my mind off Kade Wakefield.

"I can't even find next of kin for Jason Benjamin," I said, standing from my desk and tossing my pen on it. "No one, no cousins two times removed, nothing. It's like the guy never existed."

"I'm not having much more luck with people he worked with, most are either dead or have nothing interesting to tell. There is one producer who is willing to meet with us. He's coming to New York in the next two weeks, so we'll set something up," Zac offered.

"Whoa, wait a second. An actual Hollywood movie producer has agreed to talk with us?"

"Are you seriously fangirling right now?" Zac asked, shaking his head.

"It's a Hollywood producer. Which one?" As if I knew all of the Hollywood producers by name.

Zac shook his head again, but he moved some papers around and pointed at a page. "Russell Bleaker."

"Never heard of him." Okay, I was hoping for Steven Spielberg, Michael Bay or Steven Soderbergh, but I would be looking into Russell's work.

Zac pushed back from his desk, spun his chair to face me. "Milton's comment about Jason changing names, I wonder if he's onto something."

And we were back to the case. "It would explain why we can't find him."

"Maybe the forensic team has something. I'm going to run down there. How about you get us lunch?" He gave me the look, as close to puppy dog eyes as a man like Zac could muster. It was ridiculous, especially on him. I chuckled. "Fine. Sandwiches from Duke's?"

"The spicy one you got last time," Zac said, and pulled out his wallet.

"Don't want your money. I'll be back."

Duke's was a little gem in Manhattan. I'd stumbled onto it a few years ago, shared what I learned, and now, it was a cop hangout. The owner, Duke Alamode, made wicked sandwiches stuffed with meats and cheeses and offered so many different condiments, it made your head spin. Just one of his sandwiches could feed a family of four. I never finished mine, but I did try.

I definitely intended to introduce Kade to Duke's. The thought of bringing him a sandwich and our lunch ending with us on that sofa he had in his office was what was running through my head when I yanked open the door. My cop senses went on alert immediately, as my hand moved to my gun.

"Don't fucking touch that." My eyes meeting the blurry gaze of the meth head who'd shouted that warning. Only someone whacked out of his head would holdup a cop hangout. "Money in the bag, man," he ordered Duke. I scanned the shop to the half dozen scared customers in the back; my gaze shifted, and I caught Duke's eyes, before I settled my focus on the perp.

He pointed the gun at me with a shaky hand. "Over there," he ordered, to where the other customers were huddled. I moved, keeping my eyes on him. I studied him for tattoos, any identifying markers, because he was high. I wasn't risking taking him here, and I wasn't thrilled with taking him once he got outside because there were more civilians on the street. He had startling blues eyes, and with his fair coloring and his size, several inches over six feet, I would bet he had Nordic in his backyard. There was a partial tattoo on his arm of what looked like a snake, and he had a scar along the back of his neck that ended at his jawbone. I was sure we'd find his mug shot.

"Hurry up, old man," he shouted, as the hand with the gun shook, his shifty gaze going from Duke to the door.

The door opened again, and based on how young he was, I was guessing the beat cop was a rookie. He was fast, pulling his gun, but it shook almost as much as the meth head's. Shit. Just what the situation needed. Glancing back at the people behind me, I ordered quietly, "Move to that corner, go."

They shuffled, which brought the assailant's attention to us. "Don't you fucking move!"

"Take the money and go," I said.

"Shut up, cunt."

"This is a cop hangout, and it's lunchtime. You've got about five minutes before that door opens on a wall of blue. Take the money and go."

Duke held out the bag, the rookie was looking at me now. I gestured for him to lower his gun; he hesitated, but he did and even stepped out of the path to the door, but I saw the look. He was pursuing once the perp took off and, damn, but he couldn't have been on the job more than a few months…more courage than sense. Fucking hell.

"Now's your chance," I said.

He wasn't as dumb as he looked when he ran out of the store.

The rookie was ready to pursue, but looked at me for the ok. Letting the perp go, and picking him up later was my preference, but it was lunchtime, and this was a cop hangout, so there were going to be unsuspecting cops heading this way. Would the meth head panic when he saw blue and open fire? By how twitchy he'd been in the shop, I was thinking yeah. Fuck. Chasing down a fucking meth head, who was high and unpredictable, was not what I had in mind for my lunch break. But better me than the rookie.

"Call this in and get statements," I ordered, and then flew out of the shop. Running through the crowd, some of who had been pushed to the ground by the assailant, I caught up to him. He swung around, gun in hand, but I tackled him because the priority was to get the gun away, so there was no collateral damage. It went flying out of his hand. He was pissed, shoving me off him, before he landed a punch to my cheek. Stars filled my vision, but I dodged the next punch, and landed one to his gut. He took another swing, clipped my chin. I landed one to his jaw, but I think I hurt my hand more than I hurt him. I charged, using my shoulder to his gut, knocking the air from his lung, but I didn't realize how close to the curb we were. He went down and dragged me with him. Luckily for me, he hit the street with me falling on top of him and not the other way or he'd have crushed me. He flipped me; my back hit the street, as he lifted his ham-size fist. Before he made contact, he was being pulled off me. Breathlessly, I said to the beat cops that came to my aid, "I tired him out."

There was now an audience and other cops because, as previously mentioned, it was lunchtime and a favorite street for the brothers in blue. Vin from Vice grinned. "Lying down on the job, Molly?"

I rolled my eyes at his comment, but I didn't move from my prone spot on the street because, damn, the assailant was strong. As the adrenaline subsided, I felt the pain to my face. I was lucky he didn't break my jaw, but if that last punch had connected, he would have, or my nose, or both.

"You on vacation?" I glanced up at Zac, he was grinning at me, as he offered his hand.

I took it, then flipped him off, when I got to my feet. Vin fell into step next to us. "I wasn't pursuing," I said. "But there was a rookie at Duke's, a real Dirty Harry vibe."

They both understood immediately.

"I think the dude broke my face."

Vin studied me. "It might be an improvement."

I flipped him off, too, and then laughed, which turned into a whimper because it hurt to laugh. "I didn't order the sandwiches."

"Damn, you're slacking." Zac dropped his arm over my shoulders. "My treat today."

I glanced up, letting him know I appreciated the gesture, and then said, "I'm getting the most expensive thing on the menu." I glanced back. "Someone get the gun and money?"

"Yeah, it's covered," Vin said, then tugged on a lock of my hair. "Kidding aside, nice collar, Molly."

I nodded then said, "I think I'm eating my whole sandwich today. I earned it"

I didn't eat my whole sandwich, so Salem and I enjoyed it for dinner. I had what was salvageable of Frank Harris' boxes. The television was on in the background, so I saw the clip a few times. In the day of cell phones, everything was caught on tape, so I got to see the confrontation with the meth head about six times. Ethan had been over already, asking me to give him fighting lessons, provided they ended with me lying on top of him. Idiot. I grinned, and that hurt. I had some nice color blooming on my face, too. And I couldn't eat my sandwich, as it was intended, because my jaw hurt, so I picked the meat out of the roll. My phone pulled me from my research. Seeing it was my dad, I braced.

"Hey, Dad."

"Don't you hey me."

"How's Mom?"

"Molly Elizabeth Donahue. What the hell were you thinking?"

"I was right there, Dad. It was either me or the rookie who was a real John Wayne but way too green."

"He was high and carrying a gun. Was it really worth it?" Dad didn't shout, but this was as close to a shout as I'd ever heard.

"I wanted to wait, pick him up later, but that wasn't how the situation played out."

"Jesus, Molly."

I got it; as my parents, I understood they had to sit back while I put myself in danger. I tried to be smart, but sometimes, the situation determined the action. Was it a risk today, yeah, but I made the collar and got fifteen minutes of unwanted fame.

"It's my job, Dad."

He blew out a breath. I could practically hear him pulling a hand through his hair. "I know." Silence followed for a few beats before he asked, "Are you ready to retire?"

It was me who was quiet for a heartbeat before I laughed out loud. "Not yet, but I'll be more careful and will try to refrain from going hand-to-hand with any more meth heads."

"Thank you."

"Love you. Give my love to Mom."

"Love you, too. Will do. Be safe. Oh, and Gavin said you looked good."

I chuckled because he was the one who insisted I learn how to fight. "Later, Dad."

Dropping my phone, I reached for the paper I'd been reading through. Some of the research I'd found in Frank's boxes didn't make much sense to me. I wondered if the boxes weren't all on Katrina and were, instead, his filing system. So far I found nothing on Jason Benjamin. I was sure Frank had looked into him. He would have thought like the cops with Benjamin being the prime suspect. If he unrecovered anything on Jason, I hadn't found those pages yet. And maybe I wouldn't, maybe that's what the man took before he torched Frank's place.

I settled back on the sofa. People killed for countless reasons, but most of the time, the motive could be reduced to one factor, money. If we assumed Katrina Dent was murdered, keeping that quiet now by killing anyone looking into her death, was it to protect the identity of her killer or was money the motivating factor?

The news story on CyberTech pulled my attention. "It's like we're living in the movies," the anchorwoman said in awe. "Prosthetics that are made of living tissue over a metal frame. It's extraordinary."

I turned up the volume. That was extraordinary.

"The focus will be for our vets," a spokesperson for CyberTech shared. "A way to give back just a fraction of what they've given this country."

Curious, I reached for my laptop and looked up CyberTech and discovered it was a consortium, a virtual who's who in business. Two names stood out, Sinclair Rothschild and Kade Wakefield. I stood and paced, as my thoughts went in a million different directions. If we assumed money had been the underlying motive for Samantha's death, she attended a Sinclair event and ended up dead later that night. Both Rothschild and Wakefield were big time investors in the CyberTech project. Their prosthetic was being deemed the greatest technological development since the H-bomb. The announcement followed closely to Rothschild's event, so was it possible that Samantha's attendance at the event was what prompted her death? I stopped pacing. Frank had found something and was going to leak it, but was it possible what he found wasn't dangerous in the sense we were thinking, but rather drawing attention to someone who didn't want attention?

The timing of the unveiling of the century's greatest discovery and the deaths bothered me. And if there was a link to CyberTech, that opened a whole new suspect pool, those in the consortium, because the profit projections from, not just the private sector, but government bids, had limitless potential and certainly would motivate some to protect it at all costs.

Which meant Kade Wakefield just became a person of interest... again. Damn it.

CAP PACED HIS office. "We got nothing linking this theory of yours to anything," he said, looking back at me. I'd shared my thoughts on CyberTech and Samantha's death with Zac over morning coffee. He wanted me to share it with the captain.

"It might be nothing, but the timing bothers me," I said.

"Bothers me, too," Zac replied.

"Yeah." Cap pulled a hand through his hair. "Me too. What we need is someone to talk to Rothschild or Wakefield, get some background information on this project. Meanwhile, we'll do a little digging on the consortium members and see if there are any interesting skeletons."

"Molly can talk to Wakefield," Zac offered; my head whipped around so fast I pulled a muscle.

Captain looked over, his brow rising in question.

"She's got kind of a rapport with Wakefield," Zac said, eyes on me.

"He invited me to a masquerade ball, that's hardly a rapport." We so totally had a rapport, and one that was going to end in us naked, but I didn't share that.

"More than anyone else has," Captain said. "Talk to him. See if he'll share."

God, I hoped he'd share, then realized I was having sexual thoughts about Kade in my boss's office, so quickly said, "I'll call him."

"Good," Cap said. "In the meantime, keep on the forensic team, Zac. We need to find Jason Benjamin. And do some homework on the project, talk to scientists or geneticists and find out how the hell they made this possible."

"On it." I'd just reached the door, when Cap said, "Nice collar, Molly." But he was holding back a grin because I'd been sent the clip all fucking morning. "I live to serve."

He did laugh then.

Zac didn't come back to the bullpen, detouring to the forensic team. I settled at my desk, my thoughts shifting to Kade. I played with my phone. I wanted to see him again, but I didn't want it to be shoptalk. If I called on behalf of work, though, that would set the tone. I procrastinated in calling him, so I was damn surprised to get his text a few hours later, like he read my mind. Short, sweet and to the point.

Dinner tonight. I'll send the car at six.

All the sensations I'd felt on Sunday came rushing back; my hands actually shook when I texted back.

I'll be ready

I left work early, even had a glass of wine to calm my nerves as I dressed. My heart hadn't beat in an even rhythm since his text, hell, since I stepped into his office that first day; my hands shook a bit, as I pulled my hair up and applied my makeup, doing my best to cover up the bruises from the altercation yesterday. It wasn't easy buttoning my wide leg black pants and lacing up my white lace boned bodice tank, or buckling my four-inch heeled black strappy sandals because, all the while, I was imagining Kade taking them off me. I caught a glimpse of myself in the mirror and almost didn't recognize myself. I settled on the edge of my bed. I'd never felt so drawn to a person, but I *was* drawn... like a moth to a flame.

STEPPING OUTSIDE AT six, Levy was waiting for me. "Hi, Levy."

"Evening."

I settled back on the soft leather, prepared for the hour trip to Kade's home, but we drove to Broadway, to the Woolworth building. Levy held the door for me. "The elevator in the back, take it to the fiftieth floor."

If it didn't hurt to do, my jaw would have dropped. "He owns the Pinnacle penthouse?"

"Yes."

Holy shit.

The doorman held the door for me, then escorted me to the elevator and waited until I stepped onto it. "Enjoy your evening."

Oh, I intended to. "Thank you."

The doors closed, and I ran my hands over my pants. I thought I'd get a few minutes to pull myself together, but the elevator ride was quick. It stopped at the fiftieth floor, and a few heartbeats later, the doors were sliding open on Kade Wakefield, dressed in black pants and a white button-down, unbuttoned at the collar, with the sleeves rolled up. He stood there looking both casually elegant and untouchable. His gaze moved over me in a slow, appreciative sweep, before they returned to my face, settling on my cheek. His expression changed slightly, as a knot formed at his jaw.

"Welcome, Molly."

"Hi, Kade."

His lips curved up a bit at me using his name.

I stepped off the elevator and couldn't help looking around because the place was amazing.

"Would you like a tour?" he asked.

"Yes," I said, too quickly, earning a grin from him, before I confessed, "I've always wondered what this place looked like."

He touched the small of my back, the lightest touch, but it felt like a branding. He led me to the spiral stairs. At first, I didn't understand until I stood at the base of them. They went all the way up, all eight floors, because the Pinnacle penthouse was the entire green copper crown of the building. The walls were done in a soft smoky gray, the furniture was in varying shades of gray and white, and the wood floors were highly polished. A kitchen was tucked in one corner, a living room in another, a library and study. Another floor had bedrooms, another was completely open with a fireplace, a grand piano but what made it were the huge windows and the view. He took me to the French doors that led out to a balcony that spanned the one side of the building. Exquisite black wrought iron furniture with bright cushions was setup to look out at the view that was breathtaking.

"I think I'd spend all of my time out here."

He gestured to the door and led me back to the dining room, a circular room with windows around the perimeter. The table was set for two people, fine bone china, crystal stemware and silver sterling utensils. A huge arrangement of flowers, done in all white, sat in the center of the circular mahogany table that was surely an antique.

He pulled out my chair, before folding himself into the chair at my right. A man appeared pushing a serving cart. He was an older man, his dark hair mostly gray, and he had kind blue eyes. He placed a field greens salad in front of me with candied walnuts, feta cheese and hunks of strawberries.

"Thank you."

"Enjoy," he said, then smiled.

"Thank you, Benson," Kade said, reaching for the bottle of Riesling. He poured some of the pale wine in my glass and then his own. Lifting his, he said nothing, but my heart tripped at the look he was giving me, one he held as he took a sip of wine.

He lifted his fork; I did the same and had just taken a bite of the juiciest strawberry, when he said, "Do you often go toe-to-toe with meth heads?" There was a bite to his words, and looking at him, it was anger.

Shit. So caught up in him, I'd forgotten about that, and my telling bruises. Trying to diffuse the tension, I teased, "No, but anyone standing between me and one of Duke's sandwiches needs to watch out." His eyes lifted, his focus on my cheek, where the makeup didn't hide the purpling. I put my fork down and touched his arm when I said, "No, I don't usually go toe-to-toe with meth heads."

His gaze moved to my hand, before lifting back to my face. His expression smoothed out a bit, and he nodded. I went back to my salad.

"Did you always want to be a cop?"

"No," I said, earning his face. "I wanted to be a writer when I was younger, but though I have ideas, when I try to put them on paper, I can't get them to sound like what's in my head."

"Where did you learn to fight?" he asked, but there was humor in his gaze.

"My father and Uncle Gavin put me in every self defense class there was and then some. When they learned I was going to be a cop, they insisted on boxing lessons, too."

He studied me for a second, before he said, "I imagine you got a call from your dad after the video went viral."

"I did. He wasn't happy."

Another knot formed at his jaw. "No, I don't suppose he was."

"It's my job. If I hadn't gone after him, the rookie would have, and he was too young and too green."

His head snapped up at that, but he didn't share what he was thinking and instead said, "But you wouldn't have taken two to the face."

"I gave back as good as I got." Sort of.

"That you did."

I changed the subject when I asked sort of tongue-in-cheek to lighten the mood. "Did you always want to be a billionaire?"

I was happy to see it worked when his shoulders weren't held quite so rigidly. "I used to work for a diving company when I was a kid in Montenegro. When I was older, I owned that diving company and put the profits into buying a hotel. Saw the trend of Hollywood using Montenegro for movies, worked out deals to house cast and crew in the hotel, bought another hotel. It all took off after that."

That explained his accent. There was clearly more to that story because how did he go from working at a diving company to owning it? I wasn't going to press for details. Not that I wasn't interested in the details, but he'd shared a part of his past with me when the last time he closed off. I took it as a victory and moved the conversation on. I lifted my glass, met his gaze and asked, "Do you still have the diving company and hotel?"

His focus shifted. I didn't know what he was thinking, but I liked how he was looking at me. "I do, yes."

I took a sip of wine, put my glass down. "That's a great story."

"Your parents still live in Marlton?" he asked smoothly.

I didn't hide my surprise. "You remember that?"

"Of course."

So simply said, but my reaction…I reached for my glass and drained it because I didn't see this man coming, but, damn, he was getting under my skin.

He topped off my glass. "Yes, they still live in Marlton. Retired, and planning a trip to Europe." I paused and smiled. "To be fair, they've been planning the same trip for decades. I don't know that they'll ever actually go. I think it's just the idea of it they like."

He looked intense, but what he was thinking I didn't know. "Where in Europe?"

"Italy or Spain. They aren't sure," I said, flashing him a smile. His focus shifted to my mouth, and those eyes grew stormy. My voice was a little off from the lust that lodged in my throat, when I added, "See, the idea of it is the draw."

He had a thought on that but kept it to himself. "How's the investigation?"

There was the smallest part of me that recognized his interest in me could be a ruse to get me off the scent, but my gut was telling me this man wasn't involved. Did he have secrets? Absolutely, but not any that pertained to the case, so I answered him honestly. "We're hitting a wall."

Benson returned, replacing the salad plates with our dinner: grilled salmon, drizzled with a dill cream sauce, asparagus and roasted fingerling potatoes. My eyes jerked to Kade. He was already watching me. "Salmon," I whispered.

"You're on a kick."

In response, it was more than lust that moved through me. My voice was a little hoarse when I said to Benson, "This looks delicious. Thank you."

He left as quietly as he entered.

"Hitting a wall?" Kade asked, bringing the conversation back.

"Yes," I said, then lowered my fork and put my hands on the table. "I was actually going to reach out to you before I got your text."

His brow rose.

"This could be way out of left field, but I saw the report on the news about CyberTech."

Kade put his fork down, his focus completely on me.

"I could be barking up the wrong tree, but murder usually stems from greed...money."

"I agree."

"Our case took a strange turn." I shouldn't be sharing the details of the case with him because he was a person of interest, not that I thought he had anything to do with Samantha's death, but I really wanted to use him as a sounding board.

"And you're hesitant to share with me and not just because of protocol."

The man was astute.

I answered without thought. "I don't think you have anything to do with Samantha James." His expression shifted again, stirring warmth that moved through me slowly, seductively. "Even in light of our new direction, I crossed you off the list after our interview, before even verifying your whereabouts."

I couldn't discern his reaction, but something stirred behind his eyes, before he reached for his wine and took a sip. I wanted to know what he was thinking. Almost asked him, but then he said, "Whatever you choose to share won't go beyond this room."

It was a risk, but one I was willing to take. "Are you familiar with the story of the movie star, Katrina Dent?"

He looked thoughtful before he said, "Doesn't sound familiar."

"She was very big in the eighties. She died in 1989, a believed suicide. Samantha James met up with a man who was working on a story about Katrina Dent. He seemed like a fanatical fan, but he was murdered, as was his friend."

"And Samantha was killed, who met with him," Kade finished.

"Yes. Her boss, Milton Teller, used to represent Katrina Dent."

Kade caught on immediately. "Katrina Dent is the link."

"Yes, that's where we went, too, and we'd really like to find her fiancé, so he can fill in the missing pieces, but we did discover that there are those who worked the case, back in the day, who didn't think it was suicide. They were being pushed to close the case, though."

"And someone digging into her now ends up dead," Kade said. "As well as those he spoke to."

"Exactly."

"What did you want to talk to me about?"

"Well, back to motive. If it's money…" I paused, because if he was involved, I was tipping him off. I took a shot that my gut was right. "The timing of CyberTech's news and the murders bother me. Samantha was at Rothschild's event, days before the announcement by CyberTech. We know Frank found his story, but what if it's not so much Katrina Dent, but the blowback Frank's story could have on CyberTech?"

"So someone involved in CyberTech has a link to Katrina Dent." Kade didn't miss a thing.

"It's a theory. That's why I wanted to talk to you, find out what you knew about the project, background, players, etc."

"That makes me a person of interest." Like I said, the man missed nothing.

"I meant it. I don't believe you have anything to do with Samantha."

There was that look, again, before he settled back in his chair. "I was brought in two years ago. They needed capital. The testing, as you can imagine, is extensive. I was given a high level overview, but had my own people look into the soundness of the theory. They were excited, pioneering they called it. Actually regenerating a person's own tissue, being able to offer that to those who put everything on the line for their country. As soon as they gave the green light, I offered the funds."

Altruistic, and yet, he downplayed that when he kept himself in the shadows. I wondered if anyone ever really got to know him. I wanted to be the one who did, every part of him.

"The launch is scheduled in two months, a huge fanfare. All the investors will be there." I was hoping we'd have the case closed by then, but that was good to know. "What was her fiancé's name?" he asked.

"Jason Benjamin."

"I can have my people look into it." He saw my look of concern, before he added, "Discreetly."

It's not like we were having much luck on our own. And sure, it went against protocol, but I'd gone this far. "Thank you."

He studied me, for a few seconds, before he asked, "Why did you share with me? I'm sure your partner has me on the top of the suspect list."

"Zac has reasons for why he's the way he is. It's why we work so well together; we check and balance each other." I reached for my wine, took a sip before I told him, straight up, another risk, but I was in it too far now. "I shared with you because despite the possibility this could come back and bite me in the ass, I trust you. I don't know you well, but I trust you."

Chills danced down my spine. For someone I believed to be stoic, during our first meeting, the man had smoldering down. He pulled his focus like it took effort, and we finished the rest of dinner in silence.

After dinner, he took me to the library. Books lined the walls, a thick rug under our feet, buttery soft leather furniture. I settled on the sofa, he moved to the bar.

He lifted a decanter with a honey-colored liquid. "Would you like some?"

"No, thanks." I'd had enough wine at dinner. Any more alcohol and I might act on my need to taste him.

I watched him: the way his muscles flexed under his shirt and the deliberate way he moved. He turned to me, lifted the glass, my eyes drifting to his lips and how I wanted to feel them on mine. I hadn't meant to ask, but the words fell past my lips. "When you were called away on Sunday, was everything okay?"

He put the glass down and pushed his hands into his pockets. "It will be." His gaze moved down my body. "I haven't been able to get you out of my head."

It was possible to be rendered mute from lust because I was. Frozen on that soft leather sofa, staring at a man that my path never should have crossed, and yet, here I was in his home, listening to him telling me he couldn't get me out of his head. If he closed the distance, I wasn't going to be able to say no. I didn't want to.

And then he closed the distance. I could hear my pulse pounding, felt my blood rushing through my veins, heating as it did. He reached me, his stare so intense and direct, and pulled me to my feet. Before I could inhale, his mouth was on mine. Not a gentle, exploring kiss, but all consuming. His tongue pushed into my mouth, his fingers curled into the back of my head, as he held me there for his assault. And that was what it was, an assault, in the best possible way. My hands sought him, moving over his stomach, around his back, where I fisted the cotton. I moaned when his flavor saturated my tongue. His arm banded around my waist, pulling me up against his hard body. I sighed, and he took advantage, sweeping my mouth again. I felt his fingers on the lacing of my tank, and all I could think was go faster. I pulled his shirt from his pants, my hands moving under it to feel his smooth, hot skin. I felt the air on my back before he pulled from me, his hot gaze dropping to my breasts, when he pulled my tank off. He didn't touch me, even though I wanted his hands and mouth on me. He just stared his fill before he took my mouth again. His hands moved over my skin, softly, like he was blind and needed to touch me to see me. I'd never had any-one so focused on the discovery, but that's what he was doing. He was discovering me, inch by beautifully excruciating inch. My breathing grew labored when his hands moved up my stomach, his finger brushing the underside of my breast. My knees went weak when he dragged his thumb over my nipple, the softest, lightest touch, but heat pooled between my legs. His hands circled my throat, the pads of his fingers applying the littlest bit of pressure, as he kissed me deeper, longer. This was a marathon, and he was taking his time. My body was on fire. I had aches in places I didn't even know could ache. I wanted him to put me out of my misery, as much as I wanted him to keep doing exactly what he was doing, because he was killing me softly.

His mouth pulled from mine, his hands moved to the button on my pants. Our breathing matched, harsh breaths filling the silence, as he held my stare and slowly worked the button. My thoughts were on him taking his time, exploring between my legs. I drew my lower lip between my teeth because I really hoped he explored me with his mouth, too.

Slowly, he pulled the zipper down. I was completely at his mercy. He wasn't even touching me, just his fingers working the zipper, but I was caught in the spell of his making. Clay at the hand of a master, ready to be worked and molded, however he saw fit. I'd never experienced anything like it and knew he was ruining me. No other man would be able to pull from me what he was so masterfully pulling.

His fingers brushed along my stomach, my heart slammed into my ribs, as my breath caught. He moved lower, running a finger along the edge of my panties. I moaned, he growled, and then my cell went off.

Anger raged with lust. "No," I whispered brokenly. I didn't move. Was unable to get my body to react because I didn't want to. Kade moved, though, retrieving my purse and handing it to me. I stood before him topless, my pants undone, but he was completely dressed. I was a bundle of nerves, and he looked completely composed.

"Molly," I said, my voice betraying my raging emotions.

"You okay?" Zac asked.

"Yeah, what's up?"

"We got a body. I'll text you the address."

I dropped my head. "Okay."

Kade moved into me, slipped my top back on, worked the laces. Some of the heat faded because he seemed almost too calm and then he curled his hand around my chin, held my gaze on him and that's when I saw it. Everything I was feeling, buried in those eyes. He was just better at hiding it. "We're not finished, Detective."

I could only nod because we weren't, not even close.

He finished dressing me, then walked me to the elevator. "Be careful," he whispered, brushing his thumb over my cheek, before he kissed me. "Text me when you're home."

Warmth moved through me at that order. "I will. Next time, I feed you."

In answer, his lips tipped up.

The doors opened, I stepped in, didn't take my eyes off him until the doors closed, then I leaned back against the wall and cursed. I loved my job, but tonight…"Fuck."

I took a cab to the residence in the garment district. Zac and Julia were already working the scene when I arrived.

"What do we have?" I asked.

Zac glanced over, and then did a double take, because I hadn't changed. "Look at you."

"Seriously, I'm not in the mood."

"Date that bad?" he asked.

"No, it was that good."

"Ah," he said, then grinned, but he moved it along. "Looks like a robbery gone wrong."

I didn't get home until after two in the morning. There was enough evidence left at the crime scene that we were able to identify the perp, a repeat offender, had an APB out on him. I kicked off my shoes, poured myself a glass of water and texted Kade that I was home. He responded with simply: **Sweet dreams, Detective.**

I was going to be dreaming about where we left off, so my dreams were, most definitely, going to be sweet.

TEN

Kade stood in front of the windows of his office, looking out on Manhattan, but his thoughts were on last night, on Molly Donahue. He'd only wanted a taste, but a taste wasn't enough. God, she was sweet. His fingers curled into fists in his pockets, a growl rumbled up his throat. He hadn't meant to take things where he had, but after she shared so openly with him, after she told him she trusted him, even not knowing much about him, he needed a taste, and now, he wanted to finish what he started, a craving, one that could make him reckless, one strong enough to snap his control. And that made Molly Donahue dangerous because she could be a weakness, and he didn't have weaknesses.

He didn't like seeing the bruises marring her delicate skin. He'd seen the video; hell, he'd watched it a few times. It was her job, but he could admit he didn't like it.

He was surprised he'd shared his past with her. He didn't talk about his past, and yet, he had with her. It felt natural, another aspect of Molly Donahue that Kade needed to consider. As well as the fact that she was too sweet to muck around in the sewer where he once called home.

The intercom buzzed, right before the door opened on a man in a bad suit and a comb over of what remained of his dark hair. Harvey

Daniels knew how to find dirt on anyone. The deeper it was buried, the more he enjoyed the hunt. Learning what he had last night, he was curious about Molly's theory. Particularly since, he had personally sunk almost two hundred million dollars into CyberTech. If there was going to be blowback, he fucking wanted to know.

Kade gestured to the chair across from him before he settled behind his desk.

Harvey didn't waste time. Another reason Kade liked him. "Samantha James wasn't old enough to have any dirt. She was exactly what she seemed."

Kade said nothing, just steepled his fingers and listened, as Harvey detailed her life, and he was right; she hadn't lived long enough. Someone had taken that from her. He understood Molly standing for the dead because he felt the need to do the same for Samantha.

"Molly Elizabeth Donahue." He glanced up and grinned. "Now there's a looker."

Kade stopped him. She put her trust in him. He wasn't going to abuse that. "I don't need the information on her. I called you here because I have something else I need you to look into."

Harvey got that look he got when he had something else to hunt.

"Jason Benjamin, fiancé to Katrina Dent, the movie star. I'm not going to say more than that. I want everything you can find on him, and I want to know how hard it was to find." Kade pulled out a slip of paper and pushed it across the table. "I want information on these individuals, too. I need this sooner than later. An additional hundred thousand has been deposited in your bank account."

Harvey's eyes went wide, before he stood. "I'll get right on it."

Kade got to his feet. "As always, a pleasure."

Harvey was already out the door. Yeah, Kade liked him. His thoughts turned back to Molly. She was investigating a case that someone seemed hell-bent on keeping a secret. She wasn't just in the line of fire, but a target. Made an even bigger target, if her theory was right, and she was seen mingling with him. But that was something he could fix.

ELEVEN

MOLLY

I was exhausted and grateful it was the weekend. Not that my job followed weekend schedules, but I'd really like a few days to catch up on sleep. I wanted something to eat, then I wanted to go face down for a solid eight hours. I glanced at my phone, no message from Kade. It had been two days since our dinner, and outside of him wishing me sweet dreams, I hadn't heard from him. I hadn't reached out either. I wanted to. I'd picked up my phone a few times, but I was a little insecure when it came to him. He and I didn't move in the same circle and, well, I wasn't sure if his dinner dates all ended the way ours did. Well, would have, if I hadn't been called away.

I flipped on the television. Salem joined me, as I dug through the fridge for something to eat. I heard Kade's name, smiled and looked back at the television. The smile slipped from my face, seeing him with Emerson DeWitt. It was like taking a punch to the gut, which was immediately followed with anger, at myself for getting swept up. I'd spent the last two days daydreaming about our night together, checking my phone more than I'd ever checked my phone, waiting for us to take up where we left off, and he was out with Hollywood's sweetheart. I was a detective, I should have fucking seen that coming. The back of my eyes burned and that only pissed me off more.

I lost my appetite. I added some kibble in Salem's bowl, flicked off the television and went for a shower. Turning the spray as hot as I could stand, I stripped, climbed in and let the heat roll over me. Even angry, it hurt because I thought he'd felt it, too. His words *we weren't finished*, well, we were because I had never been one to share. I let the tears fall, gave in to the pain that I shouldn't even feel, because I hardly knew the man, and then I shut that shit down. Buried it where I buried my other disappointments. I'd gotten sidetracked, but Samantha James needed me. That's where my focus needed to be.

I got ready for bed, but I wasn't tired, so I grabbed the remote to watch a movie. I saw I had a message waiting. My heart jumped seeing it was from Kade.

Tomorrow night. Seven. I'll send the car.

I had gotten a thrill when he'd sent a similar text for our dinner date, but now, I wondered. Was he just used to getting what he wanted. He didn't ask because he knew the answer. Had I read him that wrong?

I replied, **I thought…it doesn't matter. I misread the situation. I think we are, in fact, finished.**

Not even a minute later, my phone rang. He didn't let me answer, before he demanded, "What does that mean?"

"It means I saw you on the television with Emerson. I don't…" I pulled a hand through my hair because I wasn't prepared to talk about this. "Like I said, I misread the situation."

"How?"

Seriously? I stood, paced and, as I did, I grew angrier. "After our day skydiving, and dinner I thought you felt it, too, so turning on the television and seeing you with Emerson, like I said. I misread the situation."

"Felt what?" he pressed, in a low gravelly voice.

"It would seem something I shouldn't have."

Silence followed. Nothing, he gave me nothing. Temper rose up to meet hurt. "Goodbye, Kade," I waited, still nothing, so I hung up, dropped my phone on the sofa, felt the fucking tears again, but refused to let them fall. I turned off the television and the lights and went to bed.

I didn't know what woke me, but then I heard the knock. Glancing at the clock, it was after three in the morning. I climbed from bed, grabbed my gun and moved to the door. Peeking out, Kade was standing there.

I didn't even think, unlocking and opening the door, because I was still working on why the hell Kade was at my door at three in the morning. Then I saw his face. He was pissed. He stepped into my apartment, closed and locked the door behind him. I stood in my tank and boy shorts, my gun forgotten in my hand, staring at Kade Wakefield in my little apartment.

"We didn't finish our conversation." His voice was deceivingly soft.

"It didn't seem like we were having one."

"What did you feel?"

"Why do you care?" I wasn't trying to be flippant, but the man had to give me something.

There was that knot at his jaw. "I took Emerson to the ballet because if you're right about your theory, I'm being watched, too."

It took me a minute to process those words because I was still on the fact that he was in my apartment. Then the words settled and some of the lust faded. I hadn't thought of that, but he was right. Anyone connected to the project was likely being watched.

"And it wouldn't do for anyone to know that a certain homicide detective has gotten under my skin, that I can't go a day…" He moved and not controlled, like usual, but restless, like a caged tiger. "Fuck, I can't go an hour without thinking about your taste and how I want more of it." He stopped pacing and looked me right in the eyes, his own looking like the calm before the storm. "I fucking want you, Molly Donahue, and I don't want anyone knowing just how much." He stepped right into my personal space. "Because that puts you at risk."

Oh my God. My whole body felt those words. My mouth opened, without the command from my brain, and answered his original question. "I felt home."

His fingers curled around my gun. He took it from my numb hand and put it on the table, and then he was on me. My tank was off and his mouth was on my breast, his tongue playing with my nipple, before he sucked that hard peak into his mouth

"Yes," I moaned, my hands working off his shirt.

My panties followed. He lifted me, dropped me on the sofa. His hands moved under me, cupping my ass, lifting me to his mouth. He sucked on my clit, before sinking his tongue deep into me.

"Oh my God."

The roughness of his five o'clock shadow on my inner thigh combined with what his mouth was doing had me writhing under him. His head lifted, hot eyes stared at me, as he pushed two fingers into me, curled them and hit that sweet spot. He sucked on my clit, and it was too much, the orgasm crashed over me. He didn't stop, tasting me with a thoroughness that had a second orgasm following the first. Then I was up, in his arms, as he carried me to my bedroom. He dropped me to my feet. I worked on his shirt, pulling it down his arms. My hands moved back up those arms, enjoying the hard muscle under the smooth skin, down his chest, over his abs, taking my time to explore each muscle in his six-pack. My fingers shook, as I worked the button on his trousers, his focus never leaving my face. I pushed his trousers and briefs down his legs, my focus shifting to his cock. My clit pulsed; a new wave of heat pooled between my thighs. His cock was thick and long, and god, I wanted him inside me. Fisting the base, I tongued the tip, before I drew him into my mouth. He moaned, as I sucked him deeper. I was just getting into a rhythm when he dragged me up his body, his mouth slamming down on mine, before he stepped me backwards to the bed. He curled an arm around my waist and brought me down on the bed. I spread my legs wider; he fisted his cock and centered it. Our gazes were locked when he pushed into me.

"Fuck, yes." I moaned. Finally.

He sank in deep then stilled, lowering himself to take my mouth in a hard kiss, before he pulled out and sank back in, a low moan working up his throat.

"Again," I groaned.

He pulled out, lifted my hips and sank even deeper. My legs tightened, wanting to hold him inside me. He picked up his pace, my breathing turning to pants, as he fucked me. Chills danced down my body, my moans growing louder, until I came on a scream. He moved even faster, he felt so fucking good, but then he was gone. Before I could object, his hands were at my waist, turning and lifting me to my knees. He ran his finger down my spine over my ass, down to my pussy, where he pushed it in. I dropped my head and moaned. He twisted my hair around his hand and pulled my head back, his mouth on my throat, his tongue running up my neck. His cock was pressing into my ass, my hips moving back to feel more of him. He growled, then moaned, before he took my mouth in a rough kiss, his hand moving to my breast, twisting and pulling on my nipple.

His thick cock slid into my tender pussy. "Ah fuck." And still, I shifted back to take him deeper, stirring pain from his hold on my hair, which only made the sensation between my legs even more intense. His hand moved down my belly to my clit, as his cock pounded into me, going so deep. The sound of skin slapping against skin accompanied our moans, as he fucked me to my fourth orgasm. My arms and legs went weak, but he held me close, his thrusts turning almost violent, before he came, the sexiest sound ripping from his throat. He pressed a kiss between my shoulder blades and tightened his hold on my hair. Pulling my head back and still being inside me, I felt that ache again. His mouth was right at my ear when he whispered, "We've only just gotten started."

I WOKE FROM the ache between my legs. It took only a second to remember the night. He hadn't been kidding, two hours and six orgasms. The man should give instruction to all other men because he knew his way around the female body. I bit my lip because I shouldn't want him again; we'd only just stopped a few hours ago, but already, I was aching for him. He'd given me four orgasms before he allowed himself one. I'd never been with someone like that. Hell, I'd never been with a man like Kade, though I doubted there were many men like Kade. It was more than lust that moved through me. I glanced over, but the bed was empty, and touching the sheets, they were cold. Had he left? I sat up, disappointment settling, until I smelled bacon. He fucked me unconscious and was now making me bacon. Where the hell had he been all of my life?

His shirt was on the floor; I pulled it on and fastened a few buttons, while I made my way to the kitchen. He'd pulled on his trousers: his bare back to me. I leaned against the doorjamb and took a minute to appreciate the sight because, damn, it was a sight.

"Coffee's on," he said, glancing over his shoulder, those gray eyes slowly moving down my body. "That shirt never looked so good."

I crossed the room, came up behind him, wrapped my arms around his waist and pressed a kiss between his shoulder blades. Remembering our rounds of sex, my nipples went hard. He knew, when he said in a rough voice, "We need to eat."

"Coffee?" I asked.

"Please."

I moved to the cabinet for two mugs, my thoughts drifting to what he'd said last night. "Do you think it's possible you're being watched?"

He pulled the pan from the heat. "I think you make a good argument, and without something else to link Katrina Dent to the recent murders, the timing alone warrants further investigation."

He plated up the eggs and bacon and brought the plates to the table. I took a minute to appreciate that he was feeding me, again, but this time, he was making the food. I could get used to it. He settled next to me. Touched my cheek with his thumb, a light brush, before he said, "Eat."

I reached for my fork, my thoughts turning back to the case. "I'd really like to find Jason."

"There's a good chance he met the same fate as his girl," Kade said.

"I know, but he's the missing link." I took a bite of the scrambled eggs that had onions and peppers. "This is delicious."

"It's just eggs," he countered.

"Well, I usually have cold pizza," I said, then grinned when he gave me a look. "How do you create human tissue?" I thought out loud.

"Stem cell research has been a hot topic. It was only a matter of time before science filled in the gaps."

"Today, it's prosthetics, and tomorrow, it's cloning, or gene manipulation, to get the child with blonde hair and green eyes." A shiver moved through me because the concept was so Sci-Fi. "I get progress, I even understand the impact CyberTech will make on so many lives, but people tend to keep pushing the frontier, always looking for bigger and better, but, sometimes, bigger isn't better."

"It's a fine line, I agree."

That got me thinking. Bigger and better…CyberTech was prepared to launch this amazing discovery, but just how much further past this discovery were they? I wasn't sure I wanted to know.

"Do you have vacation?" Kade asked.

Now, it was a chill, a very pleasant chill that moved down my body. There was a little voice in the back of my head, questioning the timing, hell, questioning him being here at all. I didn't tell that voice to shut up, but I didn't listen to it either. "I do."

"Next weekend. We leave Thursday, return on Tuesday."

"Where?"

"Somewhere I can keep you naked and in bed."

I felt those words; they settled between my legs.

"Yes?" he asked.

"Yes."

He stood, pulled me to my feet and tossed me over his shoulder. "Enough talking."

My body was on fire, but I did like the man's methods…fucking loved them.

"HE DOESN'T EXIST," Zac shared, on Monday morning. I was having a hard time following him because my thoughts were on the weekend. Kade had followed me out earlier. He'd spent the whole weekend, most of which was spent in bed. I had wanted sleep. I hadn't gotten any, but I was energized. I thought I knew good sex. I hadn't known good sex…great sex…mind-blowing sex. I bit my lip because he wanted another weekend of the same, longer this time. I wasn't going to survive four days of mind-numbing sex. I couldn't wait.

"Molly?"

My focus jerked to Zac. "What?"

"Are you here?"

Unfortunately. "Yes." I pulled my shit together, focused on the case. "Jason Benjamin doesn't exist." Then it hit. "He doesn't exist!"

"Yeah, welcome to the party," he teased. "The first appearance of Jason Benjamin was right before he started dating Katrina Dent."

"So there never was a Jason Benjamin." I dropped down on the edge of my desk. "Why would he fabricate an identity?"

"Damn good question, and since we haven't a clue who the person was who was pretending to be Jason Benjamin, and the fact that it's been thirty-one years, we could walk right up to him and not know it's him."

"He didn't have to change his name like Milton suggested, he just had to go back to his real identity. So maybe he wasn't the target, but the mastermind, which makes me wonder if maybe Katrina really was murdered."

"If she learned he wasn't who he claimed to be, that would be motive," Zac added.

"Do we have any pictures of him?" I asked. "We can get the forensic team to age him."

"Already thought of that, but every picture of him is with Katrina, and his face is conspicuously blurred."

"I wonder if Milton has pictures?" I pondered out loud.

"I'll call him."

"Jason Benjamin is looking more and more guilty, but of what?" I said.

"Katrina Dent was twenty-seven when she died."

She'd been so young.

"If we assume Jason was her age, or even a decade older, he'd be late fifties to mid-to-late sixties now. We focus on the players who are in that age bracket and run background checks to see if anything shakes out."

That was a lot of fucking busy work, but we didn't have any other choice. "Okay." I said, moving to my chair. "I'm going away this weekend. Out Thursday through Tuesday, but I'll bring my laptop, can run the searches on vacation."

I felt Zac's eyes on me, before he said, "You're going on vacation. Have aliens landed?"

I knew he wasn't going to make it easy. "I just need a break."

"You could definitely use one. Don't worry about taking your laptop. I'm just surprised you're agreeing to taking the break. Where are you going?"

It was the promise of another weekend like this last one that had me agreeing. I didn't think that was necessary to share. "Not sure."

"Just going to wing it?" he asked.

I dropped my arms on my desk and met his inquisitive stare. "I'm going away with Kade Wakefield."

Silence followed that announcement, before Zac leaned back in his chair. "Do you think that's wise?"

"He's not involved in the case. We've already crossed him off the list. He's not in his mid-fifties to late-sixties, so, yeah, there's no reason for me not to see him." That wasn't entirely true.

Zac knew that, too. Kade could be shady, and I was a cop. He didn't point that out; instead, he said, "You and Kade don't exactly move in the same circle."

Anger made my next words sharp. "Well, he's slumming."

"I was thinking the other way around," Zac said. My head jerked around. "Just be careful."

My anger instantly faded, and I replied sincerely, "I will." I turned to my computer. "Okay, so we run checks on all those involved in both the case and the CyberTech project. That's going to take a while."

"Yeah, good thing there's no statue of limitations on murder."

KADE AND I were going away, and I wanted to bring something, so I stopped at Sweet Escape on Fifth Avenue because I hadn't gotten those sticky buns out of my head. I meant to stop in the morning, but work got in the way. I was happily surprised to learn they baked them all day.

I ordered two dozen, some to eat, some to give to Ethan and some to freeze for Kade and my weekend.

I heard my name, as I waited for the young woman to box my lovelies, and turned to see an elderly man. Recognition was immediate. "Mr. Rothschild, how are you?"

He closed the distance and smiled. "The sticky buns," he guessed correctly.

"Yes. They're the best I've ever tasted."

"I agree. I eat far more than my doctor likes, but they're just too good." He stepped to the counter. The woman greeted him my name. After he ordered, he turned back to me.

"How's the case?"

"Complicated."

"Murder often is."

I didn't want to discuss the case because that was a sure-fire way to a headache, so instead, I said, "I've been seeing the coverage on the CyberTech announcement, saw you were one of the investors. How exciting."

"It is, isn't it? I thought I was in a movie the first time they showed me. The lives this discovery is going to change was worth every cent invested."

I could just imagine how much it cost, but he was right for a discovery like that, there was no dollar value too high.

"You should come to the launch. It's going to be a grand affair. I'll send you an invita—" He stopped talking, and his cheeks turned pink. "Perhaps that's overstepping." I didn't understand until he clarified, "If the social column is to be believed, you and Kade Wakefield." We were in the social column? Holy shit. "I'll send the invitation anyway, though, I suspect, if he's as smart as I know he is, you'll be on his arm for the event."

It sounded magical, another fairy tale moment, but it was still so new between us. To Sinclair, I simply said, "Thank you."

His man stepped into the shop. "Sir."

"Yes, Joshua," he said, and waved his hand.

"You'd think at my age I could slow down." He reached for his boxes. "It was nice seeing you, Detective."

"And you."

"Keep your eyes out for the invite."

"I will, and thank you."

I watched as he climbed into his Bentley, before my attention was pulled when they called my order. I ate two sticky buns before I even got home.

THAT NIGHT, I called my dad. "Hey, Molly, sweetheart, how are you?"

"Hey, Dad. I'm good." Salem joined me on the sofa. "You and Mom still planning your trip?" I teased.

"If we ever get there," he said, and chuckled.

"I just wanted to call because I'm going away for the weekend. I'm not sure how the cell reception will be, and I don't want you to worry if you try to reach me and can't."

"You're taking a vacation?" he asked incredulously. "When has that ever happened?"

"I'm actually going with a friend."

I waited. He didn't disappoint. "A friend? Do I know this friend?"

"Know of," I replied, before adding, "Kade Wakefield."

Silence followed for a few very long seconds. "The Kade Wakefield?"

"Yes."

"You're going on vacation with Kade Wakefield. Didn't I just talk to you a few weeks ago?"

"I know. It's all happening kind of fast."

"What's happening?"

"I'm falling, Dad." And I was. Falling and fast and it felt incredible. "He wasn't on my radar. I knew of him, but then I met him, interviewed him for a case, and now, I'm falling."

"And he's taking you away?"

"Yes. I've never felt like this. And I've tried. I've dated, but I just never connected, but with him, it was immediate."

"And he feels it, too." He wasn't asking. "A warning...be careful. I know you're a cop, but I'm thinking of your heart. You're a great judge of character, but this is Kade Wakefield. Before you fall all the way, make sure he's there to catch you."

He would be. I knew that down to my bones, but to my dad, I said, "I will."

Silence again, before he added, "You sound happy and that alone makes me happy. Have a good trip."

"Thanks. Love you, Dad."

"Love you."

TWELVE

Kade's car pulled up in front of Molly's apartment. She was already outside. Dressed in shorts and a tee, her hair in a ponytail. Kade recalled the video of Molly taking down that meth head, but seeing her now, she looked like a college kid going on Spring Break, the many sides of Molly Donahue.

He climbed from the car, and she smiled, even looked a little nervous, as she tucked a strand of hair behind her ear.

"Hey," she said, coming down the steps to join him on the curb.

"Good morning," he took her suitcase and handed it to Levy before he gestured to the open door. He climbed in after her. She was touching the soft leather seats and remembering her hands touching him like that had his jeans growing a little tight.

"So where are we going?"

"You'll see."

Her eyes darkened, curious and a little frustrated. It was a good look. She turned in her seat, and there was so much going on behind her eyes. "Jason Benjamin doesn't exist."

That got his attention. "Come again?"

"Yep, fabricated. He first appeared right before he started dating Katrina." Her expression changed. He didn't care for the shadows behind her eyes now.

"What's wrong?"

"I shouldn't be sharing this with you, but I want to. It feels..." Her focus turned to the window.

He touched her chin and brought her gaze back on him. "You have a habit of doing that, not completing sentences."

"Natural," she said. "It feels natural."

He kissed her, long and deep, before he broke the kiss and held her heated gaze. "So does that."

She touched her lower lip with her tongue and, fuck, but he wanted her, right the fuck now.

"I'm a cop," she said, out of the blue.

"I'm aware."

"You're Kade Wakefield."

He couldn't help the grin because, for such a confident woman, he liked that he made her a little insecure. "Last time I checked."

"An odd match," she said.

He knew what she was thinking; he'd already been thinking the same. They had no business together; it was doomed from the start, and, yet, here they were going away together because a man who prided himself on control had none when it came to her. That alone was a huge fucking warning sign.

"We give ourselves the weekend," he said.

Another shadow drifted over her expression. He didn't like it, so he kissed her, ran his hands over her body. He didn't fuck her, but he pleasured her until that shadow was gone.

They reached the airstrip, and she didn't hide her surprise. "We're taking a plane. I've never been on a private plane."

He helped Levy with the bags, then reached for Molly's hand and pulled her onto the plane. As soon as they were seated, they taxied. There were no attendants because he wanted the privacy.

"Can I get you a drink?" he asked, after they reached altitude. Her focus was out the window.

"This is amazing. No waiting." Her gaze swung around to him. "You've ruined me for commercial flights." She grinned. "Sure, I'll have a drink."

He made her a lava flow, fitting given where they were going.

He poured himself three fingers of whiskey.

She joined him. "What is that? It looked delicious."

"Coconut, strawberries, pineapple and rum."

She took a sip, and, damn, he liked the expression that followed. "So good."

She really thought so because she had two. The nerves she'd been feeling were gone. She moved around the cabin, talking. He liked how she moved, liked how she did everything with passion, from working out the details of her case, to eating the light lunch he had prepared.

"Come here," he said from his seat.

He liked that, too. She didn't question, just closed the distance between them. She knew what he was thinking when her eyes grew dark. Then she shimmied out of her shorts and his cock, already at attention from watching her, grew harder. He worked at his jeans, freeing his cock. Her gaze drifted down, her tongue appearing, as she ran it along her lower lip.

"Climb on," he ordered.

Again with that passion, she straddled him, her hands coming to rest on his shoulders. He grabbed his cock; she held his hard stare and lowered herself onto him.

"Fuck," he moaned. Her eyes closed, her head tilted back, a groan moved up her throat and passed between her parted lips. She rode him; his fingers found her clit, his focus on her face, as she moaned breathlessly, until she came, calling out his name when she did. His hips continued moving, drawing out the pleasure, before he pushed her down on his cock and groaned out his own release.

HE BROUGHT HER to his private island on Antigua. After dropping their belongings off, he took her for a sail. His Tartan 3700 sailboat was anchored just offshore. Molly was at the bow, wearing a white bikini, one of his shirts over it, her dark hair blowing in the breeze. Fuck, she was beautiful. Possession moved through him, something he knew he shouldn't feel, but, fuck, he wanted her and not just to fuck.

He watched her navigate the deck to join him. "Did you learn to sail in Montenegro?"

"Yes."

He studied her profile, watched how it changed when she smiled. "I'd never leave here," she said. Her eyes found his. "How often do you come here?"

"Not as often as I'd like."

Silence settled between them, with only the sound of the water lapping at the hull. It was some time later when Molly asked, "How did you go from working at the dive shop to owning it?"

And that was the elephant that had been in the room with them from the beginning. He'd taken the shop and not by legal means. He'd do it again, the owner had been a real sadistic prick, but it was the line in the sand, the one that pitted her against him, even if both wanted it otherwise. He didn't answer her, and his lack of answering was all she needed.

They were in the skiff heading back to shore when she said, "Thank you." Her eyes found his. "We've only just gotten here, but it's already the best vacation I've ever been on."

As soon as they entered his house, she started for the bedroom, looking back at him, when she dropped his shirt on the floor. He pushed his hands in his pockets, so he didn't reach for her because he was enjoying the show. She turned, walked backwards and pulled at the string for her bikini top. Her breasts sprung free, her top joined his shirt. She bit her lip, as she reached for the string to the bottoms. She knew like he did, they were only going to get the weekend. She didn't want to waste a second of it either. She disappeared into the bedroom; her hand appeared to drop her bottoms on the floor.

He was across the room seconds later.

KADE STUDIED MOLLY, as she looked at postcards. Her floppy sunhat was shielding her face. His focus drifted down her body to the white sundress she was wearing, though he knew every curve of her body, because he'd explored them in detail.

Her pale skin had a beautiful glow, kissed by the sun with no tan lines, because they had spent the first two days of their vacation on his private beach, where he insisted, she sunbathe in the nude. It was convenient because those days were spent fucking with breaks for eating.

He was playing with fire when it came to her. His well-honed control slipped around her. He reacted more on instinct than deliberation. He could acknowledge it was the combination of those big blue eyes and the intelligence behind them, coupled with the hard edge of the detective and the soft and sweet of the woman.

She had no idea the effect she had on him. Had no idea he'd never brought a woman to his sanctuary, the place he retreated when he needed to get away. He wanted her here, wanted to see how she fit. And she did, just like she fit him; every soft curve molding to his hard lines like pieces of a puzzle slipping together.

Her head tilted back, and she laughed, drawing his attention to her throat. Their first night together, when he showed up at her apartment, she hadn't held back, had loved like she seemed to do everything, without hesitation. She looked over, those blue eyes were wide and not at all shuttered. They warmed, before she walked to him, her fingers curling around the waistband of his jeans. "What?" she asked, as she studied him.

He didn't answer with words, but held her chin, lifted her mouth and kissed her. Her lips parted, his tongue slipped inside to taste her. She moaned, pressed closer. He broke the kiss, saw desire in those pools of blue. "Hungry?"

"Always," she whispered.

He kissed her again. "Food."

"Hmm…okay."

He reached for her hand, something he'd never done with a woman, but with her, it was just natural. She had a way of pressing against his side when they walked, like she wanted to feel as much of him as she could. He wasn't complaining because he liked feeling her soft body against his.

They passed a cove, and she stopped. He turned his focus on what caught hers. "How sweet is that," she said, the softness that entered her expression caught him in the chest. There were little kids, snorkels in hand, waiting to swim with the fish. "I think that's what I'd do if I lived here. Teaching the little ones the joys of the sea." She looked up at him, and her expression took his breath because, for as streetwise as she was, she was a fucking New York City homicide detective for fuck's sake, there was an innocence about her that stole his breath. "Can you imagine a more appreciative audience?"

He kissed her, needed to taste a little of that innocence, because he'd never been innocent. And as was her way, she pressed into him and kissed him back, without hesitation. When he broke the kiss, she asked, "What was that for?"

He didn't answer because he wasn't sure he was capable of words. Instead, he ran his thumb over her cheek, then reached for her hand, pulling her close, and continued their walk.

They were seated at an outdoor restaurant. "I've never been to the Caribbean. It really is as beautiful as the pictures," Molly said, taking it all in.

"Do you want a drink?" He liked watching her. Every thought she had was seen in her eyes. He knew she could hide them, had witnessed that during their first interview, but she wasn't hiding them now.

"Yes, a lava flow," she said, remembering their time on the plane.

His lips tipped up at the memory. "And to eat?" he asked.

"You pick," she said. "You know what I like." The innuendo wasn't lost on him.

She bit her lower lip, and, fuck, he had half a mind to pull her onto the table and fuck her senseless.

"Very well, I'll order for you." He waited because he'd learned that Molly liked to share.

She didn't disappoint when she said, "Whatever we get, we should go halfsies."

He'd never in his life shared his food, but he enjoyed watching her. Like with everything, she ate with a passion. No counting calories for Molly Donahue. If she wanted it, she ate it. "I suppose I could share," he teased.

The look she gave him was part sweet and part seductress. Maybe she did know the effect she had on him. He'd never watched anyone as much as he did her, but everything about her fascinated him. He reached for his beer, enjoyed how she studied her surroundings. Part of that was the cop in her, but she had an enthusiasm for life and didn't hide it. She was like a chameleon, able to adapt to any surroundings. He stood out. He knew that because he was unyielding, but Molly fit as an NYU detective, but she also fit here in sundresses, sandals and hats.

"You like it here." He wasn't asking.

"I do. It's so different from home, but I like the vibe. I could see myself retiring here, a little place on the beach." Her cheeks turned pink, her gaze drifting to him. "Not that I'm hinting."

He could see her here, too. Liked it more than he should, but nothing had changed. A man like him with the number of skeletons in his closet, some were bound to come back and haunt him, which would force Molly to choose between her job and him. How the hell could he put that on her? Bringing her here had been selfish. He fucking knew it, but he was a selfish man, one accustomed to taking what he wanted. He wanted her, but he knew he couldn't have her. She knew it, too. They were traveling down a dead end, ignoring the signs to turn back, but they wouldn't be able to ignore those signs forever.

"I love being a cop," she whispered. "Love being a voice for those who don't have one. Love following the breadcrumbs, tracking the bad guys, bringing them to justice. From the first day I held that shield, I was hooked." Her gaze never left his when she added, "But you make me want to give it up."

Fucking hell, how the hell was he supposed to let her go?

MOLLY'S EYES WERE closed, her body swaying to the music. She'd had three rumrunners and was feeling good. Every Monday, there was a block party of sorts. The view was amazing, hundreds of feet above sea level, the cove with the sailboats spread out before them, and the food was phenomenal. Among the offerings were seafood stew, grilled prawns, and Johnnycakes. The music had started not too long ago.

Her eyes opened and settled on him. "It's like night and day from Manhattan. I can't imagine you want to stay in the rat race forever."

He looked out at the cove. He'd never wanted to be in the rat race, but when you grew up with nothing, you clawed to get out and then kept clawing to get higher in fear of falling back into hell. Before he knew it, he wasn't that scrawny kid, but Kade fucking Wakefield. He went from one extreme to the other. He wasn't sure which was worse.

His focus shifted back to her. "No, that's why I come here."

She dropped her elbow on the table, her chin in her hand. "You look good here." Her eyes moved over him dressed in a loose cotton shirt and jeans. "Relaxed. Not that you don't look good in a suit and…" Her cheeks turned pink. "You know what I mean."

"I can't imagine you want to be a homicide detective forever."

"Certainly not after this case. The more answers we get, the more questions we have. It's sad thinking about Katrina Dent. She was in the spotlight, every move captured, and yet, no one knew anything about her. Not really." She glanced down, gathering her words. Her gaze lifted. "She reminds me of you." She reached across the table and ran her finger over his hand. "You have people who know the man behind the image, right?"

Never in his life had anyone asked him that, though he wasn't surprised she had because Molly cared, even down to the fucking street vendors that fed her. She cared about people. It was what made her a good cop, a better person. He understood Katrina Dent better than most. A rising star by the nature of what it was put you out of reach. It wasn't all it was cracked up to be, being at the top of your game.

"A few."

"If I wasn't a cop, do you think we would have met?" she asked.

He hadn't thought of that, but, no, it wasn't likely they would have. The pain in his chest that followed that realization was hard to ignore. "I don't think so."

"I don't either." She leaned back in her chair, held his stare. "So despite the obstacles with me being me and you being you, it's what brought us here." She stood, moved around the table, and straddled his lap, pressing down, her hands moving up his chest to link at his neck. His fingers dug into her thighs to hold her to him.

"I don't want this to end." She studied him and saw his hesitation, but not because he didn't want her, but because he didn't want his shit touching her. "Okay," she whispered, but there was a note of sadness in response to his hesitation. She stood, reached for his hand. "Dance with me."

He pulled her close, his hands moving into her hair to hold her gaze on him. "I don't want this to end, either."

Her eyes were wet because wanting something and having it were two entirely different things. She nodded. "Maybe one day when I'm not a cop and you're not Kade Wakefield," she whispered, before she pressed her cheek to his chest. He never fucking saw her coming, and now, he couldn't imagine letting her go. But he had to.

HER HEAD WAS thrown back, her hands fisting the headboard; her back ached, as he fucked her from behind. His fingers dug into her hips, pulling her closer, as he thrust deeper into her. A groan burned up his throat, his focus on where they were connected, her pussy milking his cock with her orgasm, her moans stirring his blood, as he fucked her harder, wanting to draw it out for both of their pleasure. His balls tightened, the fire burned up his spine into his cock. He sank in deep and came on a growl. Her breathing was as rough as his, the smell of their lovemaking filling the room. He'd just fucking come, was still inside of her, and he wanted her again. And it was because he did, that he pulled out. Seeing his cum between her legs, wetting her inner thighs, brought on a wave of possession. His clenched his jaw. She looked over her shoulder, her black hair curtaining half of her face, those blue eyes soft and trusting, and, fuck, it knocked his world off kilter. He climbed from the bed, caught a glimpse of confusion in her eyes, before he walked from the room, right out of the house to the beach, not stopping until he was waist deep in the ocean. What the fuck was he doing? And not just for leaving her in the bed, but being here with her to begin with. It was the reality that his need for her eclipsed everything else, a woman he'd only known for a few weeks. She wasn't just his weakness; she was becoming his breath.

She didn't follow him out. She wouldn't because she understood him better than anyone ever had. He had thought bringing her here he'd fuck her out of his system. He was so fucking wrong about that.

He didn't know how much time passed before he walked back into the house. She was in the kitchen, grilling up some fish they'd bought earlier at the market. Her hair was pulled up into a knot, but she wasn't wearing his shirt like she usually did. She'd pulled on shorts and a tee. He didn't like it. And fuck him for being so goddamn contrary.

After he dressed, they ate in comfortable silence, both lost in thought. After dinner, he had some calls to make. He returned to find her outside in the moonlight, her back to him, as she watched the surf. He joined her, settling next to her on the blanket.

"I get it," she whispered. "I didn't see you coming, either. From the beginning, it seemed like a dream," she confessed. "Like a fairy tale come true."

"I told you. I'm no prince." His voice was rough.

"I know you're not the prince, but you're not the villain, either. Your past gives you color and character." She turned those eyes on him when she confessed, "And I'm completely hooked."

A growl moved up his throat before he lowered her back on the blanket, slowly removed her clothes and when he sank his cock into her, he did it slowly, controlled, deliberately, savoring her and the moment. He brought her to orgasm, her eyes filled, because she knew he was saying goodbye. He loved her, marking her as his, even knowing he couldn't keep her. In the morning, she was up before him, her bags already packed.

THIRTEEN
MOLLY

I was working day and night. Needed to distract myself from thinking about Kade. Logically, I knew what he was doing, worried that one day I'd find myself smack in the middle of a tug of war between him and my job, but he really did make me want to give it up, to remove the obstacle because I'd never felt what I did when I was with him, and not just how he played my body like a maestro. He saw me, all the parts of me, even the parts I tried to hide. He saw them, and he wanted more. It was the same for me. The more I learned about him, the more I wanted to learn. We fit together; it was that simple.

My body ached for him, and my heart ached more because, even feeling it, too, he'd said goodbye. Not with words, but that last night he'd been different, touching me almost reverently, memorizing and committing every part of me to memory. I knew he was because I had been, too. The fairy tale ended, though, and I was back in real life, but like Alice tumbling down that rabbit hole, the experience changed me, getting a taste of how my life could be.

Zac and I were meeting Russell Bleaker, the producer who had worked on a few movies with Katrina. I hadn't gotten a chance to look him up, but I was grateful for the touch of excitement at meeting him because, since returning from Antigua, I'd been hard-pressed to even smile.

We met him in Chinatown, which surprised me because he was a Hollywood man, so the Plaza seemed more his thing, but the place he picked made a great General's chicken. Considering how the man ate, he was trim. Had to be pushing seventy, with a thick head of white hair and startling green eyes. He was handsome, and in his day would have stopped traffic. He'd still cause a few fender benders now.

"This is delicious," he said, helping himself to more chicken. "You want info on Jason. He was an odd one," Russell said, pointing his chopstick at me. "I didn't care for him. The charm was surface deep only. And though I couldn't prove it, not only was he using, I think he was dealing, too."

"Wait, what," I said.

"Yeah, arrogant prick. He held Katrina on a very short leash, while behind her back, he was partying and doing drugs on her dime."

Zac leaned back in his chair. "Well, shit. And Katrina?"

"She was a beautiful soul who got eaten up by the power and greed around her. It's sad to say, but she's in a better place."

"As a producer, you must have worked with Milton Teller," Zac questioned.

"No. I knew of him, but I never met him because Jason was so active in Katrina's career." Russell put his chopsticks down, leveled us with a hard stare. "Jason Benjamin was a dirt bag. He didn't just do drugs; he fucked around on her. He was a playboy and got away with it because he could be so damn charming. Katrina worked hard and that fucker enjoyed the fruits of *her* labor. I never understood why she didn't shake him off. There were men in the wings just waiting for a chance. It was like she felt beholden to him, and maybe he helped make her who she was, but that shit only has so long a shelf life." He dragged a hand through his hair. "I hate that she took her life, but I'm not surprised that she did." He reached for his chopsticks again. "The only silver lining to her tragedy was Jason crawling back to whatever hole he came from." Then he smiled. "As you can tell, I wasn't a fan."

Later that day, Zac sat on my desk. "Jason was dealing. Was that the plan from the beginning, to get into the circle of the rich and famous?"

"So how did Jason and Katrina meet?" I asked.

"And why did her parents do nothing? If Russell saw it, and he only worked with Katrina during filming, how did her parents, who still keep a shrine to her, not know her fiancé was doing shady shit, shit that, if caught, would blowback on Katrina?"

I shook my head. "Good question. And how does this play into the murders? If at all?"

Zac blew out a breath. "I have no fucking idea."

A WEEK AFTER returning from Antigua and I was exhausted. My attempt to work Kade out of my system wasn't working because every night, when my head hit the pillow, he was there. He was haunting me. As the days past, the stronger the urge was to track him down and knock some sense into him because what had started between us was worth fighting for. If I wasn't so fucking tired, I might have actually followed through on the conversation I'd repeated countless times in my head.

I hadn't yet seen him since we'd been home, but I knew that wouldn't last. Part of me didn't want to see him because who wanted to confront the one they wanted but couldn't have, but another part of me sought him out in crowds. It was poetic that when I did see him again, I was on the job, moonlighting with the vice division, staking out a popular spot for some of the city's biggest crime bosses.

I recognized the car that pulled up to the curb before Levy climbed out. He opened the back door and offered his hand. A long leg appeared, before the model who owned it, stepped onto the curb. I couldn't effectively put into words how it felt seeing her. I was working myself to death to not think about him, and he was out with one of his fucking models. I wasn't just hurt; I was pissed. Then he appeared, but instead of the delicious feelings he so easily stirred in me, all I felt was a blinding anger.

"Isn't she a Victoria Secret model?" Jimmy asked, the lead detective on the sting operation.

"Probably," I muttered, and hated the tears that stung my eyes.

"Damn, I wouldn't mind those legs wrapped around me," he said. "Fucker's lucky."

Never in my life had I been as angry as I was at that moment.

"Alright, let's see what's what," Jimmy said. One of his team was planted in the restaurant, wired, and we were listening in. This was strictly surveillance, that's what Cap agreed to, but sometimes things didn't always go the way you planned. I'd been experiencing that particular truth more than I cared to.

"He's not there," Jimmy hissed.

"Who?"

"The one we wanted. He was probably scared off."

That was helpful.

"Ah, shit." Jimmy hit the steering wheel. "Something's up."

Kade was inside, and I was fucking pissed at him, but I didn't like that he was so close to a situation where something was up. "What's happening?" I demanded.

"Carmine has a temper," Jimmy offered. We heard the shouts from across the street. "Shit." Jimmy climbed from the car.

"Carmine DeLuca?"

"Yeah. He's a hothead, and that's a packed restaurant."

"What's the plan?" I asked, as we moved toward the restaurant.

"Diffuse. It's not the first time. Nothing pulls his shit in faster than seeing the NYPD," he said, then looked at me and stopped. He yanked the band from my hair, unbuttoned a few buttons on my blouse. I slapped his hand away.

"Carmine has a thing for dark hair and light eyes," he said.

I wasn't sure I wanted to be on Carmine's radar.

We walked into the restaurant. You could feel the tension. Some customers were leaving, some looked like they wanted to leave. I didn't glance around because I didn't want to see Kade.

Jimmy dropped his arm around my shoulders, lowering his mouth to my ear. "He'll probably recognize you from your fifteen minutes." I wasn't a fan of Jimmy's. He tried to play the good ole boy, but I suspected he didn't like that I, technically, outranked him. "But there's nothing he likes more than chicks with authority. Work it," he ordered, then dropped his arm and slapped my ass.

I didn't show my anger and, instead, worked it. I felt a heat burning down my spine. I might not have gained Carmine's attention, but I had someone's. I passed their table. Carmine *was* a hot head, raging about something, but then I heard, "Hey." I felt him before I saw him, coming right up to me. Being face to face with the legend, his dark hair, blues eyes and muscles in all the right places, I could admit I was fangirling a little. "Aren't you that cop?" he said, taking a step away and looking me up and down, his focus lingering on my breasts. "Yeah, it's you." Then he smiled and, damn, he had a great smile. "Carmine DeLuca," he said, and offered his hand.

I took it. He held it tightly. "Molly Donahue."

"She's a cop?" Someone asked.

"A detective, homicide, right?" he asked.

It was a little unnerving he knew that, and kind of cool that he knew it. "Yes."

"What brings a babe like you here?"

I took back my hand. He grinned. It was a test because I knew he knew who I walked in with, so I answered honestly. "I heard the ruckus. Wondered if my particular brand of law enforcement was needed."

Now he smiled. "If you want to go hand to hand with me, Baby, I am all in."

His focus shifted to something over my head. His easy smile faded. I knew who was there because that heat turned to a full out burn.

"We got a problem?" Carmine asked.

"That's up to you." Kade's voice was too soft.

Carmine glanced at me, lingered before he asked, "She with you?"

"Yes."

I didn't hide my anger. Carmine smiled. "Doesn't look like the lady agrees."

Kade didn't want his world to collide with mine, but that was exactly what he was doing. And he was out with his fucking model.

I held Carmine's stare. "Have you cooled off?"

"I'm hot now for an entirely different reason, Sweetheart."

I understood better his popularity. I nodded, and knew I was a little pink in the cheeks because the man *was* charismatic. I then turned to Kade. His eyes shifted from Carmine to me. God, he was beautiful and pissed. I was pissed, too, but instead of putting a voice to that anger and making a scene, because I knew it would turn into one, I deliberately shifted my focus to his date. When my gaze shifted back to him, I didn't hide the hurt. His own expression shifted, so slightly, most would have missed it, but I'd studied his face and knew every nuance.

Then I walked away.

As I approached, Jimmy asked, "Problem?"

"No. We're done for the night, yeah?"

"Yeah."

"Later." But I didn't wait for a reply and walked out of the restaurant. I didn't hail a cab right away, needing to walk because I wanted to scream. Then I detoured when I saw the neon bar sign. Yanking open the door, I settled on a stool and ordered a shot of tequila. One shot turned to three followed by a beer. I was feeling pretty good when I finally caught a cab for home.

Ethan popped his head out when he heard me. "Hey," he said, but he looked weird, nervous.

"What's wrong with you?" I said, nodding to his apartment. "You smoking?"

"No, you had a visitor. He told me to tell you to call him." He pulled at his collar. "He was insistent."

"Let me guess, Kade Wakefield."

"Yeah, the dude is intense."

"Whatever," I said, turning back to my door and unlocking it.

"He told me to tell you if you didn't call him, he wasn't going to be happy."

"Yeah, well I've not been happy, either. He can join the fucking club."

"What happened?" Ethan asked.

"Life," I said and didn't hide the hurt. "Sorry he bothered you."

"You okay?"

I smiled, but knew it didn't reach my eyes. "I will be."

In my apartment, I actually entertained the idea of calling Kade, but the decision was taken out of my hands when Zac called. "We're catching the red eye to Los Angeles."

I was grateful to have a reason to push my personal life to the back burner. "What's happened?"

"Got a potential link to Jason Benjamin."

I didn't hide my surprise when I asked, "How'd you find him?"

Silence followed before Zac said, "He found us."

ZAC AND I were in a coffee house on the wrong side of Los Angeles, in a place that not even the worst of the worst seemed to want to frequent. According to Zac, how we'd been contacted had been unusual, as if Mitch Anderson was playing it safe and cautious. Perhaps that accounted for him looking like a homeless man. Though dressed as he was, nothing stood out, he absolutely blended. He had shifty eyes and telling quirks that suggested he did drugs and often. He wouldn't talk until we bought him food and then he didn't stop talking. Though it wasn't clear if he was telling us the truth or just making shit up because I wouldn't have been surprised if he pulled out a tinfoil hat.

I was on my fourth cup of coffee, but it wasn't working. I was crashing. I'd gone too long on fumes.

"I don't know what Jason's background was, but he seemed more like a marketing man to me," Mitch said, stabbing his pancake. "He could sell anything. Hell, he created Katrina."

I leaned in. "What do you mean by that?"

"Her parents introduced her to him, and the next thing you know, she's the hottest new face in Hollywood, and he's elbows deep in all of it."

"How do you know that?" Zac asked.

"Because I was there when she met him for the first time."

Well, shit. It was Zac who asked, "You knew Katrina before she became the Katrina Dent?"

"Yeah, she wanted to be a teacher. She loved kids. One day, her parents called her home from school for a dinner party, and Jason was there. I don't know. It all seemed kind of staged to me. Her parents looked nervous. I don't know why that impression lingered all these years, but that's how it felt. They didn't hit it off, Katrina and Jason. Katrina returned to school with me, livid, and then the next thing I know, she'd dropped out of school, disappeared for a while, and when she made her reappearance, she was a Hollywood star."

"Her parents pimped her out." I was incredulous.

"Yep. They saw dollar signs. Almost overnight, they went from middle class to Hollywood elite."

"Are you aware that Jason Benjamin is an alias?" Zac asked.

Mitch hadn't known by the look he gave us, but said, "That really doesn't surprise me. To say he was shady is an understatement."

"You have any thoughts on Katrina Dent's suicide?" Zac asked.

He put his fork down, looking thoughtful. "She reminded me of Marilyn Monroe. Pushed into the spotlight, not a place she wanted to be, but having others depending on her, she stayed at it for them, even though it was killing her slowly. It wasn't a surprise she had a breakdown."

"What breakdown?" I asked.

"I think it was in eighty-four, she spent almost a year in a private facility, a mental health break."

"We hadn't heard that."

"You wouldn't have. Only a handful knew. She told me." Pain moved over his face. "You'd think that would've been the wakeup call to her family, but she did four movies the year she got out, filming all over the world, and Jason was with her for every single film. To the public, he was the loving fiancé, but he was holding the leash."

Russell Bleaker had said the same.

"And her parents went along?" Zac sounded as incredulous as I felt.

"Have you seen that shrine they live in? Are they mourning or is it regret? Forcing their kid into a life she didn't want because they profited from it."

I had thought the same.

"Did you ever meet Milton Teller?" Zac asked.

"No, but I knew of him."

I was starting to get that itch, but I moved the interview on. "Katrina never married Jason. I don't imagine that sat well with him."

"No, it didn't. Even with him being the puppet master, she wouldn't marry him, and you know he wanted that because then he'd have a legal claim to her money."

I looked over at Zac. "We need to follow up on her financials." Turning back to Mitch, I asked, "What do you think happened to Jason?"

"He was an opportunist. I think he disappeared, changed his identity again and found someone else to manipulate."

"Why are you coming forward now?" I asked.

He held my stare when he said, "I'm dying. Cancer. Got a few months, maybe a year."

Shit.

"The shit that went down with Katrina, and knowing more than your average person, it never sat right with me. And Jason, he played the charmer, but looking into his eyes, there was nothing there. After

Katrina died, I kept my head down because there was a part of me that feared her death might have been more than suicide. I'm dying, so when I heard through the grapevine someone was looking over her case again, I decided I needed to share what I knew."

"Would you sit with a sketch artist?" Zac asked. "We have no pictures of Jason."

Mitch thought about it then said, "Yeah, but I'll only meet them here."

"I'll arrange it with the local authorities. They'll call you," Zac said.

"Okay."

Zac and I lingered at the diner after Mitch left. "So her parents arranged the meeting between Katrina and Jason, then sat back and let him take over. So how did the Dents and Jason meet?" Zac wondered out loud.

"And was money their motive, too? Enough to pimp out their kid. We need to look deeper into them because their behavior is contrary."

"I agree. It's almost like Jason had something on them?" Zac said, leaning up a little. "What if he did? What if the parents found themselves in a bad situation and the only way out of it was the daughter?"

"But there was no guarantee that Katrina was going to become famous," I said.

"Unless there was," Zac said. "Maybe Jason had the connections to make her famous. It sure seemed like he knew all the right players."

"I'm missing the straightforward murders. This case is making my head spin." I reached for my coffee. It was awful, but I needed the caffeine. "Mitch made it sound like Katrina really could have taken her life," I said.

"Which begs the question, if she did commit suicide, then what did Frank discover that he was ready to share with the mainstream media?"

"Maybe he learned who Jason really was or is," I suggested.

"My thought, too."

"We're here, let's make some calls and try to get in with the Dents again," Zac said, as reached for his coffee but stopped and pulled out a few bills to drop on the table. "This coffee is shit. There's better stuff at the hotel. Besides..." He studied me for a second before he added, "You need sleep."

I SLEPT FOR an entire day. Zac went to see Katrina's parents without me, took one of the LA detectives, not that he got anything from them. They not only clammed up but also told him the next time he wanted to talk with them, he needed to go through their lawyer. The gloves, it would seem, were now off.

Zac had learned from Officer Dobbs that Katrina did have a will, and she gave everything away, left nothing to her parents or Jason Benjamin. So despite public appearances, she knew what they were doing and spited them at the end, which strongly suggested suicide, having her will up-to-date, but now there was the question of who was footing the bill for the Dents' lifestyle because they didn't have a source of income. And why?

We were catching an early flight in the morning. Zac was heading out for drinks with some of the locals, but I declined the invitation. I ordered room service and was going to watch a movie because I was still trying to catch up on sleep.

I had turned off my phone, but as I waited for my dinner, I checked messages. For someone who said he'd be angry if I didn't call him back, Kade hadn't tried to call or message me. I dropped the phone on my bed. This was the same man who had resumed his dating of super models, only a week after we returned from what was, for me, the most erotic and amazing weekend. I had seriously misjudged his interest.

The knock at the door had me climbing from bed. Yanking it open, I expected room service so seeing a very pissed off Kade was definitely a shock.

He moved right into me, forcing me back, before shutting the door behind him. Déjà vu hit hard.

"How did you find me?" I asked, only partially interested in the answer, because he was here, in LA.

He didn't answer, just crossed his arms over his chest. Slowly the shock at seeing him faded, my brain reengaged. I moved away, crossing the room, before turning back to him. "Did you lose your super model? You came to the right place to find another."

"What the hell were you doing at Braciole?"

"My job."

"Your job is homicide not vice," he bit back.

"I've been moonlighting."

"Why?"

I was just too damn tired to go toe-to-toe with him. Dropping on the edge of the bed, I confessed, "Because staying busy keeps me from thinking."

His voice was softer when he said, "Carmine is dangerous."

Did he know that from personal experience? I didn't dwell on that because he was in my room, so I soaked up the sight of him and realized, I wasn't the only one who looked tired. My voice was softer when I said, "I know he is." Tilting my head, I asked, "You came all this way to tell me that?"

"I was here for business."

That was a solid hit. I nodded in understanding. "Well, thanks for the warning." It was hard to believe this was the same man I'd spent those incredible days with in Antigua. "I hope whatever business brought you out here is successful. If you don't mind..." I said, and gestured to the door.

Silence settled, but he made no move to go, the seconds stretching out. And then, he shocked the shit out of me when he said, "I grew up with Carmine in Montenegro." His mouth snapped shut before he paced away from me, dragging a hand through his hair, and when he turned those eyes on me again, there was so much going on behind them. "The man who owned the dive job was a sadistic fuck who mistreated his employees, docking their wages for no reason, molesting the women." He moved closer, his voice dropped. "I walked in on him raping one of the girls. She was no older than me at the time. Sixteen." Silence settled between us, but the air was fucking electrified. "I killed him," he confessed in a low voice, then leaned closer and said it louder, "I fucking killed him, cut him into pieces and fed him to the fucking fish." He got right up in my face. "You said I wasn't the villain. I am the villain. I know Carmine is dangerous because he and I are cut from the same cloth."

I was horrified, but not at him, at the monster that would take advantage of those depending on him, on the young. He'd killed a monster. That didn't make him one. I didn't realize tears had filled my eyes until I felt one roll down my cheek. "Why are you telling me this?"

"Because when it comes to you, I forget what I am. You make me want to be a better man."

"From where I'm standing, you can't get much better." His hands fisted, as he fought for control, but he was here, right here. I got up on my tiptoes, my gaze locked on his, when I ran my tongue along his lower lip. I'd wanted to see when that control snapped. His hands fisted in my hair, and his mask slipped. I saw the stark want and the danger, before his mouth slammed down on mine. His kiss was brutal, his fingers stirring pain, as he twisted my hair, his teeth and tongue abusing my mouth. He pushed me back against the wall, one hand capturing both of mine and holding them over my head. His other hand ripped my tee from me, then my panties. He pushed two fingers into me watching what his touch was doing. I moaned, tried to break free, because I wanted to touch him, but his hold on my wrists turned almost painful. He brought me to orgasm, watching as my body yielded to him. My legs went weak from the intensity of it; he drew me into his arms and lifted me from my feet. He placed me on the bed, and then straddled my hips. He reached for his tie; my focus on his fingers, as he deftly undid the knot, pulling the silk from his neck that was the color of the sky. It wasn't fear but a primal need that moved through me in a slow, seductive crawl, when he took both my hands, wrapped the silk around them and tied the end to the headboard. I'd never been tied up, but feeling that vulnerability and seeing the look in Kade's eyes…I'd never been so wet. I pulled at my restraints and more heat pooled. My hungry gaze tracked him, as he stood and undressed. My breathing hurt, my eyes unable to move from Kade, who looked every bit the predator. I moaned when his shirt drifted to the floor, whimpered in anticipation when his pants and briefs followed his shirt. One knee hit the mattress, and I almost came. The second knee followed, and I pulled on my restraints again, wanting so badly to touch him. He grabbed my waist, and I cried out when he flipped me onto my stomach and yanked me to my knees, my elbows pressing into the mattress and my hands fisting the silk. His hand moved down my back, over my ass. He squeezed, my breath caught, and then released on a cry when he slapped my ass. His hand moved around to my stomach and down.

"So fucking wet," he growled in my ear.

Using that wet finger, he ran it down the crack of my ass, stopping at the tight ring of muscle. My breath stilled when he pushed in just the tip.

I moaned into the pillow, then braced when I felt his cock at my pussy. He didn't slam into me like I was expecting, but sank in slowly, inch by delicious inch, until I was full of him. For a few seconds, he held himself there, and then he pulled out, sinking back in again. The pace was slow, at first, but that wild side was fighting to get free; his hips moved faster, as mine moved back into his thrusts to take him deeper. The hand at my hip moved to my clit.

A moan burned up my throat, as I turned my head to look back at him. Our gazes were locked when he pushed his finger into my ass, all the way to the knuckle.

"Oh fuck," I whimpered, my head dropping.

His finger mimicked what his cock was doing; a second finger joined the first.

"Ahh, fuck, yes." My arms ached, as I pulled on my restraint. I was mindless now. My body taking over, my moans filling the room, as the orgasm edged and then crashed over me, the fullness in my ass intensifying my release. I screamed out his name, my hips still moving, because the pain mixed with the pleasure was fucking mind-blowing.

His pulled his fingers from my ass, his hands gripping my hips, as his thrusts turned almost violent, his own orgasm coming on a groan, deep in his throat, that curled my toes. We stayed connected; our heavy breathing filled the silence, before he bent over me, untied my wrists and pulled me against his body. His hand rested on my ass. "You good?"

I glanced up into those eyes. "There isn't a word to describe how I'm feeling right now."

"It can't work," he said.

I didn't want to think about it, so I turned my focus on his body, my hand moving over the muscles of his abs.

"But I don't fucking care." My gaze jerked back to him. "I tried, but I can't let you go."

Those tears were back, my voice broke when I whispered, "I don't want you to."

"We have shit to talk about it."

I held his hard stare. "I meant what I said. I'd give it up for you. If it comes down to me choosing, it's not a choice." I straddled him, my hands coming to rest on his shoulders, my hair curtaining us. "As far as that animal, badge or no badge, I don't see a crime there. Either way, that never leaves this room."

He yanked my mouth to his, my hand moved between our bodies, fisting his cock as I sank down on him. I rode him hard then he flipped us and took over, getting us both off.

WE CALLED DOWN to room service, adding to my order. I'd pulled on his shirt; he'd pulled on his pants to open the door.

"When do you have to go?" I asked.

His eyes caught mine. "I came here for you."

"But you said…"

"I know."

I couldn't help grinning because I was just as far under his skin as he was under mine. "I make you crazy."

"Yeah, you fucking do."

"Good. Then we're even."

"Carmine is dangerous," he said. "But he's like a brother."

Remembering the man in question, that didn't surprise me. "I saw a bit of you in him." Then a thought had me stopping mid chew. "Does he know about me?"

His expression shifted, his voice a growl. "Yes."

"Hmm." I reached for a fry. "Who was the model?"

He glanced at me out of the corner of his eye. "Why? You jealous?" he teased.

"At the time, I was hurt, not jealous."

He grabbed my chin, held my gaze to his. "Smoke and mirrors." He kissed me. "Yeah?"

"Yeah."

He released me and reached for his beer. "I was there because there were rumors of another attempt on Gregory Enzi senior's life, and I was making sure Carmine didn't lose his shit. He's a bit of a hothead," he said, then waited. And I knew what he was waiting for. I was there with vice, the line in the sand clear, and we were on opposite sides of it.

"Like you pointed out, I'm not vice." I didn't know what he was expecting, but his head lowered, and he nodded once. "Hey." I got his face, and damn, but I'd never get tired of looking at him. "I don't know much about Carmine, but if he's anything like you, I know I'll like him." I touched his arm, his focus going to my hand, before lifting back to my face. "He's not their target." I probably shouldn't have shared that, but I did because I knew what I wanted. I was looking right at him.

The look I was coming to really love swept his expression before he kissed me again. "I choose you," he whispered against my lips.

Three words and I was a goner. I touched his face. "Say it again."

He didn't smile or grin, but said it almost solemnly, a vow. "I choose you."

I kissed him. It was then that I knew I didn't just choose Kade Wakefield. I was in love with him.

KADE WANTED ME to go home with him, but I took the plane back with Zac because I wanted to tell him about Kade. He took the news better than I thought.

"You're dating Kade Wakefield," he said, his expression almost as incredulous as his words.

It was more than dating, way more than dating. "Yes."

"He was in Los Angeles to see you?"

"Yes."

"Why didn't you go back with him? I'm sure he has a private plane."

"I wanted to tell you about him."

"You do realize that, though, there are no active investigations on him, he doesn't just dip is toe over the line."

"We both know what we're getting into, know that things will need to change to make it work. But he's a good man, Zac. You know me, you know I wouldn't fall for someone who wasn't."

He nodded because he did know.

"If it comes down to it, I'm choosing him."

That earned me his face. "What?"

"I love the job, you know how much I love it, but I…"

"Fuck, you're in love with him."

"I am. It happened so fast. Blindsided me, but from the minute we walked into his office, I knew."

He pulled a hand through his hair, let out a breath. "If we're being honest, I knew then, too." I wasn't surprised. Zac was an excellent detective. "You leaving the job doesn't work for me."

"I don't want it to come to that, either."

"Good. Well, if you can keep Kade Wakefield walking a semi-straight path, that's one less thing we've got to worry about," he teased, then sobered, and added, "Be careful."

"I will."

"But I'm happy that you're happy."

I reached for his hand and squeezed. It was why we worked so well together because we were more than partners; we were friends.

FOURTEEN

Whoever created his background is good, damn good," Harvey said, "It's like Jason Benjamin was conjured out of thin air. I'm not giving up, but I'd like to know who built his profile because they're CIA level good. What I have uncovered is he was handpicked for Katrina Dent. Practically custom-made for her and I mean custom-made. He had work done, his nose augmented, his lips changed, so he looked more like what she liked."

Kade leaned back in his chair, intrigued. "Who footed that bill?"

"Her parents." Harvey moved to the edge of his seat. "Her parents introduced her to Jason Benjamin, and soon, he wasn't just her beau, but he was representing her, handling contracts. I have to admit; he did a damn good job. Katrina Dent had a stellar career, traveled all over the world filming movies, and Jason was there, every step of the way."

"Was Katrina consulted about the life her parents and Jason had planned for her?" Kade asked disgustedly.

"That's what's interesting. Tony Dent had a thing for playing the ponies, lost more than he made, was in it for some serious dough and then in stepped Jason, offering him the golden goose."

"In it to whom?" Kade asked.

Harvey pointed at him. "Right question. Family was originally from Brooklyn, owed a low-level loan shark who I traced back to none other than Gregory Enzi senior."

Well fuck.

"Parents got in too deep then Jason Benjamin magically appeared, who happened to turn their child into a star."

Kade didn't like where this was going when he followed the logic. "He was part of Enzi's crew." Molly was right in the fucking middle of it.

"I can't prove any of this, just following the breadcrumbs, but that's what I think. Dent was into him for fifty large, but he had a beautiful daughter, and Enzi had the contacts. Got his foot in the door of the Hollywood elite and the money to be made from dealing drugs…certainly an incentive to make the dream a reality." Harvey shook his head. "Katrina Dent was a pawn in the truest sense of the word."

"Son of a bitch."

"Other interesting tidbit, their daughter died, Jason disappeared, and their income flow stopped until almost a year to the day when the same sum, twenty grand a month, was deposited into their account like clockwork." Harvey leaned back in his chair. "Who's paying them and why?"

"Enzi. They showed their loyalty by keeping their mouths shut for a year. Reward them with a payoff." Why hadn't the authorities, at the time, followed the money? "And Katrina's death?"

Harvey rubbed a hand over his head. "I got to say, from everything I've found it looks like a suicide. She started withdrawing from friends, missing public appearances, she even started acting differently, more closed-off and guarded."

"And Jason?"

"No trace of him. I'm still looking, but again, whoever arranged for him to disappear was good. Even for organized crime, his shit was sealed up tight. Another interesting tidbit, Katrina went away in nineteen eighty-four, a mental health break they claimed."

"But?"

"She was in the maternity ward, but there was never an announcement of a child."

"The baby wasn't Jason Benjamin's." Kade resisted the urge to pull a hand through his hell, but fucking hell.

"That's my guess. Found the woman who worked the ward, was the nurse on record for Katrina Dent. She moved back to Manhattan years ago. She's going to be at the Art Institute Gala tomorrow night."

"You're a little dangerous," Kade said.

"Yeah, but I've never been able to dig up anything on you, and I've tried."

Kade would have been disappointed if he hadn't tried, but he'd never find anything. Harvey was good, but Kade knew better.

Harvey reached into his briefcase and pulled out a file that he dropped on Kade's desk. "Info on one of the names you asked about."

"Thanks, Harvey."

He stood. "I'll be in touch when I have more."

Kade walked him to the door, offered his hand. "They'll be a bonus in your account. Appreciate the speed."

"Anytime."

"Penelope," he called from the door.

"Yes, Mr. Wakefield."

"Confirm my attendance to the Art Institute gala."

"Yes, Sir."

Upside to all this bullshit, he'd get to dress his woman again and then undress her.

He closed the door and walked back to his desk. Lifted the file and scanned the contents. "Son of a bitch."

"WHAT'S GOING ON with you?" Carmine asked Kade that night. They were on the back patio, surrounded by manicured lawns, tended garden beds and woods. He had purchased the estate in the suburbs, as a tax write off, but it had grown on him. He liked the quiet, the open space, even the history of the place that Benson went out of his way to share. "Talk to me about the cop."

"She knows," Kade said, and waited for Carmine to lose his shit.

He didn't disappoint when he stood so fast he knocked his chair over. "What the fuck is wrong with you?"

Kade's words were clipped. "How long have you known me?"

"She's a fucking cop, was working with vice."

"She told me you're not their target."

"Of course she's going to tell—"

Kade was up and had Carmine against the wall in a heartbeat. "You forget who you're talking to." His tone menacing.

Carmine shrugged him off and stalked away from him. Pacing to get a hold of his temper. "You're telling me you're looking at the big picture."

"Yes."

"You're not letting your cock do the thinking?"

"I'm going to pretend you didn't just ask me that."

Carmine stopped pacing, looked at his friend, really looked at him. "Shit, she's not just a fuck."

Kade bit back. "No."

"And she knows about DeNuzzi."

"Yes."

"And?"

"She said she didn't see a crime there."

Carmine pulled a hand through his hair. "I can't believe you're sleeping with the fucking NYPD."

"Not all, just one."

Carmine stopped pacing, looked back at his friend, then laughed out loud. Kade relaxed his stance.

"I took her to Antigua."

Carmine stopped laughing. "No shit? She's that important."

Kade returned to his seat, reached for his whiskey, took a sip. "I'm only just beginning to realize how important."

Carmine sat on the edge of the chair and dropped his elbows on his knees. "Fuck, man. Surprised as fuck it's a cop, but seeing her in person, I get the appeal."

Kade leveled hard eyes on his friend.

Carmine put his hands up and laughed. "Just an observation," he said, and then added sincerely, "I'm happy for you. So what happens now?"

Kade wanted Molly in his apartment and his bed. It was one of the things they needed to discuss. "I make it known she's mine."

"What do you think her partner and boss are going to say?"

"She took the commercial flight back with her partner to tell him."

"And what if she gets push back?"

Kade wasn't going to let that happen. They could find a way where she didn't have to give up her career. "She wants me."

"She'd give it up?" Carmine was incredulous.

"Yeah," Kade said, lifted his glass, and added, "I'd give it all up for her."

Those words rendered his lifelong friend speechless but not for long. "Well, then it's time you introduce your woman to your family."

Kade didn't miss a beat. "Why do you think you're here?"

The doorbell turned Carmine's head. "You sneaky bastard."

Kade knew there was a good chance Carmine wouldn't show if he knew Molly was coming. He was a crime lord, after all, and she was a cop, so he took the option off the table.

Benson appeared and right behind him was Molly. He hadn't told her either, but she took one look at Carmine, smiled, and crossed the patio to him. "I guess he told you," she said, in way of greeting.

"You do realize the last time we met you had me under surveillance," Carmine said.

"Yeah, but I was moonlighting. I work with the dead, not the living."

"Moonlighting?"

"To keep myself distracted."

"Really?" he said and moved closer. "Why?"

"I think you know why," she countered.

"I think I do, too, which begs the question why Kade was out with a Victoria Secret's model that night," Carmine said, both of them turning their attention to Kade.

He stood, crossed the patio, pulled Molly close and kissed her, and long enough that when he broke the kiss, she didn't remember what they were discussing.

Carmine laughed. "That won't work on me, Brother."

Benson appeared. "Dinner is served."

After dinner, Kade watched Molly and Carmine and wasn't surprised how easily they got along. She was sharing some story about her neighbor, her eyes bright with laughter. Carmine caught Kade's attention a few times during the evening, giving him his approval. He didn't need it, but he was glad to have it. And for the rest of the night, he watched the woman who had bewitched him, bewitch his brother.

HIS COCK WAS still inside her, and as much as he wanted to go another round, they had shit to discuss. He kissed her, long and hard, then pulled out of her. He didn't stay in bed because she was too tempting, looking as she did, soft and sated.

"We need to talk."

"Now?"

He grabbed her hand and dragged her from bed. "Now."

He pulled on sweats; she pulled on his tee. He led her to the kitchen, so he could put the island between them because her in just his tee was fucking distracting.

"I talked to my PI."

Soft and sated shifted. His cop was looking back now.

"He found a possible link between Jason Benjamin and Gregory Enzi senior."

She was off the stool. "What?" She started to pace. "Okay, tell me everything.

"Tony Dent liked to gamble, was in it to a loan shark for fifty grand, one who had a link back to Enzi."

Her eyes went wide. "Enzi saw Katrina, had contacts in Hollywood, made her a star, opened up a new revenue stream with selling drugs to the Hollywood crowd."

He loved watching her work. She was a damn fine detective. "Yes."

"Which explained Jason's fabricated name because he had mob connections." She pulled a hand through her hair. "So did Katrina learn who Jason was connected to? Was that what led to her death?"

"There's more. My guy found evidence that when she went away in eighty-four for a mental health break that she actually had a baby."

Her jaw dropped. "There's no record of a baby." She dragged a hand through her hair. "Why didn't the coroner note that in the autopsy?" Her focus shifted back to him. "It wasn't Jason's."

"Our thinking, too."

She was moving again, working it out. "So a young girl was forced into stardom because of money. Her fiancé was unyielding, but she found a bit of happiness, got pregnant. It would ruin her image if people learned of her baby, so they hid her away, she gave birth, they took the baby." She stopped pacing. "They took her baby." Her eyes turned bright. "How the hell did she bear that? Unless she didn't, unless she tried to find her baby, but there were those who wanted the secret kept, which points the finger at Enzi senior, the man behind the creation of Katrina Dent." She paled, realizing just how dark a road her case was traveling down. "Jason killed Katrina. Enzi would know Jason, even with a different name, so Jason carried out the order and then went back to the Enzi crew or broke free, and with Enzi having his foothold in Hollywood, and Jason having a body on him, Enzi knew he was safe from Jason talking." Wide blue eyes found his. "Frank figured out who Jason was, that's why he was killed, why Samantha and Emily were killed."

"So who is he?"

"I don't know, but I need to share this with Zac."

"There's more."

Molly had been heading for her phone but stopped and looked back at him. "One of the women who worked the maternity ward, when Katrina was there, is going to be at the Art Institute Gala tomorrow."

She moved right into him, pressed her soft curves against his hard body. "Want a job?" she teased. "Zac is going to want to be there."

"I figured." And he had. An extra half a million donation and he was granted a plus two. He wasn't going to share that with her.

"He can come?" she asked.

"As long as he's got a tux."

She kissed him. He didn't hesitate to take the kiss deeper. Then he lifted her, carried her back to the bedroom. "You can fill in your partner in the morning."

Her voice was a husky whisper. "Good idea."

THE FOLLOWING MORNING, before Kade dropped Molly at work, he sat in a personal dressing room. Two women were bringing in gowns for Molly to try on for the gala. He knew which one he liked, the black cocktail dress with a dipping v-neckline and opened back that fell just to her mid thigh. She looked exquisite in it, even more exquisite out of it.

She appeared wearing a silver gown, sheer top, with appliqués over her breasts, and a full skirt. She walked like she was on the catwalk, swaying her hips and turning to give him her back. "Yes? No?"

"Nice, would look nicer pooled at your feet."

"That's a no," she muttered and went back into the dressing room. He stood, dismissed the women, who didn't hide the looks they were giving him. He stepped into the room; she knew it was him when she stopped working the zipper. "I wondered how long you'd wait," she said, a bit breathlessly.

He reached for the zipper, pulling it slowly down, kissing every inch of skin he exposed. He pushed the straps from her shoulders, the gown slid down her body.

"Look at me." His voice was hoarse.

She turned, dressed only in her lace boy shorts. "I was right. It looks better pooled at your feet."

His gaze moved down her body; he brushed his finger over her nipple, her breath hitched. His gaze moved back to hers. "Move in with me," he whispered.

He watched her expressive face and could practically hear her internal argument, the doubt, and the worry that it was too soon, that they were rushing, but he saw when she settled on the answer he wanted to hear. Instead of giving him what he wanted, though, she said, "I have a cat."

He countered smoothly, "He's invited, too."

Her smile was blinding. "Yes," she whispered.

He wanted to kiss her, but he knew he wouldn't stop at kissing. She had to get to work, so he helped her dress, but held her chin when he added, "I want you in my apartment by the weekend."

She drew her lower lip into her mouth, her blue eyes heating with want. She didn't answer with words, but that was all the answer he needed.

FIFTEEN

MOLLY

"Holy shit," Zac said, pacing the captain's office. "Holy shit."

"How did you get this info?" Cap asked, then held up his hand. "Do I want to know?"

I'd definitely crossed a line, but considering what we learned, it was worth it. "Kade Wakefield's PI."

"And he's helping because?" Captain narrowed his eyes, then answered his own question. "It's an active investigation, Molly."

"I know, I know, but he knows about it since we interviewed him. He offered to look into Jason Benjamin, and since we weren't having any luck, I didn't see the harm."

"We can't use anything he shared," Captain warned.

"I know, but it gives us a direction to look, one I don't think we would have found on our own."

"We're going to have to pull in Vin's team, get him to do some of the legwork, maybe they even have shit on Jason and Katrina, shit they don't even know they have," Captain said.

"I agree with Molly. I think Jason killed Katrina. And since he's the only player in the wind, him killing now, to keep his secret, makes sense."

"Agreed, but I'd still like to know who the father of Katrina's baby is and where that baby is now. And follow up with that coroner. Why did he withhold the pregnancy from the autopsy report?"

"I already have a call into Jackson. As far as the baby..." I said, earning both of their attention. "There's a gala tonight and a woman who worked in the ward and cared for Katrina is going to be there."

Captain dropped down on his desk. "Whoever the hell this PI is I think he needs to work for us. I'm guessing you'll be attending this gala."

"Yes, as will Zac."

"I am." Zac looked surprised.

"Kade made it happen."

"I think we need to put Kade on the payroll, too," Captain said. "Alright talk to this woman. I'll reach out to vice. We need to find Jason Benjamin's true identity and let's find her baby." Captain moved around his desk. "Follow up with Milton Teller. He didn't know about the baby? And now that we know her parents' secret, selling their kid for fifty grand, maybe they'll be more willing to talk."

ZAC FIDGETED WITH his tie. "I want to be mad, but Kade's guy found out more than our entire forensic team."

"Why didn't Breen follow the money?" I asked. "It's Detective 101, but he didn't follow it."

"Yeah, that's a question we're going to have to ask him."

Kade appeared. "Car's here."

He'd given Zac and me time to strategize. I hadn't needed to ask. He greeted Zac then disappeared, leaving us to it. I walked to him now, slipped my hand into his, and touched my lips to his.

He responded with another kiss, hard, quick and perfect.

Zac approached, fidgeted with his tie again. "Thank you for the invite and the info."

Kade studied Zac before he said, "That hurt."

Zac blew out a breath. "You have no fucking idea," he said, and started for the door.

When we reached the gala, Zac was all business. My head was in the game, but looking around at the museum, where the gala was being held, all the beautiful people, I wanted to mingle, too. Maybe after, we could.

"We need to draw her from the crowd," Zac said. "Any thoughts?"

"I'll bring her to you," Kade offered.

He didn't wait around for a reply before he disappeared.

"I can't believe I'm saying this, but I kind of get the appeal," Zac said.

I'd just taken a sip of my champagne. It almost came out of my nose. "Warn me next time."

He chuckled. A few minutes later, a woman approached us. "Your presence is requested in the Chloe room. Out those doors, second exhibit on the right."

Zac glanced down at me when the woman disappeared. "He's good."

We entered the room that still had people mingling, but the noise level was manageable. I spotted Kade, immediately, in the corner with an elderly woman, early seventies. Camilla Mulroney was dressed in a long black gown that hugged her figure, and she still had a hell of one. Her gray hair was swept off her face and small diamonds hung from her ears.

We approached, and Kade made the introductions before Zac took point.

"We're sorry to ambush you, but we wondered if we could ask you a few questions about a patient you tended."

Camilla knew immediately. "Katrina Dent."

"Yes."

She looked a little nervous, but she surprised us when she said, "What would you like to know?"

"She was pregnant," Zac said.

"Yes, she came to us before she started showing. Stayed with us for the duration of the pregnancy. I'd never seen someone so excited about having a baby, and I worked in the maternity ward."

"Did she admit herself?"

"Her fiancé did." It was her tone that revealed she wasn't a fan of his. "For someone so highhanded, he didn't come around very often. Katrina was exhausted when she joined us, but for those seven months, she was happy, rested and so excited to be a mom."

"But she wasn't," Zac said.

"No. I'll never forget that day. They didn't even tell her. She needed a C–section, and they took her baby before she woke from the anesthesia. She never got to see her baby."

"Oh my god," I whispered.

Her gaze turned to me. "It was the most heartbreaking scene, but as soon as she recovered, he had her checked out and back to work." Anger was in her tone now.

"Why would she go back to work?" I asked. "Why agree when he did something so heinous?"

"To be honest, I think it was fear. She wasn't going back. She was leaving him, leaving the business, but he came to her one day, and whatever he said, she was packed the next day."

"So he was blackmailing her," Zac said, not hiding his anger.

"That would be my guess."

"Has anyone found you since?" I asked. "Looking for information on Katrina?"

"I would have thought so, but, no, not one person until a few years ago. Some reporter found me."

"Frank Harris?" Zac asked.

"Yes, that's him." She sobered. "I never believed she killed herself. Even with everything she'd been through, she had a thirst for life. I've always thought it was a crime that whoever killed her got away with it."

"Well, we're hoping to fix that," I said.

"I hope you do."

"Thank you for your time," I said then asked, "Do you know what happened to the baby?"

"No. I never even knew if it was a boy or girl before they were whisked away."

"Any thoughts on the father?"

"No, I just know it wasn't her fiancé's. That was a relationship in name only."

I PACED IN front of my desk, still wearing my gown from the gala. Zac had taken off his tie. It was almost midnight, but we were compiling a list. Kade had dropped us off, demanded I call him when I was ready to be picked up. He understood, didn't push, gave me what I needed. I liked to think I did the same for him. He said it couldn't work, but we did work.

Zac was at the board, as we brainstormed the baby daddy. "Milton, Mitch, Russell, they all could have been the father."

I settled on the edge of my desk. "Mitch was her childhood friend, but he didn't mention the baby. I think he would have if he'd known. And I didn't get lover from him. Speaking of, has he done the composite?"

"Got a call yesterday. He's meeting with them today," Zac said.

"Russell made a few comments that led me to believe he was interested in Katrina. Was she interested back? It's possible he's the father, but he doesn't know there was a baby."

"I agree."

"And Milton, something about him bothers me. He's been withholding shit from the beginning. He could tell us what Jason looks like, but he hasn't shared. He had to have known about the baby, at least the break she took, but he never shared."

"I agree, he's holding back, but why?" Zac said.

"Why bring Milton in at all? Jason seemed to control all of it. No one worked with Milton, though they all knew of him."

"We need to talk to him again," Zac said. "So Gregory Enzi senior gets his foot in the door of Hollywood through Jason and Katrina. His endgame is running drugs, but Jason gets caught up in the lifestyle, works Katrina to keep the lifestyle he's become accustomed to. Camilla said Katrina hadn't wanted to go back to work after the baby, but she did. And since all of this was started with her parents, people who have been dogging us from the beginning, people who are living well beyond their means, but not on their kid's dime, we need to talk to them."

"Yeah, we do, but I say we bring them here. They want to play hardball, let's make it official," I said.

"We only have circumstantial evidence."

"Well, maybe we can find a judge who was a Katrina Dent fan."

"I'll get on it. In the meantime, we need to talk to Vin. Learn more about Gregory Enzi senior. The attack on his life…was that unrelated or was our killer targeting him, too?"

I hadn't thought of that but shit, it was possible. I pointed at Zac. "That's another thing Milton is holding back on. He had to have known about Enzi back then, certainly knows of him now. I can't believe a mob boss isn't going to check in on his cash cow. And there's no way Milton didn't know who Enzi was. His job is public relations, he knows all the players. So why didn't he mention that link?"

"I'll call him in the morning," Zac said.

"Is it possible this is all about keeping the identity of Katrina's baby a secret?"

"It's definitely a theory, but why?"

"Maybe the blowback, the father doesn't want his past coming back and fucking up his world," I theorized.

"If that's the case, he won't be getting any parenting awards."

"I CAN'T BELIEVE you're leaving," Ethan said, when I visited him later that day. "It's Kade, isn't it?"

"Yes."

"You worked it out."

"We did." He looked down at his fingers that he was twisting together. "I won't live across the hall, but we'll stay in touch. We have drinks to get," I said.

He looked up, but I saw the reservation.

"We're not going to lose touch, Ethan."

"I don't have many friends in the city. I don't want to lose you."

"You won't. In fact, once I'm settled come for dinner."

His eyes lit up. "Seriously? At the penthouse?"

"Yes."

"Alright, yeah."

I joined him on the sofa. "I don't have many friends, either. This..." I said, gesturing between us, "means a lot to me, too."

He pulled me close. "Good." I held him as hard as he held me.

KADE JOINED ME later that day. I found myself glancing over often, resisting the urge to pinch myself because Kade Wakefield was helping me pack up my apartment. In fairness, he'd hired movers, and they did most of the work, but there were things I wanted to do myself, namely my clothes and personal things. It was Saturday; I had the case to think about, but Kade was very persuasive, so after fucking me stupid, he convinced me to work from home.

Zac was on point, anyway, following up with Milton and Jackson.

I stopped folding my shirts, distracted with the sight of Kade in faded jeans and a tee, one that was old, well-worn and had a whiskey label on it. His feet were bare, not something he did often, but he looked so fucking hot.

"Stop or we're never going to get this done," he said, not even turning to confirm I was staring.

"That's a good look on you. I can see you like that on your beach." He looked back now. "Though, how we spent those days on your beach, that was pretty hard to top."

"You naked is hard to top, period." His eyes grew dark. "And as much as I want you naked right now, when I fuck you again, I want it in our bed."

It had only been a couple of months. It was crazy. I wasn't just moving in with him; I was in love with him. I couldn't imagine my life without him. The thought of losing him had my legs going weak. He was across the room in a heartbeat.

"What just happened?"

Looking into those eyes, I couldn't stop the words. "I love you."

His hold on me tightened, but it was watching his gray gaze turn stormy that had me saying it again. "I love you, Kade."

He walked me back until I hit the wall, his hands moved into my hair, his focus unwavering. "Say it again."

"I love you."

He growled, before he kissed me, not hard, not rough, but deep and long and filled with promise. He broke the kiss, his breathing as heavy as my own. "I've never in my life said those words," he whispered. "I wasn't sure I knew what it felt like, but from the moment you walked into my office, there's been a pain right here." He took my hand and pressed it against his chest. "One that only eases when you're around." His mask was off now. "We never should have met, but I can't imagine a life without you." His gaze drilled into mine. "I love you."

It was my turn to demand, "Say it again."

He smiled, not grinned, but smiled, before he said in that voice I loved so much. "I love you."

He kissed me again, deeper, longer, and as much as I wanted to get naked, he was determined to wait. I fisted his tee, held his tender gaze. "We need to get this shit done."

In reply, he kissed me, again.

I LAY IN bed and watched Kade sleep. My body was pressed against his, his hand on my ass, but his breathing was deep and even. We'd packed my apartment in record time. I was going to miss Ethan, but it hadn't been hard leaving my apartment. I was rarely there with the hours I kept. But moving in with this man, we could live in a box by the river, and I'd go happily. I smiled thinking about earlier. As soon as we stepped off the elevator, he dragged me to his bed, but it didn't stop there. He fucked me on the kitchen counter, on the dining room table, the sofa in the living room, he even fucked me up against the windows. We ordered Chinese takeout, sat in the living room, barely dressed, and had a picnic. It had been the perfect day.

I was careful when I climbed from the bed. Salem was curled up next to me, but he jumped from the bed and followed me out of the bedroom. I pulled on Kade's tee and moved to the living room, standing by the windows, looking out at the city that never slept.

I faced death every day. It was what I chose to do, but there was a part of me that I'd buried deep, the part that feared what I did for a living. That fear had begun to grow stronger after meeting Kade. I knew better than most how fast it could be taken away. How one minute you're attending the event of your life, and the next, you're another statistic. For so long, my job was my life. I was good at it, and I loved it, but being with Kade, I understood now there was more to life. And that was what had that fear growing. I thought of Katrina, and as much as our lives were different, she had found happiness. I really needed to believe that. Her baby, the man she'd found comfort with, and it was taken from her.

I loved the city. If you asked me two months ago where I saw myself in ten years, I would have said exactly where I was. A family, children, for me, that was much like the fairy tale. I never really saw it happening because I never found anyone I wanted that with. And then I met Kade. He filled all the places in me I didn't know were empty, and I knew I did the same for him. Now, I didn't just think about it, but I wanted it. I wanted children with him, wanted the house on the beach with Kade in his faded jeans and bare feet. I wanted days of playing and nights of making love. And because I wanted it so much, it brought the fear that I could lose him. Learning what we were about the Enzi family, knowing Carmine DeLuca was somehow linked to them and he was like a brother to Kade. How deep was Kade in the underbelly of New York? How would those take it that he was now living with a cop?

Strong arms moved around my waist and pulled me back against a hard chest. His lips brushed over my ear. "Talk to me."

"Two months ago, I didn't even know you," I whispered.

He turned me to him; dark eyes studied my face. "Too soon?"

"No, I think I was ready for this after our first dinner together."

His expression softened, as he pulled a hand through my hair. "So what's bothering you?" He asked, but then read me like he so easily could. "You're thinking about Katrina and how fast it can be taken away."

"How do you do that?" I whispered.

"You've very expressive eyes."

"The more we learn, the uglier it gets, and with the link to Enzi—"

"You're wondering how deep Carmine and I are in."

"Yes."

He released me, but I enjoyed watching him. He wore only a pair of sweats that hung so low on his hips, I could see the top of the V. Would I ever stop wanting this man? I really hoped not. He caught me looking and said, "My eyes are up here."

My own jerked to his face, the laugh bubbling up my throat that those words came from Kade Wakefield's mouth. He grinned, but when he had my attention, he continued, "I know there's a lot of speculation about me and my business, but the Feds are going to be disappointed because there's nothing worth pursuing." He grew thoughtful. "My biggest skeleton you know, but that crime happened in Montenegro, and there's no extradition between here and there."

"If I walked in on what you had, I'd have killed him, too."

A meaningful silence followed, before Kade whispered, "I believe that."

"And Carmine?"

"Carmine is smart."

"But he's in deep."

"Deeper than I'd like."

It was thinking about Enzi that had me asking, "What's Enzi senior like?"

"I don't really know him. He's in his eighties. In his day, though, he was ruthless. I'm not surprised to learn of his part in Katrina Dent's life and death. He was old school, the kind of boss who people feared and had every right to."

"And his son?"

"Enzi junior isn't like his father. He's tough, but he's moved the family into other areas that are less volatile. Did he make his bones, has he worked on the wrong side of the law, sure, but who in that culture hasn't, but he isn't the cold-blooded monster his father is."

"Why don't Carmine and Enzi senior get along?" Then I realized what I asked and quickly said, "Never mind, that's not your place to tell me."

He nodded. "Thank you for understanding that." He pushed his hands into his pockets, which only made his sweats move lower on his hips. I crossed the room because I couldn't take another second, my hands moving over his abs, down along that V of muscle. I was going lower, but he stopped me, which had my gaze jerking to his.

"I know you're in the middle of a case, but I want you to come home with me."

I glanced around the penthouse.

"To Montenegro."

"Do you still have a family there?"

"I never had a family, but it's part of who I am."

I didn't even need to think about it. "Yes. When?"

"Whenever you can get the time."

"Okay, I'll talk to the captain." I pressed a kiss on his chest and added, "I'd like to take you to Marlton."

He lowered his head to hold my gaze. "Do they know about me?"

"Yes." That surprised him. "Before we went to Antigua, I called my dad. Told him about you, how I was falling. He told me to make sure you were there to catch me. I knew it then that you would be."

His voice was whisper soft. "Always."

Would we have always? He touched my chin. "Are we burning too hot? Like a roman candle, hot and bright, but not something that can be sustained?"

"There are no guarantees in life, Molly, but what I can tell you is I've never wanted a woman like I do you," he said, moving forward, which had me moving back. "I've never needed a woman like I do you." My back hit the window. "I've never craved the taste of a woman like I do you." He pressed in close, his fingers going between my legs. My breathing turned shallow. "I don't just want your body but your heart and your soul. I don't see that burning out."

I fisted the cotton at his hips and pushed it lower, my hand curling around his cock. He lifted me, my legs wrapped around his waist. I centered him right where we both needed him. Our eyes were locked when he sank into me.

I moan, tilted my head back.

He pulled out, held my stare. "Every part of you," he whispered, and sank in even deeper, "Mine."

I fisted his hair and kissed him, my tongue pushing past his lips, my heels digging into his ass. I ran my hands down his arms, the one going between our bodies to touch my clit. His arm was locked around my waist; his free hand caught mine and linked our fingers, before he pressed them against the glass.

We broke the kiss, but our faces were close, our eyes on each other, and when we came, it was together.

I DIDN'T WANT to get out of bed on Monday morning. Kade's attempt to energize me with a morning fuck backfired because I wanted us to stay right there, all day. He dragged me from bed, got me in the shower, washed my hair, was creative with washing my body, which led to another round of magnificent morning sex, before he left me,

151

returning with a mug of coffee that he wrapped my hand around. A hard kiss and he was gone again, getting ready for the day.

I drank the whole mug, before I dried my hair and pulled it into a knot. Entering the bedroom, I took a second because it was a pretty spectacular room, tucked off the main floor. The walls were a soft gray; there was a wall of windows with blinds that moved up into the ceiling, so nothing hindered the view. There was a massive dressing area with a walk-in closet that was bigger than my entire bedroom at the apartment. The king-sized mahogany bed with a crisscross craftsmen headboard sat in the middle of the room, dressed simply in a navy blue comforter. A fireplace and sitting area was on one side of the room, a new makeup table on the other. My heart swelled because he'd been thinking about me moving in for a while. Walking into the closet, I couldn't help smiling because Kade had organized it, but not into his and hers. My clothes were with his, my suits with his, my shirts. It was the little things that showed how much he wanted me there, but more, it shined a light revealing how lonely he'd been. The truth was, I'd been just as lonely.

Instead of taking one of my shirts, I took one of his, a soft gray one that felt like heaven against my skin. I pulled on my black pants, grabbed my boots and jacket. Entering the kitchen, Kade was at the island, mug in hand, reading a newspaper. I knew now his clothes cost a small fortune, but he wore the elegant, tailored fabrics so well.

His focus was on me, his mug stopped halfway to his mouth, as he took in my outfit. "Nice shirt."

"I wanted you with me." I said, dropping down on one of the kitchen chairs to pull on my boots. "And since it's not 'bring your sexy boyfriend to work day,' I had to improvise."

Silence followed before Kade replied smoothly, "Friday is 'fuck your hot detective girlfriend on your desk day,' so make sure you free up some time in your schedule."

My head jerked up. He wasn't smiling, but I was getting that look that was even better than a smile. "I'll make sure to clear the whole day."

"That's probably wise." He took a sip of his coffee. "You're going to need another gown."

"For what?"

"The CyberTech launch."

I'd forgotten, with everything going on. I hadn't seen the invite from Rothschild, but I was sure it was in my mail that I hadn't looked at in a while.

"It's going to be fancy, isn't it?"

Kade wasn't impressed. "Likely."

"Star studded."

"Probably." And then he caught on when his eyes found mine and warmed. "The Academy Awards."

"Bucket list item."

"So not just a gown but jewels."

That got my attention. "What kind of jewels?"

"Ones worthy of that exquisite neck."

My hand moved to my neck. He grinned. Salem jumped up on the counter, rubbing up against Kade. I watched as he scratched behind Salem's ears and was jealous of my cat. "He's made himself at home."

"Good," Kade said, putting his mug down and turning for the plate of eggs and bacon. He set it on the counter next to him. "Eat."

"You're spoiling me."

His eyes found mine. "I haven't even begun to spoil you."

I took the fork, pressed up against his side. He reached for his mug. "I'll talk to Cap," I said, around a mouthful of egg. "How long were you thinking for the trip home?

"A week."

"Okay." I finished my breakfast; he read his paper. As we were leaving for the car, I teased, "You're very accommodating."

"I'm softening you up," he countered, and hit the button for the elevator.

"You want something?"

He nodded.

"What?"

He leaned into me, his mouth almost touching mine. "Your ass."

This man was going to be the end of me, and I was so okay with that. I couldn't keep the lust from my voice. "You don't have to soften me up for that."

I swear he almost pulled me to the bedroom right then and there. Possession moved through him, his kiss was a brand, his words like gravel. "Noted."

"MILTON IS IN the wind," Zac said, standing and tossing his pen on his desk.

"What?" I said, looking up from the notes on Enzi that Vin had dropped off.

"After our last meeting, as soon as he got home, he packed up and left."

"He's gone?" I said, pushing back from my desk. I had the craziest thought. I stood, and paced, thinking through what we knew before I looked over at Zac. "No one met him when he worked for Katrina, not the producers, not her friends. Not one of them could pick him out of a lineup."

Zac knew where I was going. "You're thinking…"

I started pacing again. "Milton is brought on board as Katrina's representative, but no one recalls working with him. They all only worked with Jason, but her actual publicist, no one knows."

"He was there, but he wasn't there, because he never existed," Zac finished.

"Exactly. Milton Teller was Jason's backout plan."

Zac was pacing now. "He didn't disappear, he just assumed the identity he created." Zac looked at me. "I don't know. It's thin."

"But it works," I said. "We need to dig deeper into Milton's past, see if he actually has one."

"Yeah. We got the composite from Mitch. The computer geeks are aging it. We'll run facial recognition software on it, compare it to Milton. Send pics of Milton to LAPD for Mitch to view."

"He's likely changed his appearance," I warned.

"Yeah, and since we don't have DNA on Jason, it's not like we can compare, but Milton taking off, doesn't look good for him."

"I thought Chadds Ford PD was watching him?" I said.

"Yeah, I did, too. Got a call into Jamison to find out what the fuck happened." Zac looked at his watch. "The Dents are due any minute."

"Damn, you've been busy."

"Yeah, well, having a new direction to look, I couldn't stop thinking about it."

"How did you get the Dents to come?" I asked.

"We didn't give them an option. LAPD reopened Katrina's case, tagged it as a homicide, and they're material witnesses, as well as people of interest in our case. Their lawyer tried to get them out of it. He wasn't successful."

"Good. They need to start talking. They didn't do right by their daughter when she was alive, but they can in her death."

"Agreed."

Zac reached across his desk for his coffee. "That shirt looks a little big on you."

"Costs more than we make in a month, too," I said, then grinned. "I think we should talk to Gregory Enzi, the old man."

"I'm trying, but his lawyers are closing rank," Zac shared.

"Okay, so Enzi wants in on the Hollywood scene. The Dents are into him for fifty grand, they offer up their kid, who has that magical combination of beauty and personality. He gets one of his own to be her keeper, creates a star and keeps her there. Jason gets caught up in the lifestyle, Katrina finds someone to share the loneliness with. She gets pregnant, they don't want anyone learning about it, so they hide her away until after the pregnancy. She's scared into staying with Jason, but she starts to withdraw, not fulfilling her end of the deal. Enzi has Jason kill her and then Jason takes off, assumes the identity of Milton Teller. Jump ahead thirty years, some unknown journalist is digging into Katrina's death." I tapped my finger to my lip. "Was it possible that Frank knew about Milton. That he targeted Samantha, not because of Katrina, but confirming what he believed about Milton?" I bit my thumbnail. "I still think there's a connection between CyberTech and all of this, the timing is too coincidental. I wonder if Milton is an investor?" I walked back to my desk and jotted a note to go through the CyberTech file again. "All of this, I believe, is about keeping the past in the past."

"Meaning, the identity of the baby and the father of the baby?" Zac clarified.

"Yeah. Learning of the baby, lends credence to murder. I think someone was trying to stir shit up with Samantha, who and why, I don't know. But I think the intention of our killer isn't altruistic, just self-preservation. If Milton is Jason, the baby is a loose end that, if found, exposes the whole ugly mess," I offered.

"So, who's the baby?"

TONY AND ELLIE Dent were not the same people we visited a couple months back. He was aggressive, and she was afraid.

"Why can't you leave it alone?" Tony demanded.

"You pimped out your daughter to cover your gambling debt. I understand why you'd want us to leave that alone." I didn't hide my anger.

"How dare—"

"Enough. You are getting very close to obstruction, and we will absolutely charge you, so cut the shit. We know you owed a loan shark fifty thousand, a loan shark that had links to Gregory Enzi senior. We know you introduced Jason Benjamin to Katrina, that you even footed the bill for his plastic surgery. How did you meet Jason?"

Tony's complexion turned an alarming color, but it was Ellie Dent who said, "I can't do this anymore."

Tony's head jerked to her. "We can't…"

"Yes, we can. We're not living. We haven't been living since we traded our daughter for fifty thousand dollars." She showed spine when she turned determined eyes on us. "We owed the money. The man we owed offered us a solution. He was the one who introduced us to Jason."

"How did they know about your daughter?"

"We lived in Brooklyn, it's a tight community. Katrina used to do the local theater. She always had a presence. It was hard not to love her. It wasn't the first time she was approached to model, or to act, but she wanted to be a teacher." Tears collected in her eyes. "We took that away from her."

"And Jason?"

"He worked for the loan shark," Ellie said.

"And who was that?"

"Terence Baker."

Zac's head snapped to me, because we knew that name. He was the same man who had encouraged Samantha to interview for Kade's company. If Terence worked for Enzi, why the hell would he stir this all up? The impact on Kade, my heart sank; he was getting pulled into this shit again.

"Terence Baker worked for Enzi?" Zac clarified.

It was Tony who answered. "We never knew that for sure, but Enzi was the boss. Nothing happened in the city that he didn't know about."

"So Jason makes your daughter a star and you follow on her coattails. Tell us about Milton?"

"We knew of him, but he was very behind the scenes. Katrina spoke fondly of him, though."

Zac and I shared a look before I asked, "So you never met him?"

"No, not in person. But we spoke a few times on the phone," Ellie offered.

Our theory was thin but definitely a possibility. "And the baby?" I asked.

"What baby?" Ellie said, her back going rod straight.

"Katrina had a baby when she went away in eighty-four for that mental health break."

They were either great actors themselves, or they really didn't know about the baby. "We have a grandchild?" Tony demanded.

They had, but that child wasn't a child anymore, and they'd missed it because of their fucking greed.

"You really didn't know?" Zac asked.

"We're not complete monsters," Ellie cried. "A boy or a girl?"

"We don't know. So you aren't aware of a man, your daughter was keeping company with, who wasn't Jason?" I asked.

"No."

"Do you know where Jason is now?" Zac asked.

"After Katrina died, we never saw him again."

"Yes, but do you know who he is?" I pushed.

"Not if he walked right up to us. He'd changed his appearance before and after—" Tony caught himself.

"After what?" Zac demanded.

I guess they realized they were in too deep, so he confessed. "After she came back from that year off, she was different. We didn't know there was a baby, that actually explains so much, but she started to withdraw, was late for shoots, just wasn't the same woman. It was why they made it look like a suicide because everyone would believe it. Jason killed her, under orders, and then he disappeared."

"Orders by who?"

"Gregory Enzi."

Holy shit. "You do realize what you're saying, yes? You are pointing the finger at a known crime boss?" Zac said.

"He's been paying for our silence ever since," Tony added. "Too coincidental if we showed up dead after our daughter, and since we weren't talking, it was worth it to him to keep us happy."

"Not that we were. We haven't been happy for a long time."

I tried to bite my tongue, but I just couldn't. "Spare us the bullshit. Greed got you here, and instead of manning up and handling it, you sold your daughter. You ruined her life, you took away her dreams, you made her beholden, to not just an animal like Jason, but also Enzi, and you did all of it for fucking money. Your daughter's death is on your hands, and you can try to wash that shit away with your excuses, but you did this to her. The two people who should have protected her were the ones who sacrificed her. You won't get an ounce of pity or empathy from me. And, in fact, if I could try you in a court of law for being the worst parents ever, I fucking would." I stood, shoved my chair into the table and headed for the door. "I'm done here."

I stepped outside, leaned back against the wall, dropped my hands on my knees and tried to pull the fury in, but all I saw was that innocent girl who had been betrayed by the people who should have loved her the most.

Zac joined me a few minutes later. "You okay?"

"They're disgusting."

"Yeah, they are. I'm going to call Vin. He's going to want to pepper them with questions."

"Okay."

He touched my arm. "That had to have felt good."

My gaze collided with his. "It did."

"Let's go fill in the captain," Zac said, and started down the hall. I fell into step with him. "Terence Baker. He gets the ball rolling with the Katrina Dent shit, and then thirty-one years later, befriends

Samantha James and encourages her to interview for a job with Wakefield. Why?"

I shook my head. "I don't know. Why stir up the past when it was at rest?"

"Good question." He reached for his cell, pulled up a number. "Yeah, Vin, meet us in Darling's office. We got something for you."

VIN WAS PACING Cap's office. "They actually pointed the finger at him?"

"Yeah, figured you'd want to get in there and ask some of your own questions," Zac said.

"Hell, yeah." He stopped pacing. "It might be a good idea for you to put your investigation on hold for a few days. This kind of rattling could lead to an all-out battle within the Enzi family or another family, seeing the weakness and making a move to takeover."

"That's a good idea," Captain said, then turned to Zac. "What did you learn from the coroner in Los Angeles?"

"He purposely withheld the pregnancy from the autopsy report for the sake of the baby. With the media circus around her death, and his own reservations about what really happened to Katrina, he felt including the discovery of the baby might be signing the baby's death warrant."

Cap pulled a hand through his hair. "Well, with how this is all shaking out, it looks like he wasn't wrong about that. I've got the team working on aging the sketch. Not that I'm particularly hopeful, because if Jason Benjamin was so determined to stay hidden, he most likely got plastic surgery."

"We have a theory on Jason," I said. "We know it's a little out there but…"

"Let's hear it."

"Jason creates Katrina, acts as her agent in all matters, but brings in Milton Teller, as her official public relations representative. People know of him, but no one has worked with him in person."

Cap caught on. "You think Jason is Milton Teller?"

"He is in the wind now. It's a possibility," Zac said.

"Jesus, this case," Cap said. "Okay, look into Teller. If Jason is as good as we think, he's probably covered all his bases, but dig deep and see if something about Milton doesn't pan out. And we'll get the composite and compare it, though I doubt it will help."

"We can look into plastic surgeons, at the time, and surgeries to see if we can find something. Even just asking a plastic surgeon to compare Milton and Jason's photos to see if it's even possible they're one in the same," Zac said then turned to Vin. "We could use some of your expertise."

"Shoot."

"You know Terence Baker?"

"Yeah, he's pretty high up in the Enzi organization."

"So, he's still in the family?"

"Yes."

"Okay, so based on the Dents' confession, Terence Baker was the one who got the whole ball rolling with Katrina Dent, allegedly at the order of Enzi senior. It was also Terence who encouraged Samantha to interview for the position at Wakefield's and we'd bet money, Frank Harris, one of our victims, learned of Samantha from an anonymous tip from Baker. It isn't likely if Jason is Teller that he would have stirred up the past because it exposes him. So why the fuck is Baker stirring up something that was already buried?"

We all recognized the look that entered Vin's eyes, a cop on the verge of breaking a case wide open. "Because it's a coup," he said, pacing at the back of the room. "There's been bad blood between the father and son for years. The old man is old; the son is ready to take over. I would bet money it was the son who ordered Terence to stir it up. Create the weakness, the unrest, and use that to take his father's place. Using Wakefield was smart because of his connection to Carmine DeLuca. DeLuca is a hothead, but he's also dangerous. Coming at Wakefield would set him off, and there's no love between DeLuca and Enzi senior."

"So the son stirs up the ghosts of the past and incites DeLuca to take out his father, so he can step into his place," Cap summarized.

"Yeah."

"Alright, Vin will take point with the Dents. We'll ride the desk for a few days, until things cool off," Cap added.

"If we're riding the desk, I think I'd like to take those days," I said.

160

"Another vacation?" Zac teased.

"Why not," Captain said, "Not much for us to do until vice gets a lockdown on this shit."

"Thanks, Cap."

"Enjoy if for me, too."

Before I could reply, Zac brought the conversation back when he said, "I want to know who's cleaning up the shit Enzi stirred up."

A look went around the room before I said, "That's the million dollar question."

I WAS CROSSING a line, but if Vin was right, DeLuca was being setup, and as Kade's friend, I had to at least warn him. I went to see Kade, but he was in a meeting. Penelope showed me into his office. I stood by the windows and looked out at the city, but my thoughts were on the case and how there seemed to be multiple agendas. It wasn't a wonder we were having so much trouble nailing it down.

The door opened, voices followed. I turned, just as Kade glanced over, then took a double take. I knew what flashed through his head when his focus shifted to his desk. I felt the heat creep up my neck.

"We need to reschedule. See Penelope. She'll get you on my calendar." He didn't wait, opening the door then closing and locking it. He leaned back against it, pushed his hands into his pockets and asked, "Is it Friday?"

Despite what brought me here, now I was thinking about sex on his desk. "I have a new bucket list item."

He didn't move when he said, "I'll be sure to help you scratch that off and soon, but for now, tell me what's put that shadow behind your eyes?"

"We met with the Dents today."

Understanding swept his expression.

"They confessed to all of it. Being in debt, the plan, they even fingered Gregory Enzi senior."

I saw the sharpness behind his eyes. "They did?"

I crossed the room to him. "They also told us their loan shark's name was Terence Baker. We found his name in Samantha's things, confirmed with her parents that he was the one who recommended she interview for your public relations department." This was exactly what Kade had warned would happen, us finding ourselves on different sides of the law. "Enzi ordered Katrina's death, according to her parents. A job carried out by Jason before he disappeared. Enzi was also the one to pay off the Dents to keep them quiet. I was having trouble understanding why Terence would have stirred the shit up with Samantha when the blowback would be on the very man he worked for. Vin, from vice, filled us in."

Silence followed.

"Enzi junior wants to take over, so he's blowing shit up, so he can step through the rubble and take his father's place. Vin believes you were targeted to set off your hothead friend, to incite him to take out Enzi senior."

Kade had no reaction.

"If Vin is right, Carmine is being setup."

The silence grew heavy before Kade finally spoke. "And you're here to warn him."

"Yes."

The air was knocked from my lungs when he lifted me off the floor and crossed the room. With one hand, he swiped shit off his desk, before my back hit it, and in a few breathless seconds, my boots, pants and panties hit the floor. He undid his pants and pulled his cock free. He fisted my hair, slammed his mouth on mine, as his rammed his cock into me. His arm locked around my waist, as he moved hard and fast, almost brutally, between my legs. It was fucking magnificent.

I came hard; he swallowed my scream. He came right after me, his groan rumbled up his throat and worked its way down mine. I locked my legs around his waist, my hand covering his that was still twisted in my hair. Turbulent eyes looked down at me. "I fucking love you," he whispered.

I let those words sink in and settle comfortably in my chest. "I fucking love you."

He looked down our bodies, his expression turning primal. "I need a painting of you like this," he whispered. Hungry eyes lifted to mine. "I want to undress you, splay you on my desk and fucking feast." His cock was still inside me, so I felt how much he wanted to do just as he claimed.

"You need to warn Carmine," I said softly.

He moved his hips, and I moaned.

"We're coming back to this."

"Yes, we are." I dragged my thumb over his lip; he bit it and my pussy convulsed. He moaned. "We're taking a step back on the case, so Montenegro is an option," I offered.

"Done," he said.

"Just like that, no checking your schedule?"

"Yeah, just like that."

"If you don't…" I looked down at where we were connected, "pull out in the next second, I'm not going to let you."

He grinned, leaned closer and whispered, "I'd really like to see you try."

SIXTEEN

Kade met Carmine at Polar. It was lunchtime, but the jazz section was packed. Kade moved through the crowd to his office in the back. Carmine was already waiting, sitting behind his desk, with his feet up on it.

"Comfortable?" Kade asked, closing the door behind him.

"I am. I could really get used to this," he said. "You've got a few waitresses out there that I really need to try out." The look Kade gave him had him chuckling, as he stood. "I know, off limits. So what's up?"

"I stay out of your shit, but when that shit affects my shit. What's going on with Enzi?"

Humor dropped from Carmine's face. "What's happened?"

"Molly came to see me. They have people in custody who are pointing the finger at Enzi senior, as the one who ordered Katrina Dent's death."

"Wait a minute, take a step back. Who the fuck is Katrina Dent?"

"She was a movie star back in the eighties. Died, it was ruled suicide, but the death of the girl in the park, the two others, suggested that her death might have been murder. As it turns out, it was allegedly ordered by Enzi senior."

"Well, shit," Carmine said, and pulled a hand through his hair.

"Terence Baker, you know him?"

"Yeah, he's a asshole."

"He had a hand in Katrina's downfall, and he also played a role in Samantha James' death."

Carmine caught on immediately. "It's a coup."

"And from where the NYPD is standing, I was implicated to incite you."

"So I'd take out the old man."

"Exactly."

"I fucking can't stand Enzi senior, but you know his son is like a father to me."

"I know, but if this is all true, it's the son who stirred the shit up."

Carmine crossed the room, poured himself some whiskey and drank it down. "Your detective told you all of this?"

"Yeah, wanted to warn you."

Carmine leaned back against the sideboard. "She broke protocol to help a known crime boss." He shared something they both knew.

"Yeah, she did, so that blowing back on her isn't fucking acceptable."

Carmine's eyes went hard. "Got few who I count on, I know how to take care of those I do. Being yours, she was already on that list. Today, she earned a place on her own." Carmine put the glass down, before returning his stare on Kade. "Enzi is one, too. He took me in, he gave me legitimate work, didn't make me one of his henchmen. He's not his father."

"No, he's not, but he takes out his father, NYPD is going to be looking at you."

"Yeah. I'm okay with that because they won't find anything to link me to his death, and if it takes the heat off Gregory, so be it."

"Keep in mind the man he's looking to overthrow. He might be old, but he's ruthless, and he won't go down without a fight."

"I know, and that's why I need to talk to Gregory. He's hated his father for most of his life, but the old man is one foot in the grave." Carmine looked incredulous. "So why is he doing this shit now?"

CARMINE DROVE TO Brooklyn Heights. He didn't need an appointment, family never did. He strolled through the elegantly appointed townhouse to the back veranda, where Gregory preferred spending his time. He never understood the gardens because Gregory wasn't a flower kind of man, but his gardens were always perfectly tended and bursting with color.

The man himself was sitting on the patio, a glass of wine next to him, his focus on the horizon.

"What brings you here today, Carmine?"

Carmine joined him at the table and noticed he was holding something, but his focus shifted to the man. "Got a heads up."

Gregory exhaled and looked tired, older than his fifty-nine years. "Do you believe in ghosts?"

Carmine sat up because that was not a question he'd expect from the man he knew. "What's going on?"

Gregory shook his head and instead asked, "What brings you?"

"The cops are putting the pieces together."

Gregory reached for his wine. "Let me guess, I'm looking to take over so am creating an environment that makes it possible."

"Something like that."

"I'm not the one stirring it up. He is."

Carmine didn't hide his surprise. "Why?"

"Because he's dying and he can. Because he's belligerent and vindictive."

"I need more, Gregory. My boy's girl is right in the middle of this shit."

"I heard about that. She's the one looking into Katrina Dent's death." Gregory said, took a sip of wine. "She's close to figuring it out, too, from what I hear."

"What doesn't she know?" Carmine asked.

Gregory put his glass down, stood. Even at fifty-nine, he could turn women's heads, with his dark blue eyes and tall muscled build. "Walk with me."

Carmine fell into step at his side.

"My father wanted in on the Hollywood scene, and so he found the perfect way in, a young, beautiful woman who held that magical appeal like a modern version of Marilyn Monroe. She was often compared to her. I remember the first time I saw her. I was twenty-two, a year older than she was, but she seemed so much younger. She had hope then, still had an idealistic view of the world. He sent me to keep an eye on his project. I hadn't meant to fall in love, but I did."

Carmine stopped walking; Gregory looked back at him. "Yes, Katrina and I were lovers. From almost the minute she was unveiled. She hated it, but she knew her parents were in a bind. And she was the kind of woman who would do for others, much like your friend's girl, putting her neck out to help known criminals." He opened his palm to reveal the small gold coin. "She gave me this. Her marker," he said and smiled. "Her promise that her future belonged to me and mine to her." The smile fell from his lips. "She got pregnant. I was taking her away, to hell with my father and the fact that I'd be putting a target on both of our backs. The woman I loved was carrying my child. But my father had friends everywhere. He found out, beat me to an inch of my life and took her baby. She went through that alone because I couldn't get to her. She lost her baby and me. And still she tried to do for others, but her heart wasn't in it anymore. She wasn't Katrina Dent, the superstar. He broke her. I broke her. But it still wasn't enough for my father. She was an asset, one that wasn't turning enough of a profit, one that would be more valuable dead, so he had her killed."

Gregory fisted his hands, his face going hard. "I tried to find Jason to repay the kindness, but he always was a weasel, had an uncanny ability of shifting to be whatever was needed of him. I never did find him, and I fucking looked."

"And the baby?"

"A son." Pride filled his voice. He gestured to the gardens. "These are for her. She always wanted gardens, a family. And I wanted her."

"Where's your son?"

"Hiding in plain sight," Gregory said. "And don't ask me who because I won't tell you. But that's what this is all about. I'm not the one stirring it up. My father is. Because it isn't enough to have killed the woman I loved, to keep me from my son, to take away my happy, he needs to take out my son, too. That won't happen." His expression was hard but determined. "I'm protecting what's mine. I couldn't do it for Katrina, but I will for our child."

Carmine dragged a hand though his hair. "So you're cleaning up after the fallout."

That earned Carmine Gregory's hard stare. "No, I'm taking out my fucking family. Lighting the fuse to watch it explode. I didn't order those deaths, and I realize they aid in my wish to keep the past in the past, but they were someone else's children. I'm not so heartless that I would order that."

"Your father is heartless enough."

"Defeats his purpose." Gregory plucked a yellow flower from the stem, twirled it between his fingers. "Whoever is behind it has something to lose if the past is stirred up."

It all came back to the same fucking person. "Jason Benjamin," Carmine deduced.

Gregory replied, without taking a breath, "Which brings us full circle...a fucking ghost."

CARMINE WAS IN unfamiliar territory, but tit for tat. He called Kade letting him know he was coming. When he arrived, his friend and girl were in the kitchen. She was sitting on the counter; he was standing between her legs. Kade looked happy; they both did. Kade's eyes drifted to Carmine. "Hey, Brother. Want a drink?"

"Yeah," Carmine said, crossing the room to them. "Detective."

"Carmine."

He glanced down, then looked up at her through his lashes. "Thanks for the heads up."

He saw the unease behind her eyes, but she smiled and said, "You're welcome."

Kade handed him a whiskey; he drained the glass. "It's why I'm here, to return it."

Her blue eyes went wide.

"If you can sit on this information for a little, I'd appreciate it."

"We were going away for a week, is that long enough?" she asked.

Carmine's focus shifted to Kade. "I'm taking her home," Kade offered, moving back into his woman. Carmine wasn't a jealous kind of man, but he envied his friend that he'd found what he had with his detective. Carmine wasn't sure he'd ever be so lucky. Gregory had found it, too, and it was taken from him. Carmine's expression turned dark.

"Gregory Enzi, the son, and Katrina Dent were lovers. And he confirmed that Jason Benjamin killed Katrina on his father's orders."

It took a second for the news to penetrate, and when it did, Molly's jaw dropped. "Shit." Then she said again, "Shit. Enzi is Katrina's baby's father."

"Yes, a son, but he won't say who. His father is the one stirring shit up; Baker is acting on command from Enzi senior to get at Gregory's son."

"Why?" Molly asked, not hiding her horror.

"Because he's a fucking vindictive dick."

Molly's face paled, as her detective mind worked it out. "It was Gregory junior behind Samantha, Frank and Emily's death."

"No. Those deaths work in his favor, but he would never order the death of the innocent. The one behind those deaths is the one player in this mess who still has something to lose."

She answered immediately, "Jason Benjamin."

"Yeah. You find him, you find your killer of not just those now, but Katrina as well."

Her mind was working; he could see she wanted to share with her partner, even glanced at her phone, but as he watched, she reined it in. "That probably wasn't easy," she guessed, then said, "Thank you. I'll wait until we get back to share with my partner."

"Thank you." Carmine started for the elevator.

"Are you hungry?" she called after him.

He glanced back. Kade added, "There's plenty, man."

He glanced at the elevators, then back at the two, and wasn't ready to return to his empty apartment. "Yeah, thanks. I am."

Molly kissed Kade, then jumped off the counter. "I'll set another place at the table."

SEVENTEEN

MOLLY

"Oh, fuck." My head dropped, my hips moving back into his thrusts. The fullness in my ass, as he fucked me there stung, but his fingers were curled into my pussy, hitting that spot. My elbows dug into the mattress, his fingers dug into my thigh, but it was his moans that had me matching his rhythm.

"You feel so fucking good," he groaned, his cock pulling out and sinking back in.

I moaned, fisted the sheets, felt that knowing chill, and with his cock in my ass, the orgasm was mind blowing, his name ripping from my throat when I came. His hand moved from my pussy, grabbed my hips, as he fucked me deeper, before he stilled and came, the sound that came from him made me wet again.

He bent over me, and with his cock still in me, I whimpered because, fuck, he felt so good. "You okay?" he asked.

"Okay?" My head turned, our eyes met, and I grinned. "And you thought you had to soften me up for this."

In reply, he kissed me. Gentle and savoring, and following that fucking, the contrast made my clit pulse. The many sides of Kade Wakefield between the sheets, I loved every one of them.

"I have a bucket list item," he said, kissing me again, harder this time. "Keeping my woman tied to the bed, so I can fuck her whenever I want."

I almost came just from the suggestion. I wasn't going to survive this man. I liked when he bound me. He didn't do it often, but I loved giving over that control to him. "Let's do that today," I suggested enthusiastically.

He grinned. "Got somewhere to be today. Tomorrow. You naked and tied to this bed."

"Well, I'll need to pee."

He grinned. "Fine, but only for that."

"And you have to feed me."

He looked downright wicked. "Of course."

Just the anticipation was causing my body to heat in all the right places. "Deal."

His eyes narrowed, but I saw the hunger and the victory. "Deal. Hungry?" he asked against my lips.

"Yes, I could eat, too."

He chuckled and moved his hand down my body, but it was how he did it. Unconsciously done, but he was claiming me with his touch, and I loved that he was, because I was his, absolutely all his. He pulled from my ass, and I moaned, missing the fullness, even the pain.

He climbed from the bed and worked off the condom; I watched him walk toward the bathroom gloriously naked. "I need a painting of that," I called after him. We were in a luxurious hotel in Montenegro, one owed by Kade.

"Get your ass in here, woman. We need to shower."

"Bossy," I shouted back, but I was already off the bed and halfway to the bathroom.

TINGLES MOVED THROUGH me, remembering earlier and wanting a repeat. What an introduction to Montenegro. I reached for my wine and took a long sip.

"Something on your mind, Detective?" Kade asked, but he knew exactly what was on my mind.

"Never done that before." Took another sip of wine, before I added, "Want to again."

There was that wildness banging to get out. "Noted." Said so soft and low, heat settled between my legs.

"Am I ever going to have enough of you?" I thought out loud.

"Not if I can fucking help it," he replied smoothly, but I heard the steel behind the words.

A comfortable silence settled between us, before I said, "I'm happy you wanted me to see your home." I reached across the table and traced the vein in his hand. "But I suspect there's more to it."

He held my stare before he said, "You once said you didn't read me so well. You're wrong."

The waitress returned with plates of appetizers, featuring prosciutto and local prawns. He waited for her to leave, served me some of the delicacy, before he reached for his whiskey, took a sip. "As you know, I grew up here. I don't have a family outside of Carmine. He's my brother. He's proven that time and again."

"The man," I whispered, the monster he killed that had Kade believing he was a villain.

"Yeah, family," he said. "I had a problem, and he stepped in. No questions asked." He lifted my hand, brought it to his lips. "You've done the same." He grew thoughtful, before he added, "This case of yours has brought back a lot of shit I buried. In a sense, I'm glad because I've been going through the motions for a long time. Always trying for more, so I didn't find myself back in the gutter. But you think about Katrina, who had so much, but not what she wanted. My life has been one of reaction, everything I've done has been a reaction to how I grew up, the man who was fostered by this place." He looked around, before those eyes came back on me. "But not you. You've opened my eyes that as rich as I am, I'm not as rich as I thought. Or at least I hadn't been."

Tears hit my eyes, but what a thing to say. "It's that way for me, too," I confessed.

"I know," he said, then smiled, which turned devilish when he added, "I'm planning on stepping back." He brushed his lips over my fingers, before he released my hand. "Letting those I've put in positions of power have more of it." He looked every bit the villain when he added, "I'm going to become a man of leisure."

That wasn't possible. He might slow down, but he wouldn't stop working. It wasn't who he was, but I loved that he wanted to. "And what will you do as a man of leisure?"

"Ideally, fuck you all day."

Those words had the effect he wanted, as more heat pooled between my legs. "That would mean I'd need to be a woman of leisure."

"No, we'd just use your desk in the bullpen."

That thought shouldn't turn me on, but it did. "And your desk," I added.

"Fuck, yeah."

I took another long drink of wine to calm my libido. And as turned on as he made me, it was my heart that ached in the best possible way. He brought me here to show me his past, his beginning, but he also brought me here to let it all go, to move forward, to start a new beginning with me. It wasn't a wonder that I was so totally and completely in love with him.

WE WALKED THROUGH a section of Montenegro that was so different from the opulence of where we were staying. Poverty, an underbelly of it, that was as much weaved into the tapestry of the place as the magnificent views. "This is where I grew up. On these streets."

Not in a home, not under a roof, but on the streets. My heart broke, my hand reaching for his, because I needed the connection. Looking up at him, his focus was on our surroundings, there was a touch of disbelief. "I forget sometimes what it was like," he whispered.

"What was it like?" I asked, knowing he needed to purge.

"Hungry, all the time. Dirty, only bathing when it rained, or when I jumped into one of the lagoons. Ruthless as I got older. There's a hierarchy, even on the streets. The bigger you are, the more people want to tear you down. You learn to fight in order to survive." Bitterness touched his tone. "Miles away, people are tossing out untouched food, while here, there are those willing to kill each other for something to eat."

But he'd overcome it. He hadn't just gotten out; he'd thrived. "You got out, Kade."

"So many don't."

He started to pull me away when I noticed the crowd ahead. "What's that?" I asked.

"The community center," he said.

"Can we take a look?"

He hesitated but led me to what was the hub of the area. Inside, people gathered to talk, some were reading, some knitting, but it *was* a community. There was a table setup in the back, mountains of food, and a steady line of people. My heart filled, as did my eyes. "You did this."

"Someone had to."

He grew up in hell, but he wouldn't let others. "You weren't going to show me this."

"It's not enough," he said.

I looked around the room to the happy, smiling faces. "I think if you asked them, they would disagree."

HE TOOK ME to the dive shop, the place it all started. I was expecting a little shack, and maybe at one time it had been, but now it was a state-of-the-art diving facility with a fleet of boats, top of the line diving equipment, and all of it was affordable, not catered to just the rich.

"What was your job?" I asked, as we walked down the dock toward a boat.

"Took people to wrecks," he said, as we reached a boat, and he held his hand out to me.

"Are we going to a wreck now?" He had asked that I wear a bathing suit. I figured we'd be swimming, but diving would be even better.

"Not exactly," he said, then grinned.

I went to the bow of the boat and took a seat on one of the cushions, while he spoke to the driver. Before long, we were cutting through the crystal blue water. It was beautiful, the freedom of flying over the water. I'd never been on a boat, even growing up in New Jersey, but I loved it.

Kade used the time to teach me everything I needed to know about the equipment.

When we reached our destination, we were so far out, you couldn't see land. I looked around, before turning to Kade. "We're here?"

"Yes."

He tested my equipment before he helped strap it on me. Then he went through everything he taught me again and had me repeat it. He was an excellent teacher, but it was concern for me that had him being so thorough. It was the little things that had me falling even more in love with him.

He checked his equipment before he got suited up.

The diver's flag went up. The kid who drove the boat helped me onto the diver's platform. Kade hit the water first, then I followed.

"I want you to try breathing. I'll go under with you. Remember slow, even breaths," he said.

"Okay."

He put in my mouthpiece, before his own, then we dove. I had a moment of panic that my air was completely dependent on the mouthpiece and tank, but seeing the beauty around me, I didn't panic for long. Kade gave me the thumbs up, and I gave it back. And then we were diving deeper. The water was so clear, we could see for what seemed like miles. Schools of fish swam past, darting in patterns, like they were being chased. I noticed a sea turtle, pointed him out to Kade. We dove deeper, and I spotted a rock covered in bright pink anemone, little orange and yellow fish diving in and out of cover. Suddenly, all the fish disappeared. I looked around, just as Kade came up next to me, took my hand and pointed.

A shark. As I watched, he swam closer, close enough I could see his black eyes, but he didn't attack. He swam around leisurely.

Kade had given me another bucket list item. I looked over at him. He was already looking at me. I squeezed his hand, and for the next half an hour, we swam with sharks.

EIGHTEEN

Kade woke, turned to see Molly still asleep. The sheet had slipped, exposing her breasts. He tongued her nipple, a soft whimper escaping her mouth. His hand moved down her body, getting lost under the sheet. He grinned against her breast to feel she was wet. He tongued her nipple again, then sucked the peak into his mouth.

She moaned; her hips lifted into his touch.

He kissed down her stomach. Moved the sheet, as he kissed her pelvic bone, before moving lower. He felt her eyes and glanced up, she was looking down her body at him, her lip caught between her teeth. He kissed her, then lifted her ass and pushed his tongue into her pussy. Her taste exploded on his tongue. He growled and sucked on her clit, then ran his tongue through her folds, sinking back into her pussy. He worked her up to orgasm and then over it. He lingered between her legs to lick up every drop she gave him, and then he moved up her body and kissed her, sweeping her mouth with his tongue.

"So fucking sweet," he whispered. "Now pee, cause you owe me the day."

She wanted it as much as he did because she was in and out of the bathroom in minutes.

"On the bed," he ordered.

Her eyes went wide when she saw the bindings.

"Been wanting to do this since the first day you walked into my office."

He saw, as well as, smelled her arousal. "You wet for me?"

She dropped her head on the pillow. "This is going to kill me."

"But you'll die happy and very satisfied."

He bound both her wrists, her eyes narrowed when he started on her ankles. He stopped, studied her and asked, "You okay with this?"

She swallowed, but it looked painful, before she nodded. The restraints were long enough for her to bend her legs, but he could tighten them if he wanted. He stepped back to appreciate his woman, spread eagle and bound for him. "Now that I need a painting of." He moved around the bed, fisted his cock and started stroking. "So fucking beautiful."

Her hot eyes were on his hand. He continued to stroke, her tongue ran over her top lip. He used the hand stroking his cock and touched her mouth with his thumb; her tongue swiped his finger. Using that wet thumb, he brushed her nipple. Her breath caught on a moan. Her eyes drifted to his cock again. Fisting the base, he moved his hand up and watched, as she pulled at her restraints. "I want you," she whispered.

He climbed onto the bed, held himself over her, their gazes locked, and then he kissed her. Slow, deep and long. Her body was writhing under him when he broke the kiss. He turned his attention on her breasts, feasting on her like his favorite meal, because she was. By the time he reached her pussy, she was so fucking wet and sensitive that she came almost as soon as he touched her. He was so fucking hard, but he continued to feast until she was sated. Then reached for the condom. She squirmed because she knew what was coming next. He fingered her pussy, then moved lower to that tight ring.

"Oh god," she moaned, and lifted her hips.

"You want me to fuck you here?" he asked.

Her reply was almost broken with want. "Yes."

He didn't need lube, used her own heat to prep her entrance. He lifted her hips, and she helped. He grinned at her enthusiasm. Holding his cock, he pressed into her, feeling the resistance. Her breathing was coming out in pants, her nipples were hard, her pussy wet and getting wetter. He pushed forward, breeched the ring and bit back a moan because, fuck, she felt so goddamn good, gripping his cock like a velvet vice.

Her head dropped back, and the sound that came from her almost had him ramming into her ass, but he entered her slowly, giving her body time to adjust. Her knuckles were white with how hard she was fisting her restraints. When he was fully seated, he bent over her and kissed her hard on the mouth. The movement adding more pressure on her ass, causing a moan to escape that he swallowed. He then settled back, his focus moving down her body to where they were connected. He pulled out and sank back in, slow at first, but she felt so fucking good, the grip on his cock so tight that, soon, he was thrusting into her ass.

"Don't stop. Please don't stop. I'm going to come," she moaned.

He fingered her clit, before sinking two fingers into her pussy.

"Oh god, Kade," she cried, as she came, her pussy convulsing around his fingers. Her back arched, and she clenched her ass, squeezing his cock so hard, he felt the burn starting at his lower back, before moving into his balls, and then he was coming and so hard, he couldn't stop the harsh moan that burned up his throat.

He didn't move, his breath labored, his eyes on Molly. He'd never get enough of her. He pulled out of her, climbed off the bed. She was so sated; her eyes were growing heavy. "You're going to fuck me to death," she said, but didn't sound at all upset by the fact.

"Not to death, but we can get close," he teased, then pressed a kiss on her lips before he went to take care of the condom.

AS PROMISED, HE fed her and gave her breaks for the bathroom, but the rest of the day, she was bound. It wasn't even so much the idea of restraining her, though he did like her spread out like a smorgasbord for him, but it was the trust that she was giving him. Putting herself completely at his mercy and trusting that he wouldn't abuse the privilege.

He'd fucked her with his mouth, his cock, and his hand. He'd fucked her mouth, her pussy and her ass, and still, he wasn't sated. He knew when it came to her, he never would be. He also knew life was too fucking short, and when you found what you wanted, you took it.

He wanted her. She was still coming down from the orgasm he'd just given her so didn't react, right away, when he slipped the first binding from her wrist.

"What are you doing? You still have…" she glanced at the clock. "Two hours."

He freed her other wrist, then worked on her ankles.

"On your stomach," he ordered.

She didn't hesitate, having no idea what he was doing, but trusting him. He started at her shoulders and worked his way over her body, massaging her muscles that had to be sore. She moaned in appreciation. She was boneless by the time he finished.

"Molly."

Her one eye opened. "I feel this day needs to be a monthly event, maybe weekly."

He climbed from the bed, pulled on his sweats and disappeared into the dressing room, before returning. She was sitting up, cross-legged on the bed, his focus moving to her pussy, for a second, before lifting back to her face. He sat on the edge of the bed and looked at the woman he never saw coming and couldn't imagine a life without. His voice was low and rough. "I can't promise you the fairy tale, and I sure as shit won't be the prince, but I will love you every second of every day. I will fuck you almost as much, and I will never let you doubt for one second that taking a risk on this villain wasn't worth it."

"Kade." Her voice broke, her eyes filled, when he opened his hand to the ring, a five-carat, emerald-cut blue diamond set in platinum.

"Marry me, Molly."

Love looked back at him, as tears rolled down her cheeks. "Yes."

He slipped his ring on her finger, kissed her deeply, pushed her back onto the mattress, and this time, he loved her slowly.

THEY RETURNED FROM Montenegro two nights ago and had gone right to bed, spending most of yesterday sleeping. Today, Kade was up at five because they both had work. He didn't climb from bed immediately, enjoying the sight of Molly sleeping, his focus moving to his ring on her finger. He didn't know it was possible to feel so much, but this woman touched every button. He used to live to work, but now, he was living for her. He wanted all her smiles and laughs, all her tears. He wanted to see her round with his child. He wanted all of it. Fuck, he wanted the goddamn fairy tale. Him, Kade Wakefield, brought to his knees by a New York homicide detective with beguiling eyes and a heart of gold.

He wanted to wake her, wanted to sink into her sweet body, but she was exhausted. He grinned because he was the reason she was exhausted. He'd let her sleep, though, because she was heading back to work and needed to be awake and at her best.

He climbed from bed, got ready for work, and then made his woman breakfast.

"Time to get up, Baby," he said, an hour later.

Her eyes opened, and like she always did, she smiled at him. Her hand lifted, like the memory of his proposal had been a dream. Her smile grew wider. "Sapphire?" she asked.

"Diamond."

She sat upright, almost spilling the coffee he held for her. "Diamond?" Her gaze moved from the ring to him. "This is a diamond?"

"I think we covered that."

"Holy shit. I hope I don't lose it."

"I'll buy you another one."

"No," she said softly. "This one, it has to be this one."

Before Molly, he wouldn't have understood that, but he did now. He kissed her, then handed her the coffee. "You have ten minutes to eat, then you have to get dressed."

She rested back against the headboard. "I love that you take care of me."

"Good, because I won't stop."

"Not asking you, too, though you could add more bacon to my morning breakfast."

He glanced back from his dresser and grinned. "Noted."

"I don't want a big wedding."

He turned to her, pushed his hands into his pockets. "Okay."

"I want the dress and the cake and the flowers and those we love there, but I don't need hundreds of people. I mean, if you need to because of your—"

He settled back on the edge of the bed. "Fuck no. Our day, whatever you want."

"Any idea when you want to make it official?"

He glanced at his watch. "The government offices are all opening at nine."

She laughed, the sound carried around the room. "No, I want to see you in a tux, waiting for me to walk down the aisle to you." She took a sip of coffee. "And I want to put Katrina to rest."

"Then we wait for you to close the case."

"I have to fill the others in on what Carmine shared."

He tucked a strand of her hair behind her ear. "I know." He brushed his lips over hers, tasted coffee and her. "Seven minutes to eat."

NINETEEN

MOLLY

How did you come about this information?" Cap asked me, after I shared what Carmine had revealed about Enzi and Katrina. I'd crossed the line, but it was done.

"Carmine DeLuca told me."

Zac blew out a breath. "Shit."

"It's a little unconventional, I get that, but it's information that confirms what we already know."

"It's a fine line you're walking, Molly," Cap said.

"I know."

Cap stood, walked to his window. "An arrest warrant was issued for Enzi Sr. The Dents are now in protective custody. Still haven't located Milton and we're waiting on the blood bath, but as of yet, it's been quiet." Cap turned from the window. "Too quiet."

"Enzi's gone under?" I asked.

"Yeah, and according to Vin, when he strikes, it's going to be ugly."

"He's going to go after his son," I said.

"And anyone linked to him," Zac added.

My heart dropped because that made Kade and Carmine both targets.

Cap looked at my hand. "Is there something you need to tell us?"

It wasn't how I intended to share, but it was so us. "I got engaged."

"No shit," Zac said. "To Kade Wakefield?" As if there was someone else. Clown.

"He's a good man, Zac. Carmine DeLuca is, too."

I got a look from both of them.

"Despite what he does, he's a good man."

"You know what you're doing?" Cap asked.

"I didn't set out to fall for Kade, but I did. And yeah, I know exactly what I'm doing."

"Then I guess the only thing to say is congrats, Molly," Zac offered sincerely.

Cap surprised the hell out of me when he walked around his desk and pulled me into a tight hug. "Happy for you." He pulled away but held my arms. "Be smart." Then he smiled. "But be happy."

He looked as awkward as I felt when he let me go. "I will and thanks." I moved the conversation back to the case. "Enzi is a monster."

"He's not the only one. We still got Jason Benjamin out there," Zac said.

"We need to flush them out," I said. "Bait them."

Cap and Zac shared a look, but neither shared with me. "We'll get them," Cap said and moved around his desk again. "We're closing in, and they know it."

"WE'RE DOING LUNCH every day," Kade said, as he pulled his cock from me. We'd started at his desk but moved to the sofa.

"I like this plan," I said, watching as he tucked himself back in his pants, before he strolled across the room, returning with a wet towel. Settling on the sofa, he cleaned me.

"I'm going out for drinks with Ethan tonight. I want you to come."

His gaze met mine. "No, you haven't seen your friend in a while."

So like him to be thoughtful and not just to me but also Ethan. "I love you."

"You better."

"I offered him dinner at the penthouse, too, so how about we get a drink then come back." I touched his face. "I want you with us."

He turned his head and kissed my hand. "How do I argue with that."

"Don't cook, though. I'll help you."

"Deal."

My thoughts drifted to the case. Maybe it was taking the week off, but I wasn't so sure about some things. Using Kade as a sounding board, I shared. "So we think that Milton Teller might be Jason Benjamin."

Kade's expression shifted to surprise. "Why?"

"We can't prove it yet, but no one ever actually saw Milton. They knew of him, his reputation, spoke to him on the phone, but of all the people we talked to, no one had ever seen him."

Kade pulled my panties back up my legs. "You think Jason didn't disappear, he just assumed Milton's identity, a man he created?"

He helped me to my feet, reached for my pants.

"Exactly."

He pulled my pants up my legs, kissed me over the cotton of my panties, before standing, looking me in the eyes, as he fastened my pants. "That's an interesting theory."

"He's in the wind."

Those eyes went sharp. "Is he now."

"We've got plastic surgeons looking at the composite we have of Jason and pictures of Milton to see if it's possible they're the same person because we know that Jason Benjamin didn't exist, prior to him entering Katrina Dent's life."

He pulled his hands through my hair. "That's a very interesting theory and certainly explains why Jason has been so hard to track down."

"We'll see."

"You don't sound convinced."

"I don't know. We're missing something, but knowing that it's, very likely, one person responsible for not just Katrina, but Samantha, Frank and Emily, we're getting there."

"Tonight try not to think about any of it. Enjoy your time with Ethan. I'll stop at the market on the way home, pick up steaks."

"And potatoes. Ethan loves potatoes." I grinned. "So do you."

He chuckled. "And potatoes."

"THIS PLACE IS amazing," Ethan said of Polar, as we took a seat at one of the tables. "Your man owns it?" He asked, his focus shifting to my hand. "He is your man now, right?"

I glanced down at my ring. "Yeah, he is."

"That happened fast," he said, but added, "You look happy, though, so I can't complain."

"I am happy. I didn't realize what I was missing until I met him, and now, he's everything I want."

"I'm happy for you. For both of you."

The waitress arrived; we put in our order before I asked, "What's new with you?"

"Same ole, same ole. Someone moved into your apartment."

"Oh yeah."

"She's really great. Feeds me a lot."

I chuckled. "That sounds familiar."

"Yeah, but we eat early."

"Why?"

"Cause she's seventy-two."

My mouth opened then closed, and then I laughed out loud.

"So did you solve the case?" he asked, before taking a drink of the beer the waitress dropped off.

"Not yet, but soon." I hoped.

"You think you're going to stay with it?" His question surprised me because it was only recently that I was asking myself the same.

"I don't know. Why do you ask that?"

"Because I've seen you pre-Kade and post. You lived for your job, but I think, in part, that was because you were looking for something. You found it with him. And honestly, how long can you stare down death?"

"You're very intuitive, Ethan."

He blushed.

"I've been thinking about taking a step back. I love the job, but I didn't realize how much the job asked of me." I took a sip of wine.

"I won't do anything until we solve this case, and then we'll see." I touched his hand. "After our drinks, we're going to the penthouse for dinner."

His eyes went wide. "Seriously."

"Yep. Kade is cooking, but I'm going to help."

"The billionaire is going to feed me." Ethan leaned back in his seat and linked his hands behind his head. "I can live off of that for a while. The street cred is going to be off the charts."

I chuckled. "You're ridiculous."

We had two drinks and decided to catch a cab home because we were both starving. We stepped outside; the nights were warm, hot even, and after the two drinks, I was overheated. I stopped to take off my jacket, as Ethan moved to the curb to flag a cab. I heard the pop, my hand immediately going to my weapon. I saw the car speed off, caught a partial tag, and then I saw Ethan on the ground.

"No!" I ran to him, dropped down at his side. "Call 9-1-1," I shouted. My hands were shaking, as I ran them over him. His eyes were wide with fear and pain. "You're going to be okay," I said, yanking open his shirt to see the bullet hole. Blood was pouring out of it. I ripped the bottom of my shirt off, stuffed it into the wound, and applied pressure. Tears were blurring my vision. "Call 911," I shouted again.

A man dropped down next to me. "They're on their way."

"Stay with me, Ethan." His eyes were open, but growing glassy. He tried to talk, but nothing came out. "Stay with me."

I heard the sirens just when his eyes closed. "Ethan!" I put my head near his mouth, but I couldn't feel breath. I felt for his pulse, but I didn't feel one. "No!" I started compressions, which had the blood pumping out of his wound. Tears were rolling down my face; the sirens grew louder. I gave him a breath, felt again for a pulse and felt nothing.

"Don't you leave me. Don't you fucking leave me."

Two paramedics appeared. "We got it. How long have you been doing compressions?"

"Not even a minute."

I never in my life felt as hopeless as I did at that moment. My friend was bleeding out on the sidewalk, and there wasn't a damn thing I could do.

"I'll call Mr. Wakefield," the man at my side offered. I was numb, my focus turning to him, but not understanding him. "Mr. Wakefield?" he asked.

"Yeah."

"We've got to move," the paramedic said.

"I'm coming with you," I said, and flashed my badge.

"Alright."

"What hospital?" The man asked.

"Sinai." The paramedic called back.

Ethan flat-lined twice on the way.

"IS THERE ANY news?" I asked the nurse for the tenth time.

She was sympathetic when she whispered, "No, but as soon as we have some."

I moved away from the desk, pacing the waiting room. The doors opened, and Kade appeared, moving toward me in long strides, but it was the look on his face. He thought I'd been hurt, too. The tears that hadn't stopped welled again. I was pressed up against his chest, his arms holding me so tight, it hurt.

"I couldn't stop the bleeding," I said, then said again. "I couldn't stop it."

Kade said nothing, just held me to him.

"There was so much blood. I couldn't get it to stop. He was bleeding out, right there on the street. Someone shot him." Then the rage came and I pushed at Kade. "He was shot, right in front of Polar. A fucking drive by." Then I remembered the tag. "I have to call Zac. I have a partial tag."

Kade took my face in his hands. "Molly, look at me." I was falling back on what I knew, the facts, the evidence. "Molly." Kade's voice was harsh. My eyes found his. "I will call Zac. Give me the tag number."

His one arm held me to him, and I was grateful because my legs wanted to give out. He called Zac, told him what happened, gave him the number. I wanted to see the nurse again. He wouldn't let me.

"You're in shock, Baby," he said, soft but firm.

"Someone shot my friend," I said, softly at first, and then I screamed it. "They shot him!"

He pulled me close, held me as I cried. He looked over at the nurse. "How long will he be in surgery?"

"Hours."

He took my face again. "I'm going to take you home, get you cleaned up and then we'll come back. Yeah?"

"I have to talk to Zac."

"That can wait." He didn't leave room for argument.

I didn't remember the drive home. I walked right into the bathroom to the sink. My hands wouldn't come clean. Scrubbing the blood off, it just smeared. Tears pooled, but my anger was stronger, rage burned through me. My hands were raw, but still, I saw the blood.

"Molly."

"It won't come off."

His hand covered mine, as he turned off the water. "I have to get it off."

"Molly."

I turned to him, pushed him away from me. The screaming in my head spilled from my mouth and echoed around the bathroom. He made no move to stop me when I used him to let the frustration and pain out. I stumbled back, hit the wall. Before I slid down it, he was there...holding me up. His hand curled around my chin. "Tell me what you need, Molly."

I held his intense stare, my breathing coming in hard pants, the anger giving way to the pain. I fisted his hair, pulled his mouth to mine. He didn't respond, at first, until I begged against his lips, "Please."

Twisting my hair around his hand, he yanked my head back, those eyes I loved stared back with concern, before his mouth slammed down on mine. I clawed at his clothes, but his arm banded around my waist, holding me to him, as he consumed me with just his kiss. My muscles loosened, my body giving in to him. He pulled at my jeans, dragging them and my panties down my legs, my tee and bra followed. He turned the shower on, stripped, then pulled me under the spray before pressing me against the wall. His hand moved down my body, his fingers played with me. His mouth replaced his fingers.

"Oh god." I fisted his hair, spread my legs wider, and moved my hips to take him deeper. His fingers dug into my ass, as he brought me swiftly to orgasm, before he stood, turned me to the wall and ran his hand up my back and between my shoulder blades. He pressed down, bending me at the waist. He placed my hands on the wall and pushed my legs apart. In the next breath, he was slamming into me.

"Yes!" I scream.

He wasn't gentle. I didn't want gentle. "Harder," I begged.

He fucked me almost brutally; his hand fisted my hair, pulling my head back again for his ruthless kiss. I came so hard it brought new tears to my eyes. He broke the kiss, our gazes locked. It hit me on the way home. Where Ethan and I had been, the shit that was going down and the realization that someone had mistaken Ethan for Kade. New tears fell. "If it was you," I said brokenly.

His voice was a harsh whisper because he knew, too. "It wasn't me."

He pulled out of me, drew me against him and held me, as I broke down. Three months ago, I didn't know him, and now, I wouldn't survive the loss of him.

He washed me and then dressed me. An hour later, we were walking back into the emergency room. Zac was there. "Shit, Molly," he said, crossing the room and pulling me close. "I'm sorry."

Kade moved to the nurse's station.

"He's going to pull through. He's young and strong," Zac said.

I looked up at Zac. "We were at Polar. Kade owns that."

Zac caught on instantly. "They thought he was Kade."

New tears fell. "Yeah."

"I'll call Vin. We'll fucking find out who's behind it."

Kade returned, took my hand. "He's still in surgery." He touched my hair. "Do you want coffee?"

"No," I said, moving closer to him. I had to think, I had to focus on something other than Ethan on the ground. "They thought it was you. Enzi senior is making his move." My eyes jerked to Kade. "Carmine."

But Kade already had his phone out.

Zac had left. I wanted to be out there looking for the one who shot Ethan, but I wouldn't leave him. It was hours later, when the doctor joined us.

"He's made it through surgery. He lost a lot of blood, and the next twenty-four hours are critical, but he's young."

If Kade didn't have his arm around me, I wasn't sure I'd still be standing. He wasn't out of the woods, but he was fighting. "Can I see him?"

"He's very sedated. I'd rather you wait for the morning."

I wanted to argue, but Kade's lips were at my ear. "You need sleep. I'll bring you back after you've gotten a few hours."

I nodded.

"We'll be here at eight. She will see him then." He wasn't asking. The doctor nodded.

By the time we got home, I was emotionally and physically drained. I walked into our bedroom, began working on my clothes, then dropped onto the edge of the bed and started to cry. Ethan was going to be okay. I kept telling myself that, over and over. He was going to get through this. But, if I was being honest, what had me on the verge of a breakdown was Kade had been the target, and the reality it could have been him bleeding out on the sidewalk. That he could have flatlined…that I could have lost him.

I couldn't breathe. I tried to draw air into my lungs, but I couldn't. Kade appeared, on his knees in front of me, his hand on my chest. "Breathe in, Molly. Come on." He put my hand on his chest. "Follow me, Baby. Breathe in and out, that's it."

My lungs burned, as I drew ragged breaths in and out, the panic attack narrowly avoided.

"I can't lose you," I said, on a broken whisper.

"I'm not going anywhere."

"I won't survive it."

He pulled his hands through my hair. "You would. You're stronger than you believe."

"Would you survive the loss of—"

"No." He reached for my tee and yanked it over my head. My bra followed. He stood, brought me to my feet and dragged my jeans and panties down my legs. He pulled the covers down. And when I was settled, he stripped, climbed in, and held me close. I wrapped my arm around his stomach, pressed my face to his chest and fell asleep.

WHEN I WOKE in the morning, he was still holding me close. I lifted my head; he was already awake. "You need to eat, but we can get something on the road," he offered.

I pressed a kiss to his chest, ran my hand over his stomach, up to his neck. I shifted and kissed him, my lips lingering. "I love you so fucking much." He fisted my hair and pulled my mouth back to his. His hand moved to my ass, but I was already moving to straddle him. My hand disappeared between our bodies, grabbing his cock, lifting up, his fingers dug into my thighs, as I sank down on him. We both moaned. His hand traveled up my body to my breast, pulled on my nipple, twisted.

"God, you feel so good." I sighed; my hips found a rhythm, Kade finding it with me, his cock going so deep. I fisted the headboard, rode him hard, his finger finding my clit, tweaking it.

"Yes," I moaned, his hips pushing up into me. I felt the chills right before the orgasm, my head falling back, as I rode the pleasure.

Dark eyes watched, as he continued jerking his hips, until I rode it to the end, and then he flipped me, grabbed the headboard with one hand, my hip with the other and fucked me hard and fast until he sank in deep and came on a groan.

His hand curled around my hair, his kiss hard and rough and so fucking perfect.

WE STOPPED AT Duke's for breakfast sandwiches, not that I was hungry, but Kade made me eat, pointed out that I hadn't eaten since breakfast the previous day. We arrived at the hospital and were taken right to Ethan's room.

He had tubes coming out of him, the machine beeping his heart rate, and he looked so pale, but he was awake.

"Hey," I said, hurrying over to his side.

"Hey."

"Do you need some water?"

He shook his head.

"You're going to be okay," I said, reaching for his hand.

"I was shot," he said it almost like a question.

"Yeah, outside of Polar."

"Gonna have a scar," he said.

"I'm sorry..."

He squeezed my hand. "Street cred, Molly."

It took me a second before I laughed then cried, dropping my head on his bed. He really was going to be okay.

I WANTED TO go to the station, but after we left the hospital, Kade had other plans. He took me home. I hadn't realized how much I had needed to see my parents, until they came hurrying out of the front door, as we pulled up. I was immediately enveloped by both of them.

Kade was helping my mom with the coffee. Dad and I were at the table.

"How's Ethan?" Dad asked.

"He's okay. He's going to be okay," I said, repeating that to myself, often, because he really was going to be okay.

"Good." Dad leaned back in his chair and pulled a hand through his hair. "Scary shit."

Mom and Kade joined us, Kade taking the seat at my side. "This is Kade," I said. "Not the way I planned on you meeting, but..."

"Kade has been keeping us informed about Ethan," Mom shared.

My focus shifted to Kade, my heart swelled. I hadn't known he was doing that but wasn't surprised. I took his hand, kissed his palm. I didn't say anything, I didn't need to, and for a few seconds, it was just the two of us, so much said without words.

The soft sound from my mom turned my focus back on her. "That was beautiful," she whispered.

I knew we'd moved fast, but after what happened with Ethan, I also knew that it was right and that I'd always be crazy out of my head for this man. I didn't want to wait, didn't want to give it time. Life was too short, last night was a reminder of that. "We're engaged, and I know this is the first time you're meeting…" I looked up at Kade. "But when it's right."

Mom was up, moving around the table hugging me. "Oh, Molly. I'm so happy for you." She then turned to Kade, who stood when she did, and hugged him. "Welcome to the family."

"I'd like a few minutes with Kade," Dad said, walking from the room. Kade touched my chin to lift my mouth for his kiss. "I'll be right back." I watched him follow my dad.

"You're in love," Mom said, her voice a little dreamy.

I pulled my gaze from Kade. "I am, Mom. It happened so fast, but I do love him."

"Anyone with eyes can see it's mutual." Her hand covered mine. "I'm so happy for you both."

"I'm thinking about giving up the job."

She didn't hide her reaction. She loved the idea. "You need to do what's best for you. You know that."

"I love the job, but my priorities are shifting."

"That's normal."

It hurt to draw a deep breath, thinking about last night and how it could have been Kade. "Once this case is solved."

She looked confused before she asked, "Last night wasn't related to your case, was it?"

"I think, in a sense, it was." And I suspected the blood bath Vin warned about was coming. What I wasn't sure of was who'd be behind it.

"Oh dear."

"Yeah." We both heard the door before the booming voice. "Where's my niece?"

I stood, just as Uncle Gavin entered the kitchen. He pulled me into a bear hug. "You good, Sweetheart?"

"Yeah." Then I saw Kade watching me from the doorway. "I'm good." And with Kade, I was.

IT WAS LATE. Kade hadn't left my side since Ethan was shot, but Carmine had called earlier. Carmine was his family, and they had shit to discuss, and not just our engagement. He wanted to push it off, I told him to invite him over. He'd still be here, and I wasn't going anywhere. They were now in the study talking, but I was going through Frank's papers. We were missing something. My cell rang; seeing it was Zac, I answered it.

"Just talked to Jamison from Chadds Ford PD. The party line, an internal miscommunication that had the car on Milton pulled."

"Sounds suspicious."

"Yeah, Jamison thought so, too. Likely, Milton paid someone to lose the tail. Jamison is looking into it. Not that it matters."

"Why?"

"Milton Teller became Milton Teller in the seventies. Before that, he was Randy Drew, who had a juvie record that was sealed. Manslaughter, but he was found not guilty and his record expunged. We're going through known associates of Randy Drew to see if anything pops."

"How much do you want to bet Jason knew that? Knew that Milton had changed his name and used that fact for his benefit, the reason he was selected as Katrina's representative," I said.

"I think so, too." Zac said. "How's Ethan?"

"Falling in love with his nurse."

He chuckled. "Good. Alright, get some sleep. I'll see you in the morning."

"Night, Zac."

I dropped my phone on the bed. So Milton wasn't Jason, but still, he disappeared. Paid someone off and ran, which meant he knew who Jason was and was afraid. Considering Jason seemed to be cleaning house, he was right to be afraid.

I climbed from bed. Milton had cooperated in the beginning, genuinely upset about Samantha, sincerely interested in helping. So him fleeing was a total one eighty. My blood started to race because I would bet money he hadn't known what happened to Jason after Katrina died, and probably, hadn't seen him since her death, but something changed. He saw him. Holy shit, Milton saw Jason, recognized him and took off.

I'd seen Milton at both the NYPD fundraiser and Kade's masquerade ball. The fundraiser had been before we visited him that first time, but the masquerade ball...I started from the bedroom. When we'd seen Milton at St Regis, he'd been less inclined to help us. Nervous...scared.

If we compared the list of people at Kade's party, to the names we'd collected during this case, ones linked to not just Katrina Dent but also CyberTech, because I was still convinced there was a link, I'd bet money we'd find the new identity of Jason Benjamin.

Reaching Kade's office, I knocked.

His deep voice responded immediately, "Come in, Molly."

Carmine was standing at the window looking royally pissed.

"Is everything okay?" I asked.

Kade crossed the room to me. "It will be."

Carmine wasn't far behind Kade, and despite being livid, he pulled me to him for a hard hug. "Congratulations."

I hugged him back. "Thanks, Carmine."

"I'm sorry about your friend, but glad he's going to be okay."

He really was a good man. "Thank you."

He released me; I didn't let him get far. "If I can help, just say the word."

He almost grinned, looked at Kade. "If you hadn't put a ring on her finger, I would have."

Kade ignored him, his focus on me. "Did you need something?"

"Milton isn't Jason. Milton was a kid by the name of Randy Drew, who changed his name because he had a juvenile record."

I didn't miss the look Kade and Carmine shared, but I moved past it.

"When we visited Milton, the first time, he was eager to help, surprised and sincerely upset about Samantha. The next time we saw him, he was less helpful, even scared, and then he ran. I think he saw Jason. I think he recognized whoever Jason is now, and he fled." I paced to the window. "I saw Milton at the cop fundraiser, but that was before our first visit to him." I looked back at them both. "But there was another event that had the who's who in attendance."

"Fucking hell," Carmine said."

Kade's focus never left me. "Jason Benjamin was at my fucking masquerade party."

ZAC AND CAP shared a look, when I shared with them my theory. "Fucking nice detective work, Molly," Cap said.

"So we go through the lists and find the names that pop," Zac said.

"Kade is sending over the list to his party," I said.

"If you're right, Jason Benjamin has been hiding, in plain sight, this whole time," Cap said.

"And why not. Who's going to look for him," Zac said. "If the Enzi family hadn't stirred the shit up, his identity would have stayed hidden."

"Yep."

"We need Vin because our cases are intersecting," Cap said, reaching for his phone, then stopped. "Something about the other night bothers me. If senior is targeting his son, looking to hurt him, why go after Kade and not Carmine? From what I understand, Carmine is like a son to junior."

My heart and stomach dropped at the mentioning of that night, but I pushed through it. "I don't know."

"Unless..." Zac said.

Silence followed. "Unless what?" I asked.

Cap finished Zac's thought. "Unless Kade wasn't the target."

Took me a minute, the night coming back. I had stopped to take off my jacket. I went numb. "They wanted me."

"Not Enzi behind it, but Jason. Knows we're getting close. Targets you because of your connection to Kade and Carmine, which would trigger, well, all hell breaking loose in the Enzi organization, not to mention Kade's reaction," Captain theorized.

"Giving Jason time to disappear again," Zac finished.

I wasn't stupid. I didn't want a target on my back, but I'd rather it be on me instead of Kade.

Vin appeared at Cap's door. "Enzi senior is dead." His eyes speared me. "And we got an eyewitness."

Zac asked before I could. "Who killed him?"

"Carmine DeLuca."

TWENTY

Kade looked out at the city. From his distance above it, it was easy to believe there wasn't a vein of ugly that ran through it. But the city was like life; you couldn't have beauty without the ugly. Kade was tired of wading into the muck. The taste he'd gotten in Montenegro of how sweet his life could be, he wanted that every fucking day. He was going to pursue her like he would an acquisition. It would be the biggest, most important deal he'd ever struck, but he wanted a life with Molly in Antigua. They were going to focus on life and leave death and the ugly behind.

But first, he had to ensure her safety, and there was only one way to do that. They needed to fucking clean house. Needed to remove the threats, Enzi senior and all those who followed in his ways, and they needed to remove Jason Benjamin. His thoughts shifted to Ethan, his hands fisted in his pockets. She'd been so fucking close. It hadn't been Enzi targeting Kade; it had been Benjamin targeting Molly. He wouldn't get a fucking second chance.

His cell rang. It was Molly.

She sounded frantic when she asked, "Where's Carmine?"

"What's going on?"

"I just got a heads up from vice that Gregory Enzi senior was murdered last night." Unease moved through Kade. Her voice dropped to a whisper. "Someone is trying to make it look like Carmine did it. He has a temper. I don't want him doing something stupid before I can stop this before it starts."

He knew what she meant, and the hit of emotion rocked him. "You're going to be his alibi."

"I am his alibi."

"Molly."

"There's right, and there's wrong. I don't give a shit if there's blow-back. He didn't kill the man because he was with you all fucking night. Yes, I'm his goddamn alibi."

She was prepared to hang herself out to dry with her own to protect a known criminal, a killer, and despite her words of it being the right thing to do, she was doing it for him. God, he fucking loved her.

"I'll find him. Molly?"

"Yeah."

"Thank you."

"He's your family," she said. "I'll call you when I get this shit situated."

He found her later, after locating Carmine and practically cuffing him to his desk in his office. To say Carmine was pissed was an understatement. Molly was in her captain's office, a man dressed in street clothes, the same one he'd seen that night at Braciole, was screaming in her face. She didn't flinch, didn't move. Her partner stepped in front of him; her captain put his hand on the irate officer and pushed him against the wall.

"I can't believe you're alibiing that dirt bag," the man yelled.

"I am because he didn't do it." He watched Molly grow angrier, her cheeks turning pink. They did when he fucked her. This sight was almost as good. "And the fact that you're throwing out accusations at me." She got into his face. "My record speaks for itself. You may not approve of whom I choose to spend my time, but that's my fucking business. And I'm not about to watch a man get railroaded when I know he couldn't have possibly done what he's being accused of. Stop being a fucking hothead and let us fucking do our job."

Another man stepped into the office and, from the body language, clearly the irate officer's superior. "Cool the fuck down, Jimmy. Molly alibied Carmine; he's alibied. It's homicide's case. Let them work it."

Jimmy shook off the captain, started for the door. He caught sight of Kade and his face darkened. "She's fucking his best friend. Good alibi, Vin."

Kade was across the room, had the man against the wall. "You want to question my ethics and those I associate with, by all means, but you're crossing the fucking line questioning hers."

"Kade," Molly said. "Please. He's not worth it." He heard the pain in her voice.

Kade released him. Jimmy hid his embarrassment with bluster, when he shouted, "Fucking cuff him. That's assault."

The man who had joined the gathering last stepped out of the office, pushed his hands in his pockets and said, "I didn't see anything."

Molly's partner leaned against the wall. "Me, either."

"See what?" her boss said.

"This is bullshit," Jimmy hissed.

The big guy moved in. "What's bullshit is you coming down to my floor, calling out one of my detectives, based on nothing more than your fucking temper." He pressed the guy back against the wall with nothing more than a stare. "I'm a patient man, but I'm losing it quickly. Get the fuck off my floor, and when we solve this case, I expect you to apologize to Molly."

Vin grabbed Jimmy and pushed him along. "Sorry, Molly," Vin said.

She nodded.

"A word," the big man said, then Kade realized he was talking to him.

The door closed, but Molly and Zac were on the other side of it.

The man moved behind his desk, but he didn't sit. "Donald Darling," he said.

"Kade Wakefield."

"She's like the daughter I never had," Donald said. "Love her like one, too."

Kade nodded.

"Don't know much about you, and from where I'm standing, not my business to. Her stepping in, knowing the blowback from vice, means you mean a lot to her. I don't know your relationship to Carmine and don't want to know." He studied him, for a second, before he added, "Don't betray the trust she's clearly put in you."

He could get pissed at being dressed down, but considering the man's motives were about protecting Molly, how could he?

"Never," he replied honestly.

Silence followed before Donald said, "That's all I need to hear. Nice meeting you, Son," he said, and offered his hand.

"Likewise, Sir," Kade said, then added, "Now there's something I'd like to discuss with you."

A half an hour later, Molly was on him, as soon as he opened the door. "What was that about?"

"You done for the day?" he asked.

She glanced at her watch. "I can't work the Enzi's case, so, yeah, I guess I could be done for the day."

"Good."

She collected her things. He pulled her out of the station and into the car. His mouth on her before the door even closed. He dragged her onto his lap, his hand down her pants. She moaned, moved her hips into his touch, as their tongues warred. He wanted to fuck her, but that would have to wait until later. He brought her to orgasm, broke the kiss to watch her ride it, then brought his fingers to his mouth and licked her taste off.

Their heavy breathing filled the silence. He pulled his hands through her hair, held her gaze on him. "You did that for me."

"Yes," she whispered.

"As soon as this case is over, we're getting married, so plan fucking fast."

Her face went soft. "Deal."

KADE DROVE MOLLY to the hospital to visit Ethan, demanding she not leave until he arrived to pick her up. She and Ethan were going to watch a movie. He put a man on them, just to be safe.

He drove to the corner, picked up Carmine, who was waiting.

"Warehouse," Carmine said, when he climbed in. He glanced over at Kade. "She's going to be pissed you went behind her back."

Kade's fingers dug into the steering wheel. "Benjamin took a shot at her." Hard eyes turned to Carmine. "He doesn't get a second chance."

They reached the condemned warehouse, just outside of Brooklyn, parked next to the other car in the shadows and headed inside. Zac and Darling greeted them, as soon as they entered.

"I can't believe I agreed to this," Darling said.

Carmine was ahead, unlocking the door, flipping on the lights. In the middle of the room was a man bound and gagged.

"Fucking hell," Zac hissed. "He's a goddamn senator."

"He's a corrupt goddamn senator," Carmine clarified.

Kade crossed the room to Laurence Breen and yanked the gag from his mouth. His enraged stare was on Zac. "You're a fucking cop."

"Yeah, so is he," Zac said, pointing to Darling. "You were once, too."

Kade interrupted them. "You covered up Katrina's death. And don't try to deny it because I have a file that will discredit any bullshit you might try to shell out. All we want to know is the identity of Jason Benjamin."

Kade saw fear, before the man shut it down. "I don't know."

"The fear in your eyes would suggest otherwise," Kade said, moving closer to the older man. "This Benjamin took a shot at my woman, got her friend instead. I know you know who I am, and I know you're smart enough to know Benjamin isn't the only one you need to fear, so I'm going to ask you again. Who the fuck is Jason Benjamin?"

"I don't know."

Kade held in his temper, strolled around the man. "You let a young woman's murder go unsolved for thirty-one years, and worse, you fucking profited from her death, rising up the ranks in the political world and all it cost was your soul. You should be in jail, but they..." he gestured to Zac and Darling, "have agreed to let you go free. You will, of course, resign your position, and I'll keep my file, as an incentive for you to stay on the straight and narrow. I think we're being more than fair. Who's Benjamin?"

"I don't know. I haven't seen him in thirty-one years."

"Okay," Kade stepped back, "Carmine, he's all yours."

Breen's head snapped to DeLuca.

"Your reputation seems to have preceded you," Zac said.

Carmine cracked his knuckles. "You might want to wait outside for this."

"Fuck. Fine, but you have to protect me."

It was Darling who answered, walking across the room. His large hands fisted. "Protect you? You should have protected Katrina Dent. Now fucking talk or I'll forget I'm a goddamn captain and beat you to an inch of your fucking life."

KADE WATCHED AS Molly dressed. The backless silver dress rested at the small of her back, the shimmering material hugging her hips and falling to brush the floor. Her hair was up, her neck exposed. The only jewelry she wore was his ring. He walked up behind her, ran his hand up her back, around and under the soft material to her breast and pressed a kiss on her neck. Her head fell back on his shoulder, and a moan passed her lips.

"You look exquisite," he whispered.

Her eyes opened, love and desire stared back. It was tempting to pull the gown off and fuck her in only those silver heels, but they'd do that later. He stepped in front of her, her eyes moving to the black leather box he held before lifting to his. "Not as exquisite as your neck, but the best I could do."

He opened the Harry Winston box. Ninety carats of sapphires in alternating shapes of emerald-cut and oval-cut were surrounded by sixty carats of brilliant-cut diamonds. He loved watching her, the expressions that moved over her face.

Her voice was huskier when she whispered, "It's the most beautiful necklace I've ever seen."

Lifting it from its resting place, he put the box on the dresser and moved around her, securing it around her neck, before kissing her shoulder.

Her hand covered it, her eyes moving to the full-length mirror. His arms slipped around her waist. Their gazes met in the mirror. "My life really has become a fairy tale," she whispered.

He had some ideas on how to make that fairy tale even better, but first, they needed to hunt a ghost.

TWENTY-ONE
MOLLY

It felt like we were at the Academy Awards. The necklace from Kade hung heavy around my neck. It was magnificent. Camera flashes went off around us, as we walked up the red-carpeted steps of The Met, where the CyberTech launch was being held. Kade hadn't let go of my hand, keeping me close to his side. It was where I wanted to be, so I pressed in closer.

As soon as we entered, a waiter appeared with a tray of champagne. Kade handed me a glass before we mingled with the scientists and capitalists who had made the CyberTech discovery a success.

Kade saw me to our table, kissed my cheek and said, "I'll be right back."

I looked up at him and smiled. "Okay."

Glancing around the room, I felt the tingle because these were the same people from Kade's party. My eyes moved through the crowd because I'd bet money Jason Benjamin was here.

It was while I scanned the crowd that I noticed a few from the NYPD, dressed in tuxes, stationed around the room. A sinking sensation settled in my gut. Something was going down. Why the hell didn't I know about it?

I turned in my seat, caught sight of Kade. He was talking to Carmine. Unease moved through me because I had a feeling I was the only one not in the loop. Why the fuck wouldn't they include me? I answered my own question. Kade realized the attempt on him had really been on me. He went behind my back. On one level, I understood and appreciated what he was doing. Even loved him for it, but I was a fucking detective. It was my job and my case.

I reached for my phone. I was sure Zac was here, and damn it, if they were bringing down Jason, I was going to be in on the fucking bust. I left the table, pulled up his number and was so pissed I didn't appreciate I wasn't alone until I felt the barrel of a gun against my back. "Make a scene and I ruin that pretty dress." He pulled the phone from my hand and dropped it on the floor. He nudged me with the gun and demanded, "Move."

My anger grew, being caught off guard, but, as the reality of my situation settled, fear crept in. I didn't want to go with him; my feet were rooted to the floor. I wanted to make a scene, but feeling that cold steel against my back, and the thought that he could pull the trigger and, just like that, my fairy tale was over, I kept my cool, but that fear I kept buried came bursting out, the idea of never seeing Kade again, that our story ended like this, that he'd be left to pick up the pieces had my eyes burning. I wasn't going to let that happen. I had something to fight for, to live for. I had to play along, needed to wait for the right moment, and hope like hell, there was one.

I started to move; my feet felt like lead. I wanted so desperately to look for Kade, to get his attention, but the room was so crowded, and the man pressing the gun into my back wasn't wasting time. And I realized, in that moment, that this was exactly what Kade had been trying to prevent. He had gone behind my back because he wanted me safe, he wanted the case closed, and he wanted a life with me. And I'd let my temper and ego walk me right into trouble. And I was in trouble because I was unarmed and alone and was sure this man was taking me to Jason Benjamin, bringing me face-to-face with the cold-blooded killer responsible for so much death.

He took me out a side door and down a hall. There was so much activity, no one noticed us. We moved through the crowd practically unseen. And with each step that took me away from the Kade, the stronger the feeling grew that I wasn't going to see him again. We stepped outside; he stayed to the shadows, until we reached a car. I couldn't get in that car with him; it was blind panic now because I knew what awaited me with Jason. History was repeating itself. Like Katrina, I was more valuable to him dead. Even if I got shot, I had to get away. I was just about to make my move when a sharp crack to my skull had everything going black.

When I came to, I was tied to a chair. I pulled at my wrists, but I was tied tight. My head was killing me, and I was pissed, but I looked around, trying to get my bearings, looking for exits, ways out. Fear rose up to meet anger. The shadows moved, right before a man stepped from them. I didn't recognize him, but he was unraveling, the gun he held shaking in his hand.

"It's all going to hell," he said, turning to me. "It wasn't supposed to go down like this. Stir shit up, but fuck."

I felt the blood drain from my face. "You're Terence Baker."

He stalked over to me and pressed the gun to my forehead.

Terror raced through me leaving numbness behind. My breath caught waiting for him to pull the trigger. The only thought in my head was Kade. I closed my eyes, bringing up his face.

He moved away from me, as he talked to himself, like he hadn't just put a fucking gun to my head. Anger hit then, as did determination.

"He killed him," Terrence said, pacing again. "He fucking killed him." He turned wild eyes on me. "He was going to kill me, too. Told me if I brought you here, he'd spare me." I pulled at my restraints again, violently, this time, from both anger and fear. He really was serving me up to a monster. "Don't you fucking do that," he said, pointing the gun at me again.

Wanting to distract him, so I could work on my restraints, I asked, "Who wants me?"

I heard the shot, the surprised look on Terence's face, before he dropped dead from the bullet to the head.

My head whipped around, as I struggled to breathe, staring into the darkness, trying to see who was there. A heartbeat later, Sinclair Rothschild stepped from the shadows. "It's no way to treat a lady. I do apologize." Right behind him, holding the smoking gun was his man Joshua.

I was shocked speechless. It took me a second before I was able to get words to form from my incredulous brain. "You're Jason Benjamin?"

"I haven't been Jason in a long time."

I glanced behind him to his man, so not just his right hand, but also, his own personal hit man. And I had thought during that first interview how I'd like a man like Joshua, and now that thought brought a chill.

I studied Sinclair, who, I could admit, I kind of hero-worshipped, the man who Zac never bought into the hype. To think this man, who had done so much good, was also responsible for so much death. I was in the presence of Katrina Dent's murderer, Samantha, Frank and Emily's. Remembering what Terence said, he'd killed Enzi senior, too. How many others were there?

"You killed Katrina."

Joshua brought over a seat for Sinclair and then stood behind him, his focus on me.

"I did. I was very young back then, got a taste of the good life, and I can admit, I got carried away." He folded his legs, brushed some dirt off his pants. "I didn't want to kill her, but I was ordered to and, well, you didn't know Enzi. He was a ruthless son of a bitch. If I hadn't killed her, he'd have had us both taken out."

"How'd you do it?" I kept him talking, in the hopes that Kade now knew I was gone and was looking for me.

"No one will find you, Detective. I'm sorry things have to end this way, but I was backed into a corner." Before I could ask him to clarify that horrifying statement, he said, "Katrina wasn't the same after she lost her baby and Gregory. She started drinking more, so I waited until she'd drunk herself numb and then helped her slit her wrists. I think she wanted to die." Another chill moved through me, what a fucking sociopath. "I waited with her. Stayed until she died, so she wasn't alone." His gaze leveled on me. "I'm not a complete monster."

"You can tell yourself that, but you are a monster. Though I suspect it wasn't you who killed Samantha and the others. You got your man here to do it."

"Joshua is very loyal to me. I've done everything in my power to become a better man, to right the wrongs of my past. I have done far more good as Sinclair Rothschild than bad as Jason Benjamin."

"And does that help you sleep better at night? Telling yourself that all your good deeds erase the bad ones? Tell that to Samantha James' family, to Gregory Enzi."

For the first time, I saw a bit of the evil that lurked under the surface, as well as the anger. "That journalist should have left the past in the past."

"Frank Harris," I said. "He didn't, so your boy there was willing to take out a whole apartment building of innocent people to hide your secret."

"Joshua can be a bit dramatic, but his heart is in the right place."

A horrible thought occurred to me. "How did you meet Joshua?"

Sinclair smiled. "He's not Katrina's son if that's what you're thinking."

Relief hit because Gregory Enzi had been through enough; he didn't also need to face the horrible reality that his son was a monster.

"Joshua was a struggling young man when I found him. I gave him a home. It's amazing the loyalty you can gain by showing someone starving for a affection a little compassion."

Anger burned through me, thinking about Kade and how a man like Sinclair could have found him, preyed on his pain and neglect, turning him into a killer.

"You used his pain, played on it and turned him into a monster. You won't be getting any awards."

There was that darkness again, looking back at me from old eyes.

"Why did you want Terence to bring me here?"

Surprise moved over his expression. "You don't know?" He smiled again, but it was on the wrong side of happy. "Your fiancé and the others figured out who I was. They were planning on taking me tonight at the launch." He leaned closer and dropped his voice. "They didn't share that with you?"

He knew damn well they hadn't.

"I have no intention of being taken into custody. It's not the first time I've had to move on. Sad, because I quite like Sinclair Rothschild, but I think maybe I'll go somewhere tropical next. I'm old and don't really handle the cold winters, as well as I used to."

"You didn't answer why I'm here?"

"It all started with a young woman. I like the symmetry of it ending with one, too." He was so blasé when he spoke of killing me. Like I was nothing more than an insect. The man really was a monster. I pulled on my restraints, almost wildly, because I didn't want to die. I wanted the fairy tale with Kade. He continued, "You're the common link to all those who took my life away from me. Killing you will cause the most damage."

Rage burned through me that this man could paint himself, in any way, the victim, when he was preparing to kill me, when he had killed so many others. Shock was setting in, my body going numb because there was no way out for me. My eyes moved to Kade's ring. How close we had come. It was in that moment that I knew how Katrina had felt, how Gregory Enzi had felt. To come so close to your dream, to taste it, to know it was there for the taking and to have it yanked away from you. I'd have quit my job, moved to Antigua with Kade. I would have spent every day of my life at his side. And now, he would have to spend every day of his without me. The tears fell freely.

Sinclair stood, he even looked sad. "I'm sorry things had to end this way. I was rather fond of you." Joshua stepped up to me, and there was nothing going on behind his eyes, a complete void. I didn't beg, even though I wanted to, I didn't scream or yell. I just closed my eyes, brought up Kade's face. "I'm so sorry," I whispered.

"Drop it." My eyes flew open; Joshua spun around. I almost knocked the chair over, trying to see the owner of that voice. Sinclair turned, just as Gregory Enzi stepped into the light, and pulled the trigger. My gaze dropped with Joshua's body. Enzi had shot him right between the eyes. My brain was struggling to catch up. A second ago, I was facing down death, and now, my savior was none other than Katrina Dent's lover. I couldn't lie; I was almost giddy. It was shock, but I might just live through this.

Sinclair didn't even look at his downed henchman, so much for compassion.

"How did you find me?" Sinclair's voice betrayed him. He was scared.

"Milton called me. All these years, you were right there. I never knew, neither did he, until two homicide detectives came to see him with a story about a young woman's death and a link to the death of another young woman. And like me, he knew you were involved. Still didn't know your face because you've changed it. And then, he saw you at the masquerade ball. A man your age feasting on sweets, almost compulsively, something you've always done. That was when he did a little digging and realized exactly who you were."

Go Milton.

Gregory moved to me, worked on my restraints, keeping his gun and attention on Sinclair. It was shock, but it was a bit surreal that my rescue was at the hand of a reputed crime boss. It was poetic justice, though, that it was Gregory to bring down Jason Benjamin, because I knew exactly what he'd taken from Gregory, because Kade and I had what he and Katrina once did. He got my one hand free. I worked on my other, as he moved closer to Sinclair.

"You never should have come back here," Gregory snarled.

"This is my home, too."

"You didn't have to kill her."

"If I hadn't, he would have sent someone to kill us both. I didn't have a choice."

"There's always a choice. You didn't kill my son." Gregory's voice turned harsh. "You were my best friend."

My head snapped up, and my heart ached, seeing the pain cross Gregory's face. He'd lost his girl at the hand of his best friend?

"You shouldn't have fallen in love with my assignment."

I got my wrist free and retrieved Joshua's gun. I needed a phone to call Kade and backup.

"And you should have chosen your brother over your job."

"I've spent my life trying to make up for that night," Sinclair said.

"No, you've spent your life doing what you've always done, looking out for yourself. If your good deeds didn't benefit you, you wouldn't have done them. You've been a selfish bastard your whole life. And that night, you took my life. You stood over my girl, that beautiful, sweet, innocent woman who allowed herself to be used for my father's and your gain, and you killed her. And then you ran and hid, like a fucking coward. Returned as this..." he waved the gun at him, "a lion in lamb's clothing. Fooling the world that you're all about doing good, when you're nothing but a cold-blooded killer, what the world sees me as. How fucking ironic."

Gregory reached into his pocket and pulled out his phone. He pressed a button, held the phone to his ear. "Sending you an address. Jason is here. Molly is, too."

He texted the address and dropped his phone back in his pocket.

"Go outside, Molly, and wait for your fiancé," Enzi ordered.

"He's not worth it. Let him rot in a cell. Death is too good for him," I said, moving closer to Enzi not away.

"He needs to answer for what he's done."

"He will," I said, stopping at Enzi's side. "I will see to it that he spends the rest of his life in prison."

"He'll find a way out of it. You don't know him like I do."

"Think of your son," I said, saw his reaction and forged on. "Your father is dead, and he'll be locked away. You didn't get the life you wanted with Katrina, but you can have one with your son. And Carmine. You have family, don't let him take that away from you, too."

Gregory focus shifted to me. "You remind me a bit of Katrina," he said softly.

"What a compliment," I said truthfully.

He lowered his gun. What happened next, happened so fast. I caught a movement out of the corner of my eye and saw Sinclair pulling a gun. It was instinct, stepping in front of Gregory, and leveling my gun on Sinclair. Two shots fired. I felt the heat before I felt the pain, but my eyes were trained on Sinclair. He died with a look of surprise on his face.

I fell into Gregory, he caught me, lowered me gently to the floor. He was pulling off his jacket, ripping off his shirt. His voice was harsh. "Why the fuck did you do that?" His hands were shaking, as he pressed them to the wound. "You're going to be okay. Do you hear me? Fight Molly."

My vision was going black around the edges. I heard the voices coming closer, felt Kade before I saw him. He dropped down next to me, but it was the look on his face that had tears welling and spilling down my cheeks. I tried to talk, tried to tell him I loved him, but nothing came out. We'd come so close, so fucking close. His face was the last thing I saw before the blackness took me.

TWENTY-TWO

Kade paced the waiting room, barely holding on to his control. He'd never get the sight out of his head, seeing Enzi hovering over something, knowing before he even reached her, that it was Molly. The blood blooming on the silver, dulling the sparkles, her big blue eyes filled with pain.

He dropped in a chair, his head going in his hands. He didn't know how he'd go on without her. They were only at the start, the beginning. It couldn't end this way. Why was she brought into his life, only to be taken from it?

The waiting room was filled, a wall of blue, because one of their own was fighting for her life, and they were here to show strength, support and love.

Someone took the seat next to him. "She's going to get through this," Carmine said softly.

Kade nodded, but his heart was breaking. He'd heard the doctors. It wasn't good.

"She took the bullet meant for Enzi."

Kade's head snapped up at that.

"She'd talked him out of shooting Jason, but Jason pulled a gun. He said she moved on instinct, training her gun on Jason and stepping in front of him. Said it was the bravest and fucking stupidest thing he'd ever seen."

Tears burned his eyes. He wanted to be pissed at her, but she was just being Molly. The woman who had walked into his office that day and stolen his heart, before he even knew she had.

A doctor came out, looking around the crowded waiting room. Kade was out of his chair. He knew before he even reached him that something was wrong. "We've managed to control the bleeding and repair the damage from the bullet, but she lost so much blood."

"Is she alive?" Kane demanded

"She's slipped into a coma. She could come out of it tomorrow, next week but…"

"What?"

"Based on the severity of the damage, it's more likely that she won't come out of it at all. I wish I had better news for you."

Kade stepped back, his legs went weak, and he stumbled, hitting the wall and sliding down it. He never in his life cried, but he did then. Dropped his head in his hands and broke down.

SIX MONTHS LATER

HE WALKED DOWN the corridor, he walked every day, to the private room at the end. He stepped inside, felt the familiar pain that was a constant companion these days. His beautiful Molly had a tube down her throat doing the breathing for her. Her black hair was brushed back off her pale face.

He settled on the chair, took her hand. "You going to show me those eyes today?" he whispered. "Need to see them, Molly. Squeeze my hand, Baby. Give me something."

A little piece of his heart broke every day. The doctors wanted to take her off the ventilator. Her parents, too, were reaching their wall, unable to stand the thought of keeping her going, when she was already gone.

She wasn't gone. He would know if she was gone. He would feel the loss of her, would recognize it from the unbearable pain that he felt pushing at the edges to get in. She was still here. She was screaming for them to hear her. To not give up on her.

"I know you can hear me, Baby. I know you're still in there. Come back to me, Molly." His voice broke. He dropped his head on her stomach. "Fucking come back to me."

KADE STOOD IN his penthouse, looking out the window, but not seeing it. He didn't want to be here because it didn't feel like home without her. Nothing did, but that fucking hospital room. He let the pain fill him. Fuck, he couldn't do this. She'd touched every single part of his life, colored it with that beauty that was uniquely hers. How the fuck did he go back, how did he leave the color and go back to black and white? Every day that passed, the more unlikely it was that she'd come back to him. He dreaded the day he'd have to make the decision, the one that took her away from him.

Salem rubbed up against his leg. He reached for him, holding him close to his chest, and scratched behind his ears. "I know how you feel," he whispered. "I miss her so fucking much, too."

KADE STARTED WORK on the house in Antigua. When Molly woke, they were moving. He might have to fight her on it, but they were both going to live lives of leisure. She wasn't going to be more than a few feet from him again.

He didn't know someone had come into his office, until he heard, "What are you doing?"

He glanced up and saw Carmine and Gregory.

"Molly and I are moving to Antigua, so I'm working on the house to make it bigger."

They settled on the chairs across from him. "Kade, man," Carmine said.

"I think a bigger kitchen." He grinned, thinking of the times he cooked, and Molly watched. "She likes people feeding her." He liked fucking her on the counter. "Definitely more counter space."

"Kade."

Silence settled, for a few tense minutes, before Kade stood, turned to the windows. "I know what you're going to say. Everyone is saying the same thing. And I'm trying really hard here to keep my shit together because the best fucking thing that ever happened to me is currently being kept alive by a fucking machine." He turned then and didn't hide the pain. "That incredible woman is lying in that bed. And I know everyone thinks I need to let her go, that I have to put her body to rest because her mind and her soul are already gone." His breathing grew ragged. "How do I do that?" His voice broke. "How do I let her go? Give up the very air I breathe, the very reason my heart beats. I'm supposed to watch, as the machine stops, as her breathing slows until that line goes flat. I'm supposed to sit there and watch, as my present and future drift off with her?" He swiped everything off his desk and roared, "How the fuck am I suppose to do that?"

"You'd be surprised to know you have the strength." Gregory's voice was whisper soft. "And it's going to fucking hurt, a pain that feels like you're dying right along with her. You'll question everything you believe, and then you'll get so fucking pissed. And it will be years that you go through the motions, and you never will really get over it. You'll carry the pain with you every fucking day, but a time will come, when you think of her and you smile at the memories. A time will come when remembering her brings you comfort and not pain. And you'll realize that you're keeping her alive by remembering her, by loving her."

"It's not enough," Kade said brokenly.

"I know it's not, Son, but you were the lucky one because, for a time, you drew a star from the heavens, basked in her light and her love. She gave that to you, just you. And to find her again, you just need to look up."

HE HADN'T LEFT her since agreeing to pull the plug. His felt the numb taking over and knew that it would consume him when she was gone.

The waiting room was filled with people. He'd stood in the corner and watched as her friends and family said their goodbyes. Zac and her captain actually cried. That vice cop got teary eyed. Even the fucking hot dog and gyro vendor had come to see her. All the lives Molly Donahue had touched.

When the room was cleared, he moved back to her side, took her hand and brushed his lips over her ear. "I never believed in the fairy tale, but you gave me one. Allowed the villain to love the princess, and I do. Fuck, Molly, I love you with everything I am. Sparkle down at me, Baby, let me know where you are because I'm going to be looking for you every fucking night."

The doctor stepped into the room, her parents behind him. He said nothing, just waited quietly for Kade to give the signal. His heart shattered in that minute, but he nodded his head. He didn't leave her side, held her hand tightly, as the doctor switched off the machine.

He never took his eyes from her beautiful face, so he didn't realize the commotion going on in the room, until the doctor said incredulously, "She's breathing on her own."

"What does that mean?" Kade demanded.

He felt her hand move in his, his head whipping around to her. Her eyes jerked under her lids. "Molly, Baby, open your eyes." His tears dripped on her cheek. "Please, Baby, let me see you."

Her eyes fluttered opened, saw him, her hand moved in his, before she slipped back into sleep.

"What just happened?" Kade looked back to see Molly's parents crying and the doctor smiling. "Tell me!" he roared.

"She heard you," the doctor whispered. "She came back."

For the second time in his life, his legs crumbled, as he fell into the chair at her side, dropped his head on her stomach and let the emotions out.

TWENTY-THREE
MOLLY...TWO WEEKS LATER

Mom hugged me hard, and then Dad hugged me again. They hadn't stopped hugging me since I woke up. "I'll see you soon," I said.

Dad touched my cheek. There were tears in his eyes. He'd been having trouble with words, which was why he was resorting to hugging. He found some then. "You scared us, Molly."

I'd scared all of them. I was just beginning to understand how much. Zac cried, when he showed up in my room, after clearly running to get to me. He took one look, dropped on the chair at my side, his head hit my stomach, and he cried, like shoulders shaking cried. It was the first time I'd ever seen him breakdown.

Ethan and I had a talked one night. He had a unique perspective because he'd been there. We'd always been friends, but we'd formed a bond that night.

I tried to comfort all of them, tried to get them past the horror, but in their shoes, I knew it was going to take time.

"I'm here." I glanced up at Kade who hadn't left my side, not just in the past two weeks, but I was sure in the last six months. "I'm going to be a woman of leisure."

Kade's beautiful eyes smiled, but I saw the shadow behind them, the pain. It broke my heart.

216

Dad's eyes got bright. "I want you to do what's best for you, but I can't lie. That makes me so damn happy."

I hugged Dad, again, and reached for my mom to pull her into it. "I can't imagine what these last months have been like for you, but I'm okay. You'll see. We'll get past this."

"We know," Mom said, placing her palm on my cheek. "It's just going to take some time."

We said our goodbyes; Kade touched my chin with his thumb. "I'll be right back."

He walked my parents to their car. I was discharged earlier. People had been coming and going all day. Vin had brought sandwiches from Duke's, left a stash for me in the fridge. Cap had pulled me aside earlier and told me he thought of me as a daughter. And then he broke down. Captain Donald Darling sobbed. Tears filled my eyes, remembering, but I was okay, and I think today had been cathartic for everyone. Salem rubbed up against my leg. I picked him up, hugged him hard and kissed his face. "I missed you, fur ball." Tears gathered in my eyes because I had come so damn close. Salem squirmed. I kissed him again, then let him go.

Considering the length of my coma, the doctors were surprised at how well I was able to get around. I was weak and needed some physical therapy to build up my muscles, but I was okay.

The same couldn't be said of Kade. My eyes filled with tears because he hadn't just had to make the decision to let me go, he was in the room. The pain that stole over me, just thinking about it, almost brought me to my knees, but he'd had to live through it.

And since I woke, he hadn't stopped. I got it, I'd be doing the same, he'd been given a second chance, we both had, but he was burning himself out. The elevator doors opened, he stepped out and crossed the room right to me.

"Let it out, Kade," I whispered. I touched his cheek, my gaze moving over his face. "Let it out. In your shoes, what you've been through… let it out."

His jaw clenched.

"I heard you."

Hard eyes softened. "I heard you. I was trying to get back to you. It was like I was in quicksand, and the harder I tried, the deeper I sank."

Tears filled my eyes. "I heard the goodbyes and knew I couldn't go. I couldn't leave you." I took his hand, pressed a kiss in his palm. "You were never the villain, and I'm not much of a princess, but I do love you with everything I am."

He pulled his hand from mine and stepped back. "I was watching you die," he said, in a harsh whisper. "I had to prepare myself for your death." His voice grew louder. "A lifetime without you. How the fuck was I supposed to do that, Molly? All the years I'd have to face without you. Letting you go, letting my fucking heart go. Fuck!" he roared, pacing away from me. "I almost went mad. I think if you had died, I would have. We collided, you and I fucking collided, but the best fucking things happen when two forces collide. I don't want a lifetime with you, I fucking need it."

He stalked back to me, right into my space, his hands in my hair, his mouth a breath from mine. "Every fucking breath is yours." His mouth slammed down on mine, tongues touched, and I moaned, even as my eyes burned, because we almost lost this. His fingers tightened in my hair, as he took the kiss deeper, his tongue sweeping my mouth, savoring and remembering. We were both breathless when he ended it.

"I really do want to be a woman of leisure," I said.

He looked intense, but his voice was soft. "Are you sure?"

"Yes. I was already thinking about it before all of this, but now, I know that I want every second of every day with you."

He showed me how much he liked that when he kissed me breathless.

"ARE YOU SURE, Molly? Maybe you should give it some time before you make the call," Cap said. Kade had brought me to the station. I had to walk through a wall of people wishing me well; there were presents and flowers all over my desk. I cried, was crying a lot these days. I was going to miss them. These people were my family, but so was Kade, and I wanted my life with him.

"I was already heading in this direction, Cap. I love the job, you know how much I do, but I want Kade, and I want a family. And, after all this, how fast it can be taken away, being given a second chance, I don't want to waste a second."

"I can't say I wouldn't want the same in your shoes," Cap said softly. "But the door is always open."

"Thank you." The tears started again.

I turned to Zac. "I'm going to miss you, partner," he whispered. "You're the best partner I've ever had."

Zac wasn't a hugger, but I hugged him, and he hugged me back. "Be careful."

"I will," he said, his voice rough from tears. "The case is closed, but I thought you'd like to know that Milton fled to Kevin McKenzie's."

It was so easy to slide back into being a detective. "Desiree's dad. So that's where he was."

"He changed his name because the altercation he'd had, as a kid, was defending Kevin against a hate crime."

"What kind of hate crime?"

"Gay bashing."

Well, shit. Milton seemed so gentle, but good for him for standing up for his friend. Then I recalled our talk with Desiree and how she had said Milton had taken her on because her father and Milton were friends. Understanding dawned. "They were lovers."

"Yeah, but for a man who wanted to work in public relations, he couldn't have manslaughter on his record, while molding the image of those paying him to do so. And, even expunged, we know all too well that if someone wants the information, badly enough, they'll get it."

"So Milton really had been there, just behind the scenes. At least Katrina had him."

Zac rubbed the back of his neck. "And Mitch Anderson died, but not before we were able to share with him that his information helped us break the case."

"Good. I'm happy to hear that. And Samantha's parents?"

"We gave them closure, but that's a pain they'll always carry." His eyes got a little bright. I knew he was thinking about me. I reached for his hand and squeezed it. I loved these people, this job, but I really was ready to start the next chapter with Kade. Despite the nostalgia, I couldn't keep the joy from my voice when I said, "Wedding invites will be going out soon. Block some vacation time."

Cap and Zac both looked at each other, before looking back at me. "Vacation time?"

I grinned. "Vacation time."

They followed me out of the office. Vin was making his way down the hall. "I heard you were here." He looked behind me, understanding moving over his face. "You're leaving."

"I am."

He stopped in front of me, tugged on a lock of my hair. "You are one tough cookie, Molly Donahue. You ever want back, there's a place for you in vice."

I wiped at my eyes, because I was tearing up again. "Thank you, Vin."

He pulled me into a hug. "Take care of yourself," he whispered.

"You too." I stepped back, reached for his hand and squeezed. "Wedding invite, vacation time…" I gestured to Zac and Cap. "They'll fill you in."

It was harder than I thought it would be, turning and seeing them watching me. I had spent the last six years here; my life had been this building and these people. And then, I turned and saw Kade, standing by my desk, and suddenly, it wasn't so hard because he was what I wanted.

He closed the distance, took my hand and pulled me up against him. "You good?"

"I am."

He glanced back, lifted his hand to the others, then turned me toward the door.

"Let's get Duke's for lunch," I suggested. "And we need to swing by and pick up Ethan. We owe him dinner."

"He's already at the penthouse. Apparently, he's moving in."

I laughed out loud at Kade's tone.

"I'll talk him down."

"You better." His eyes were hot, and damn, but I missed that look. We hadn't had sex yet. I wanted to. I'd even tried to seduce him a few times, but the man could be stubborn.

"I want access to you whenever and wherever, so I'll definitely talk him down." I pressed in closer. "Maybe that can be sooner than later."

He had a thought on that, but didn't share, and instead, pressed a kiss on my forehead. I wasn't going to fight him on it, not yet. I understood. In his shoes, I'd be feeling the same. It wasn't about me being hurt; it was about control and him losing it. He still hadn't really let it all out, all the shit he went through. He needed to. If he didn't soon, I was going to force his hand.

"There's somewhere I'd like to go," I said.

"Anywhere."

"It'll require your plane."

"Anything you need, Baby."

JACKSON KILBURN GREETED us with a smile. He showed us into his apartment, and like the first time, we settled in his living room.

"I was happy to get your call. I'm hoping you've got good news."

"Yes. You were right about Katrina. She was murdered, and it was at the hand of her fiancé."

Tears filled the older man's eyes.

"Jason Benjamin was killed, while being brought into custody, and Katrina's official cause of death has been changed to murder."

He took my hand into his old ones. "Thank you. You have no idea how much comfort you've brought me."

"Well, here's a little more for you. Her baby wasn't Jason's, but a man she loved dearly, and that man and his son have been reunited."

"Oh, that makes me so happy." He settled back on the sofa. "I'm an old man, and I've been ready to go, but I've been waiting, hoping to put things right. Thank you for giving me that."

"We stopped at the market on our way here," I said, gesturing to the cooler. "Would you allow us to cook you dinner?"

"I would like that very much." He tried to stand; Kade helped him to his feet. "Thank you, Son." He started for the kitchen. "I've a nice bottle of wine I've been saving for just this moment."

We spent the afternoon and evening sharing stories of the job. We talked about Katrina. When we left Jackson, he looked at peace. He died in his sleep that night. Kade and I stayed in Los Angeles for his memorial, and when we learned he had no one, we arranged one. Zac flew out, as did Carmine and Gregory Enzi. He was laid to rest on a sunny spring day in the same cemetery Katrina Dent had been buried, thirty-two years earlier.

I WAS OUT shopping for wedding gowns with my mom. It was the only reason Kade wasn't with me, and still, he grumbled about it. My heart wasn't into the gown search, though, because I was worried about Kade. Mom was pulling gown after gown from the designer rack, but I wasn't looking. She dropped down next to me. "What's wrong?"

I exhaled on a sigh. "It's Kade." I turned into her. "How bad was it?"

Her face dropped, a shadow moved behind her eyes. "It was bad, Molly," she said, and took my hand. My heart twisted, but I had to hear it, needed to know.

"Tell me."

"He wouldn't give up. Even when everyone else…" she wiped at her eyes, "Even when your dad and me couldn't take it anymore, he wouldn't give up. He said he'd know if you were gone. That he still felt you." She pulled in a hard breath. "When he finally agreed to pull the plug, he didn't leave you. Stayed with you day and night." She squeezed my hand. "He came face-to-face with your death. Your dad and I did, too, so I know how he was feeling, but you were his future, that long, beautiful road ahead of you, and he had to let it go. I honestly don't know what would have happened to him if you hadn't come back to us."

"How do I get him to let it go? He still hasn't. Not all the way. It haunts him."

"You're his breath, Molly. Breathe life back into him."

MOM AND I postponed wedding dress shopping. Instead, I stopped for something on the way home.

Kade greeted me. "How did it go?"

"It didn't." His smile dropped. "I need something."

"Anything, you know that."

I took his hand and walked to our bedroom. Dropping it, I stood at the base of the bed. "I'd like you naked, and, on the bed, and I want to restrain you with these," I said, pulling out the cuffs.

He pushed his hands into his pockets, that mask was firmly in place. "I don't think that's a good idea."

"Do you trust me?"

Anger swept his expression. "You know I fucking do."

"Then trust me."

Several tense minutes passed before he kicked off his shoes, one then the other, his socks followed. It wasn't sexual; it wasn't foreplay. He was angry, but so was I. He unbuttoned his shirt and pulled it from his body. His pants followed and then his briefs. He stood before me completely naked, and I looked my fill because I had missed him. "You're beautiful," I whispered.

A slight softness entered his hard eyes. He turned for the bed, my gaze moved to his ass. He climbed on, lying in the middle. I moved to him, wanting so badly to kiss him, to straddle him and take him deep into me, but we had to do this. I closed the one cuff around his wrist, fed it through the slat of the crisscross headboard and caught his other wrist. Hot eyes looked at me. Heat pooled between my legs, seeing the dominant Kade restrained, but that he trusted me to give me this...I fucking loved him.

"You can break free." I gestured to the headboard. "We both know that." I moved to the foot of the bed, his eyes followed me like the predator he was.

"You're angry with me," I said, walking to the other side of the bed, settling on the edge. My hands itched to touch him, even just a stroke over his cheek, but I didn't touch him. That's not what this was about. "There's a part of you really fucking pissed at me because I walked away from the table that night." His arms flexed, the headboard squeaked.

"That's not what's fueling the rage, though. You're pissed at yourself because you weren't there. Someone shot me, and you weren't there."

The bed shook, his body flexed, his muscles hard.

I stood, reached for my shirt and pulled it over my head. My bra followed. I had a scar; it ran down my stomach about four inches. One he was careful to avoid when he touched me. I saw the pain in his eyes now, his gaze drifting over the souvenir of that night.

"I almost died," I said. "And for six months, you had to watch me straddling the line between life and death." I touched my scar. "I can have it removed, get plastic surgery to cover it up." My gaze met his. "But I survived. And I did because you wouldn't let me go. I don't know how to get you to understand that. I was lost in the darkness, and then I heard your voice. You were there with me, right there with me, Kade. I'm out of the dark now, but you're still there." I touched the cuff. "Sometimes bad shit happens, and you aren't always going to have control. You weren't the one who left the table that night and you weren't the one who put the gun to my back. But you were the one who called my name in the dark, the one who didn't stop calling, until I could find my way back to you. You saved me. You brought me back to life." Tears were rolling down my cheeks; his eyes were wet. "It's your turn to hear my voice, to follow it, to come out of the dark, because I'm waiting, and I miss you so fucking much."

He pulled on the cuffs. "Unlock them."

My heart dropped, but I reached into my pocket for the key and undid them. He moved from the bed, stalking away from it. Every muscle in his body was tense. His hands fisted. I waited because this was the calm before the storm.

Just his head turned, one dark eye looked back. "I almost lost you." His voice was nothing but gravel. He was across the room in a heartbeat, had me up against the wall in the next. His hand curled around my throat, his eyes locked onto mine. "You brought color to my world, not going back to black and white."

His hand moved down my body, his eyes followed his hand. He touched my scar, ran his finger down the length of it and then he kissed it, before running his tongue along it. He moved back up my body, grabbed my hair, pulled my head back and looked into my eyes. "I want forever."

Before I could draw a breath, his kissed me. Not hard, not rough, but slow, like it was the first time. He nibbled at the corner of my mouth, ran his tongue along my lower lip. He pulled back, brushed his thumb over my cheek, and then he was kissing me again, deeper, longer. I moaned, parted my lips, my hands moved to his chest, moving down and around, over his ass. He kissed me breathless, before he lifted me and walked across the room. He pulled my jeans and panties off, before he drew me close, and climbed onto the bed. He lowered me back onto it, ran his hands up my arms, lifting them over my head. I felt the cold metal on my wrists. "Oh god," I whimpered. After cuffing me to the headboard, he moved his hands down my body, his mouth followed. He played with my breasts and tongued my nipples, sucking me into his mouth, before kissing lower. He lingered on my scar for a bit, before continuing south, kissing his way down. He inhaled deeply, looked up at me, his fingers digging into my hips to lift me to his mouth. He pushed his tongue into me, and I cried out, but he didn't linger. He moved back up my body, laced his fingers in my hair, his other hand moving between our bodies. He entered me slowly. "I want your smiles." He sank in deeper. "I want your tears." I bit back the moan, as he filled me. "I want the happy and the sad." He sank in deep, then groaned. "I want your kisses and your orgasms, every day for the next hundred years."

I wrapped my legs around his waist to hold him deep inside me, my words spoken softly, as I vowed, "I'm yours forever."

He kissed me long and hard, then he spent the night taking and giving kisses and orgasms.

"YOU'RE SURE YOU'RE okay with this?" Kade asked.

He sold the penthouse, but not his estate, because we'd be back to visit. We packed up our things and were moving to Antigua. Salem was in the carrier next to us on the plane. He wasn't happy.

"Yes, I'm sure. I want this, you and me, the island, you in faded jeans and bare feet. When I think of my life of leisure, that's where I see us."

He kissed me hard and fast. "That's where I see us, too." He took my hand, played with his ring. "Two weeks."

We were getting married in two weeks. Invites had been sent; airfare handled for all of our friends and loved ones. My dress was among my things, a lace mermaid dress with an open back. It was simple and elegant. I couldn't wait for Kade to see me in it, couldn't wait for him to take me out of it, because we'd be starting our lives as husband and wife.

We arrived in Antigua, drove to the docks, took the waiting boat, and when the house came into view, the memories came flooding back. Those days we spent here had been the best of my life, and now, here we were, making this island home. Kade helped me from the boat, holding Salem's carrier. He reached for my hand, but I was studying the house. "It's bigger."

"I've made a few changes."

"When?" I asked.

I felt him go tense and knew the answer. "I wanted our life here, so I made it a home."

He started up the dock; I didn't follow him. He looked back. I whispered, "Wherever you are is home."

With his free arm, he pulled me close and kissed me. "And you are mine."

We shared a moment, before I said, "Show me what you've done."

We walked up the backyard, and I noticed the porch was now screened in.

"That's new."

"For Salem. He can enjoy the outside, without going outside."

I turned into him. "You thought of Salem."

"Of course, but it'll also come in handy for kids."

Love moved through me at the thought of kids with this man.

We stepped inside, and it really was like coming home. Kade let Salem out of his carrier. He immediately started exploring. Kade pulled me to the kitchen. He'd added more counter space, a bigger stove and fridge. Ceiling fans stirred the tropical air. "This is beautiful."

"Several new counters to fuck you on."

I felt those words, but said to him, "You didn't really have that in mind when you designed it." But seeing the devilish look on his beautiful face, he absolutely had it in mind. He showed me the two new guest suites and another room, just off the master bedroom. A nursery. I had thought to wait for kids, but seeing the home he'd made for us, for our family, maybe we shouldn't wait.

He then pulled me into our bedroom. The one wall had been removed, and French doors, three sets of them, opened to a private patio with a wading pool. Tropical plants enclosed the little paradise, like a secret garden. The room was all light and airy, but it was the bed that had my full attention.

It was massive, covered in pillows, sitting under a ceiling fan, but it was the rings attached to the frame, four of them that had heat pooling between my legs. Kade stepped up to one. "Had them added just for you."

I reached for my shirt and pulled it over my head. "I think we need to try them out."

I WAS ON my back, arms bound, and Kade was kneeling between my legs, his cock driving into me with deep hard thrusts, his eyes on where we were connected. I moaned, my body jerking from how hard he was fucking me. "Don't stop." My head dropped back, another moan ripped from my throat. His finger moved to my clit, his groans and the sound of our skin smacking together had me struggling against my restraints because I wanted to touch him, even loving being unable to.

"Yes, oh, oh, yes, fuck…Kade!"

"That's it, Baby, fuck, you feel so fucking good." He moved deeper and faster until he came, his voice raw when he groaned his release.

He didn't move, didn't pull out. His breathing was more like hard pants, as he looked his fill. "Fucking love how you look." He brushed his thumb over my nipple. "Don't need you bound, but I love you letting me bind you."

"Don't need to be bound, but I love being bound for you."

He didn't respond with words but brushed his thumb over my other nipple, down my body, over my scar, until he reached between us. He touched my clit, sank in deeper, before he brought it to my mouth, ran it over my lower lip, then pressed the tip between my lips to meet my tongue. I tasted us. He then brought that same thumb to his lips and licked our taste off. He pulled out of me, reached over and undid my wrists, then pulled me up against him, chest to chest, heart to heart. No words were spoken, but none were needed. Then he kissed my nose. "I need to feed you."

"Maybe we can try out the new counter."

His smile was breathtaking. "You read my mind."

I STOOD LOOKING at myself in the mirror. My wedding dress was perfect, hugging my figure and just brushing the floor. I was going barefoot. My hair was swept up in a knot; I wore a little mascara and lip-gloss, but with my tan, I didn't really need makeup. The only jewelry I wore was my ring. I was getting married today. A day I dreamt about, a day that almost didn't come.

There was a knock before Gregory Enzi stepped into my room. He'd been to see me in the hospital, but we hadn't really talked, not about that night. He didn't come closer, just stood by the door. "I said it that night, you remind me of her. What you did for me, and for her, exposing the truth behind her death..." He closed the distance, his focus intense. "I'm in your debt. You ever need anything, absolutely anything, I'm a phone call away." He studied me before he whispered, "You look beautiful." He touched my cheek. "Congratulations."

He walked out of the room before I could respond, but a smile touched my lips, because maybe they were both now at peace.

"Hey, Partner."

"Zac." I met him halfway for a hug. "I'm so glad you're here."

"I wouldn't miss it." He lowered his head, looked up and grinned. "I think I could be tempted to retire here."

"You are getting up there in years. You should seriously think about it."

"I'm only thirty-six, three years older than you."

I grinned.

"You look happy," he said.

"I was always happy, but with Kade, it's just a different kind of happy."

"Well, it's a good look on you. I won't keep you, a line is forming out there." He kissed my cheek. "Enjoy the moment, savor it, Molly. It took a lot for you both to get here."

God, I missed him. "I will." He started for the door. "Zac."

"Yeah."

"You should really think about retiring here."

He flashed me a smile. "I intend to."

Ethan walked in. Zac and he shook hands. "You're looking good. How you feeling?" Zac asked.

"I'm doing good. Thanks, Man."

"Good luck with your maid of honor duties," Zac teased.

"Man of honor," Ethan said, trying to sound stern, but not pulling it off. Zac chuckled, looked back at me, winked and disappeared out the door.

"I can't believe you're getting married today." My focus shifted from the door to Ethan. He was wearing linen pants and a white shirt, so different from his all black look. He looked incredible. "And that you live here, though, I understand the appeal because this place is amazing."

I was determined to get those closest to us to move out here, too. Not immediately, but some day, all of us together again. I'd really like that. "You should think about moving here."

"It's crossed my mind," he said

"Yeah? There's a hospital on the island. You and Sandy, sun, sand."

Sandy was the nurse who'd cared for him when he'd been shot. He no longer had women coming and going because he'd found the one. "We'll definitely think about it because she's loving this place." He glanced at his watch. "Man of honor duties. Ten minutes," he said, then added more softly, "You look beautiful, Molly."

"Don't make me cry," I said. "Thanks for being my man of honor."

"Thanks for asking me." The door opened, my mom peeked her head in. "I'll see you out there," he said as he kissed me, and then kissed my mom, before he disappeared out the door.

"Oh Molly. There has never been a more beautiful bride." She touched a strand of hair that had fallen from my knot. "I don't have to ask if you're happy because I can see you are. I've never seen you so happy. And that man out there would move heaven and earth for you. He would pull down the moon if you wanted it. Hold on with both hands, Molly. Life is a rollercoaster, as you well know, but the ride is so much sweeter when you have someone to ride it with."

I started to cry; she did, too. Then we hugged. "I love you, Mom."

"I love you, too."

Dad walked into the room. He kissed Mom, before she left, then turned his attention on me.

"You're not my little girl anymore."

I felt a new wave of tears burning my eyes. "I'll always be your little girl."

"You've grown into a beautiful, strong woman. It's not easy for a father to give his daughter away because there is no man who will ever be good enough for her, but Kade is as close as a man can come."

"Oh, Dad." The tears fell again.

"I love you, Molly."

"I love you."

Dad wiped at his eyes, then offered his arm. "We should go. Your future husband is getting impatient."

I reached for my bouquet of white peonies and took his arm.

The wedding was on our beach. White chairs were setup right on the sand. Dad and I reached the patio; my heart was like a jackhammer behind my ribs. We stepped outside, the steel drum music started. People stood. I didn't see anyone but Kade. Standing at the end of the aisle, he was dressed in a linen suit and white shirt unbuttoned at the collar, and his feet were bare. The breeze off the water stirred his hair; those eyes I loved were burning into mine. The distance closed, and then he was there, taking my hand from my dad, holding it so tightly in his. I didn't hear the words from the minister, I didn't remember saying my vows, but I remembered slipping my ring on his finger, remembered him slipping his ring on mine, and then he framed my face with his hands. In that moment, it was just the two of us, the world faded.

"Every breath, every beat…yours forever," he whispered.

"Forever," I whispered back.

And then, my husband kissed me.

IT WAS LATE. Our friends and family had all retired to the hotel. As soon as the guests left, Kade brought me to our bed and fucked me hard and fast and then loved me slow and gentle.

We were in the kitchen. Salem was on the counter eating some grilled fish we put aside for him. I was in Kade's shirt, on the counter, drinking a lava flow. Kade was in sweats feeding me grapes. I couldn't stop looking at his hand and the ring, a simple platinum band.

I touched it. "I love this," I said, my gaze lifting. "Mine."

He kissed me, ran his tongue over my lips, and then reached for my hand that wore his rings, the diamond and a simple platinum band. He kissed them. "Mine."

"That first day when I walked into your office, did you think we'd find ourselves here?"

"On some level, yeah." He walked to a drawer and pulled something out. It was my business card.

"You kept it?" My heart did a long slow roll.

"You left my office, and I felt like I'd just been in a hit and run." He dropped his hands on the counter on either side of me. "Two objects in motion." He moved between my legs, grabbed my ass and yanked me to him. "Pulled together by fate." He kissed me. "Stirring heat." His tongue ran down my neck "And all that friction." He laced his fingers through my hair. "And love, so much fucking love." He dragged his thumb across my lips. "You crashed into me and gave me forever." He lifted me from the counter, headed for our bedroom, and whispered, "Starting now."

EPILOGUE
MOLLY...THREE YEARS LATER

Kade and I took the first year of our marriage to travel. We traveled to Egypt to see the pyramids, Europe to visit castles and Daytona where Kade got to drive the five hundred in a car he borrowed from William Bryon. We visited Montenegro a few times a year, but we didn't stay in Kade's hotel. We preferred an Inn, not far from where Kade grew up. He bought the land, offered them some capital, but the rest was handled by the employee-owned staff, an authentic taste of Montenegro. It was one of my favorite places to visit.

Mom and Dad finally got their European vacation, spending a month right after Kade and I got married in Montenegro, and now, they returned every year. We dove an old ship off the coast of Cancun, The Isabella, and learned that not only was there a beautiful but tragic love story about the captain and his wife, but that the two, who found it, had their own version of a fairy tale, a treasure hunter and real-life, modern day pirate. They lived in the Caribbean somewhere and locals say sometimes you see their ship, a massive sailing yacht with an honest-to-god Jolly Roger flag waving from the one mast. I scanned the horizon for them often. Maybe one day, I'd see them.

After that year, Kade and I realized we needed to work, and so, two years ago, we both found jobs on the island.

Kade walked into the bedroom, a mug of coffee in his hand. Salem was with him, jumping up on the bed to rub against my side. I scratched behind his ears.

"Time to get up, Baby. We've got work." He settled on the bed, kissed me long and deep, then handed me my coffee. "Decaf," he said, his hand moving to my flat stomach.

I was pregnant. We just found out. Kade was already working on the nursery.

He kissed me again, nipped at my lower lip, those gray eyes staring into mine. "Ten minutes."

Ten minutes later, we were walking down our dock to the skiff. We motored to the mainland, docked. Kade helped me from the boat, kept my hand as we walked the pier to the shack called Molly's. There were already fifteen little kids in their bathing suits and floatation devices waiting. I had commented that day on how I'd love to take little kids snorkeling, and my husband didn't just remember, but made it happen. We were open four hours a day every Monday, Wednesday and Friday. We didn't need the money, used what little we charged to put back into the business, it was the joy of seeing their happy faces as they explored the unknown that was so rewarding.

"Are you ready to see Nemo?" I asked.

A resounding cheer followed.

"This is Mr. Kade. He's a great teacher, so let's listen, as he shows you what you need to know about swimming with the fish."

A hand flew into the air. "Yes, Sweetheart."

"I heard my mommy talking, and she wanted to know if Mr. Kade gave private instruction."

I bit my lip to hold back the laugh and looked at Kade. It wasn't the first time. For a kids' excursion, there were a lot of mommies who watched from the sidelines. Kade's focus moved to those women when he said, "No."

I lowered my head and chuckled.

I loved watching Kade with the kids, knew he was going to be an amazing father. He had so much patience, and he didn't talk down to them. It was like they were his board of directors, just smaller and cuter. When he was comfortable that they were ready, we put our snorkels on, and for the next hour, enjoyed their faces as they got a glimpse into life under the sea. When the hour was over, our happy customers gifted us with smiles and waves.

After the last group finished, Kade and I were cleaning the equipment. I put the snorkel I'd just cleaned back in the shack, my eyes falling on Kade, whose back was to me. He only wore jeans and tees on the island, no shoes. I loved him in suits, but I loved his new look, too, because it was his choice. "You're going to be a wonderful father."

He turned to me, and for a man so confident and sure of himself, I saw a little doubt. "Never had one, but I hope so."

I walked right into him, my arms moving around his waist. "The way you love me, so completely and unconditionally, I know so." Then I batted my lashes. "Do you give private instruction?"

I saw the look, because that shit annoyed him, but annoyance gave way to heat. "For you, fuck yeah."

Even after three years of marriage, and a very healthy sex life, he still could cause those butterflies.

"Let's finish here, so I can feed my woman."

We finished up, locked the shack, then strolled up the pier to the small food stand that sold the best seafood stew on the island. "Hey, Ethan. Two large bowls," I called.

Yes, Ethan had moved to Antigua. He and Sandy lived not far from the hospital, where she worked, and Ethan had found his calling as a cook. His stand always had a line, like the one now, but we never had to wait.

"Family and she's pregnant. Give me a minute," he said to his customers. To us he said, "Sit."

He scooped out two bowls from the huge stainless steel pot he had simmering over an open fire, grabbed the rolls he made special and brought it over to us.

"You're a little late today," he said, then glanced at Kade. "Beating the mommies away?"

He placed our food on the table.

"Fuck you," Kade said.

Ethan laughed out loud. "Yeah, that's got to be a pain in the ass, all those women falling all over you. Torture," he said, rolling his eyes and pushing his hands into his pockets.

"Only woman I want falling all over me is already wearing my ring."

The teasing stopped. "I hear ya, man," Ethan said. "So did you hear about the case Zac picked up?"

I was happy, I loved my life, but I still got that chill for the hunt because I really did love being a detective. "No, what case?"

"Jewel heist that ended in murder. Victim was from Monaco, a link to the royal family."

"Holy shit."

"Yeah, he was pretty jazzed," Ethan said. He started back to his customers, calling from over his shoulder. "Enjoy. Oh, and I'm working a new recipe. I need a guinea pig."

I raised my hand. "That's me."

I caught Kade studying me throughout lunch, but he said nothing while we ate. He waited to share what he was thinking when we were heading to our second job. We docked, he turned off the engine, but he didn't move to get out of the skiff.

"You miss it," he said softly.

I wasn't surprised by his comment because the man read me like a book. I was honest when I said, "I miss putting the pieces together, but I don't miss chasing down meth heads and coming face-to-face with a barrel of a gun."

His jaw clenched, thinking about my shooting. He pushed his hands into his pockets. "Consult."

"On the case?" I couldn't lie; the idea had crossed my mind.

"Yeah. A fresh set of eyes to look over the case file."

I liked the idea, but I wasn't sure Cap would go for it. "You think Cap would be okay with that?" I asked.

"I don't see why not, but it can't hurt to ask, and if you need to make an appearance from time-to-time, we already visit Manhattan a few times a month to check on my shit, we coordinate our schedules."

"All the parts of detective work that I like and none of the bad," I said, not hiding my excitement.

Kade pulled me to him. "We'll call later."

I wrapped my arms around his neck, my voice going a little soft, because I loved this man so fucking much. "You're always taking care of me."

"And I always will."

He kissed me, hard and fast, and then he smacked my ass. "We've got work."

We walked up our dock, but we didn't head to the house. We took a path that ran alongside it, leading to a building hidden behind tropical trees. Reaching the big double doors, Kade unlocked and pulled them open. He hit the lights. We were building a sailboat. It was the second boat commissioned, an original Kade Wakefield design. I did more watching than working because he loved it. A man who had once said his life was one of reacting, he was now choosing, and it made me so damn happy.

Then he pulled his shirt off, glanced back and tossed it at me. That was one of my working conditions, he had to work shirtless, just those faded jeans and bare feet. Yeah, I spent more time watching than working.

KADE WAS MAKING dinner. I was in our bedroom, putting some papers in the safe, and noticed the box. I reached for it, opened the lid. It was the necklace Kade had bought me, that exquisite necklace. I'd only worn it that one time. Bad memories were linked to it. I ran my fingers over the sapphires. It was time to make new memories.

I stripped out of my clothes, secured the necklace around my neck and slipped into my silver Louboutin strappy-heeled sandals. I studied myself in the mirror, my eyes moving to the scar, as I traced it with my finger. I dropped my gaze to my stomach. My hand covered the baby growing there. That's what life was all about, making new memories.

I walked to the door and called, "Kade, Baby, they still fit."

He looked over and then did a double take. Those stormy eyes moved down my body and back up again. The pan was pulled from the burner, the heat turned off, and my husband was across the room sweeping me off my feet. "Dinner is going to be late."

Dinner wasn't just late, it was ruined, but I'd always liked cold pizza. Sitting on the counter, my husband between my legs, sharing a slice, I loved it even more. Kade had said on our wedding night that I'd crashed into him. That first day, we'd crashed into each other, knocking us off our original paths, so we could find a new path together. Who'd have thought something so ugly would lead to something so beautiful, but it had because we were living the fairy tale.

BRIAN GAINES WON the election to become the forty-sixth president of the United States. At the podium, during his acceptance speech, he held a small gold coin for luck that was given to him by his father, a coin gifted to his father by a woman Brian had never met, Katrina Dent, his mother.

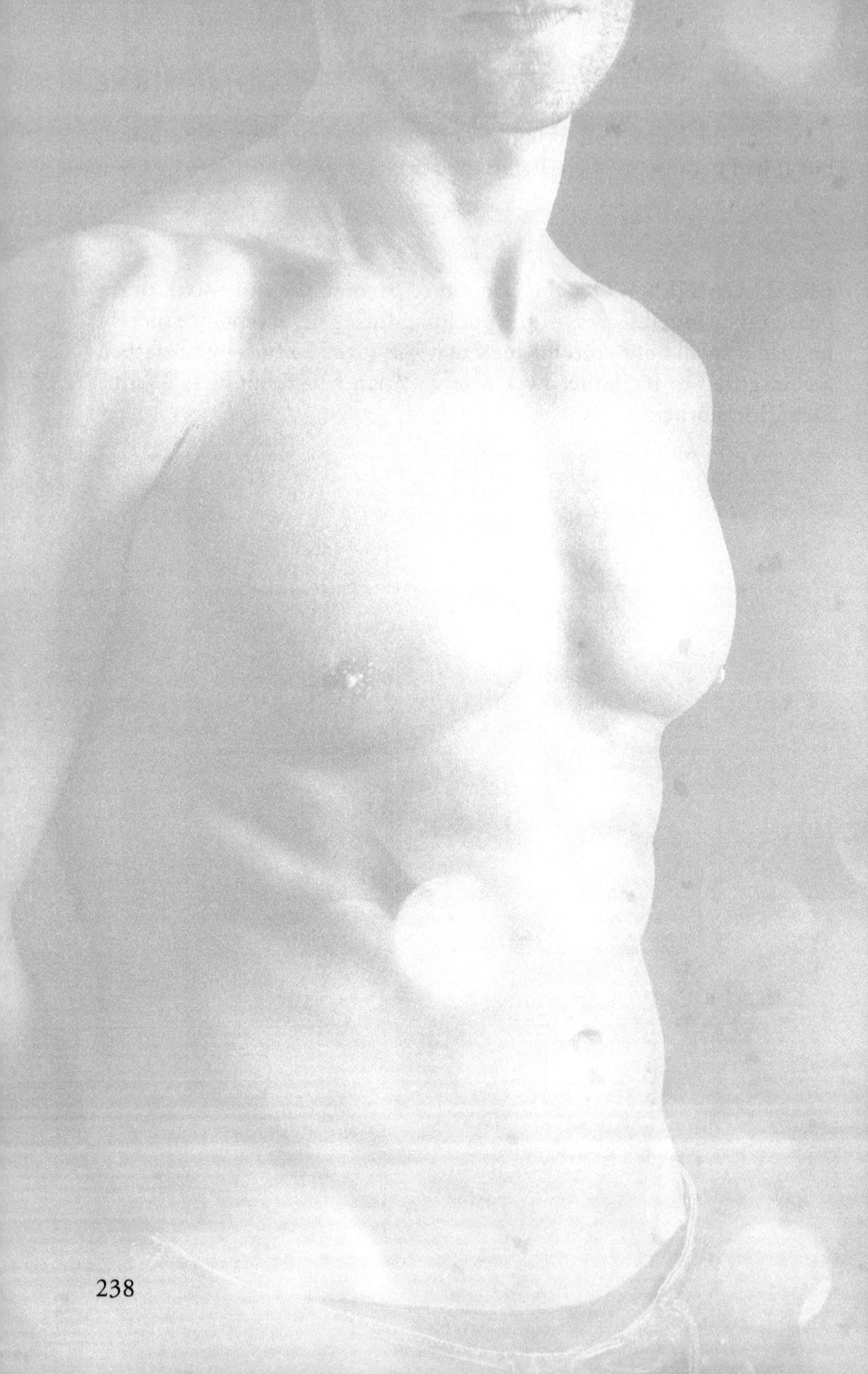

OTHER TITLES

ELUSIVE

I didn't set out to be a pirate.

Life for me was about surviving the ugliness that people knew existed but didn't talk about.

I lived in hell.

Then I saw her.

I knew I couldn't keep her, but for just a little while, I had found heaven.

Eight years later, I can't get her out of my head.

It is a mistake sailing to her island.

It is a mistake reaching out to her.

She doesn't recognize me. Or maybe she does.

Closure, it is all I'm after.

Then my past comes back to haunt me.

She's thrust into my ruthless world. An angel.

A romantic who has a journal that leads to a shipwreck and a lost treasure.

She wants to find the ending to a love story that is over two hundred years in the making.

I want to help her find it.

I didn't set out to be a pirate.

I didn't set out to fall in love with an angel.

I did both anyway.

LETTING GO

I met Brock Callahan at eleven, fell in love at fifteen and lost him at eighteen.

One moment, one single instance can change the course of your life, but I picked myself up, brushed myself off, and took that first step knowing it would be the hardest.

Years later, tired of existing but not living, I quit my job in Manhattan, sold my condo and moved to a log cabin in Wyoming.

When I wake in the bed of Killian Reid, mistaken for a one-night stand, I never imagined I'd fall for the man.

But I did.

Not at first; a slow fall, so gradual I didn't realize I was no longer falling. I'd been given a second chance at a happily ever after.

And then Brock Callahan walks back into my life.

BEAUTIFULLY DAMAGED

Ember Walsh is a trusting soul with the quiet beauty of her late mother, who perished in a mysterious car crash when Ember was three. A little tomboyish from being raised by her father, Ember packs a punch when a stranger gets pushy with her in a bar, catching the steely blue eyes of a tall, gorgeous tattooed man—Trace Montgomery. Still damaged from her last disastrous relationship and warned off the bad boy by friends, Ember fights the smoldering heat that Trace sparks in her when he begins shadowing her like a dark angel.

Burdened by a lifetime of horror and heartbreak, amateur fighter Trace doesn't want to want Ember. His deep self-loathing keeps him from having any meaningful relationships, but Ember is an itch he can't scratch. The two push and pull, slowly crumbling their walls, seemingly brought together by fate, because the turmoil that haunts their pasts is interlinked in undeniable ways. But can these two fighters finally lay down their arms?

HIS LIGHT IN THE DARK

My first memory was of a slap, hard across the face: the sting on my cheek and the jarring of my bones as I slammed back into my bed. It was my dad who had hit me.

I had been four.
Most of my memories were much of the same and no one ever saw, no one ever fought to help, no one ever cared.

Then we moved.
My new neighbor cared, rescued the twelve-year-old I had been from a beating. Always thought I'd suffer the nightmare alone, I was wrong.

Mace Donati saved me that day in all the ways a person could be saved.
And his daughter, Mia, she became the friend I had always wanted, my conscience when my own faltered, the light that led me home when I had lost my way.

The girl who grew into the only woman I would ever love.
But when you realize you're more like your father than the good people who took you in and gave you a home, the only way to return their kindness is to let them go.
I let them go, got so far lost in the shadows I couldn't remember who I was anymore. Mia never gave up on me. She fought for me, kept the light on so I'd find my way back.

And when I did, life threw us a curveball. I had to hurt Mia in order to save her.

But when my past comes back to haunt me and I almost lose her, I'm ready to fight for *her*: fight to find a way back into her heart while keeping the demons from my past from finishing what they started.

ABOUT THE AUTHOR

THE BEAUTIFULLY SERIES...
Beautifully Damaged
Beautifully Forgotten
Beautifully Decadent

THE HARRINGTON MAINE SERIES...
Waiting for the One
Just Me

LOST BOYS SERIES...
Devil You Know
Demon You Love

SHIPWRECK SERIES...
Elusive

THE IVY BLACKWOOD CHRONICLES SERIES...
The Gathering

STANDALONES
Our Unscripted Story
Savage: The Awakening of Lizzie Danton
His Light in the Dark
A Glimpse of the Dream
Always and Forever
Collecting the Pieces
Letting Go

STAY IN TOUCH

Website:
http://www.lafiorepublishing.com
Facebook:
https://www.facebook.com/l.a.fiore.publishing
Reader Group:
https://www.facebook.com/groups/lafemmefabulousreaders
Twitter:
https://twitter.com/lafioreauthor
Instagram:
https://instagram.com/lafiore.publishing
Goodreads:
https://www.goodreads.com/author/show/6553058.L_A_Fiore
Amazon:
http://www.amazon.com/L.A.-Fiore/e/B00BDAHVMG
Email:
lafiore.publishing@gmail.com

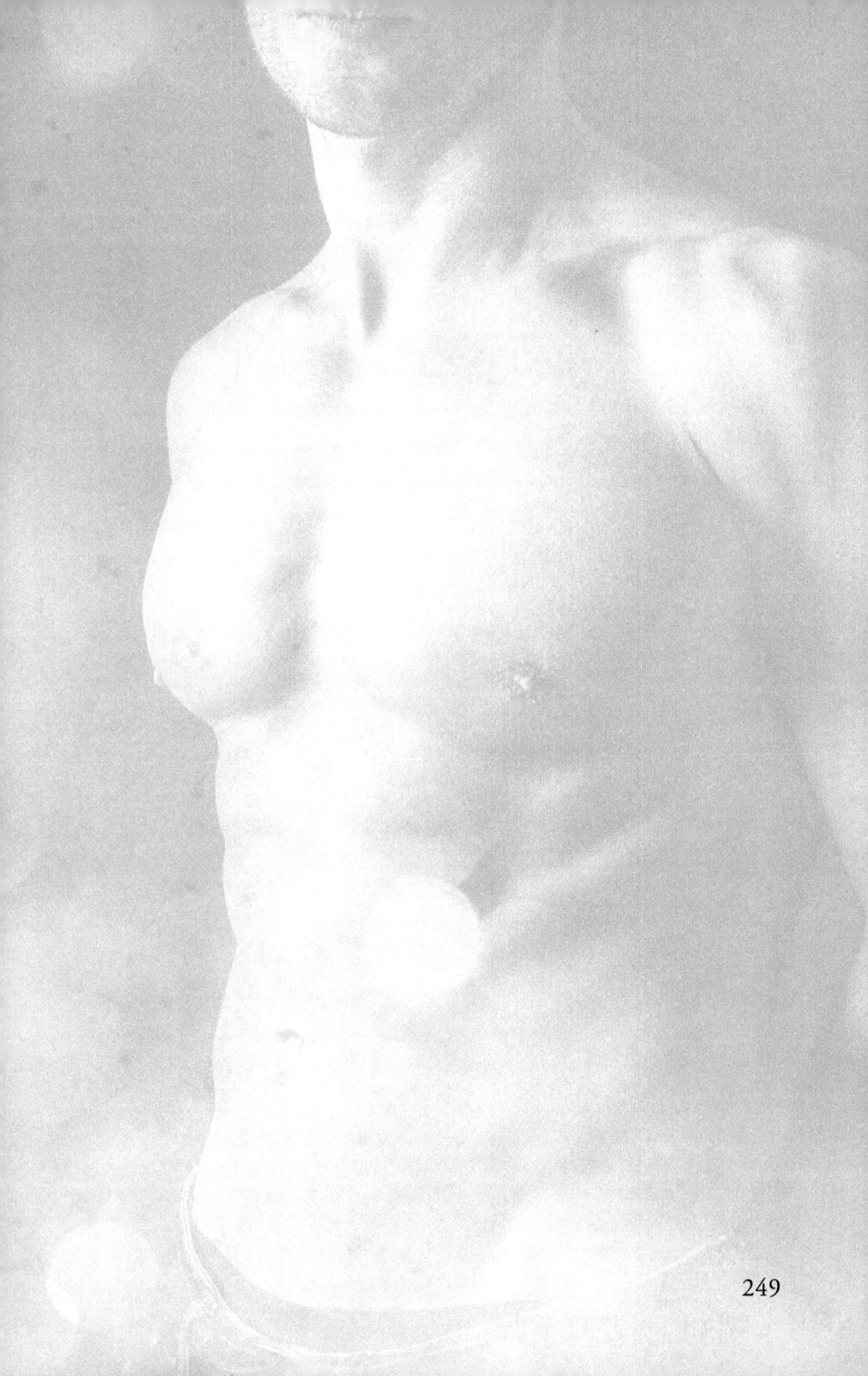